D0710942

David Wishart studied Classics [...] taught Latin and Greek in sch[...] retrained as a teacher of EFL. He lived and worked abroad for eleven years, working in Kuwait, Greece and Saudi Arabia, and now lives with his family in Scotland.

Praise for David Wishart:

'Ancient Rome's shrewdest and most sardonic detective . . . the best balance of mystery and history yet.' *Kirkus Reviews*

'More twists and turns than a roller coaster . . . fast-paced and professional.' *Historical Novels Review*

'Drawn with great dash, and the one-liners are as good as ever. Genius.' *Good Book Guide*

'Wishart takes true historical events and blends them into a concoction so pacey that you hardly notice all those facts and interesting details of Roman life being slipped in there . . . Salve! To this latest from the top toga-wearing 'tec of Roman times!' *Highland News Group*

'It is evident that Wishart is a fine scholar and perfectly at home in the period.' *Sunday Times*

'A real gripping mystery yarn with a strong vein of laconic humour.' *Coventry Evening Telegraph*

DAVID WISHART

Food For The Fishes

HODDER

First published in Great Britain in 2005 by Hodder & Stoughton
A division of Hodder Headline
First published in paperback in 2005 by Hodder and Stoughton
A Hodder Paperback

1 3 5 7 9 10 8 6 4 2

A CIP catalogue record for this title is available from the British Library

ISBN 0 340 82739 4

Typeset in Plantin Light by
Phoenix Typesetting, Auldgirth, Dumfriesshire

Printed and bound in Great Britain by
Clays Ltd, St Ives plc

Hodder Headline's policy is to use papers that are natural, renewable
and recyclable products and made from wood grown in sustainable forests.
The logging and manufacturing processes are expected to conform to
the environmental regulations of the country of origin

Hodder and Stoughton
A division of Hodder Headline
338 Euston Road
London NW1 3BH

DRAMATIS PERSONAE

CORVINUS'S FAMILY AND HOUSEHOLD

Bathyllus: the major-domo
Perilla: Corvinus's wife
Priscus, Titus Helvius: Corvinus's stepfather
Vipsania: Corvinus's mother

THE MURENA FAMILY AND HOUSEHOLD

Catia: Chlorus's wife. Their daughter is Hebe
Chlorus, Titus Licinius: Murena's elder son
Gellia: Murena's wife
Ligurius, Quintus: Murena's manager
Murena, Lucius Licinius: the victim
Nerva, Aulus Licinius: Murena's younger son
Penelope (Licinia): Murena's daughter
Tattius, Decimus: Murena's partner and Penelope's
  husband

BAIAE

Diodotus: a doctor
Philippus, Lucius Licinius: a businessman and gambling
  hall owner. Murena's ex-slave
Saenius, Quintus: a retired lawyer
Trebbio, Gaius: a drunk
Zethus: the wineshop owner

For Roy, nuper rudiarius. Ah, well, end of an era . . .

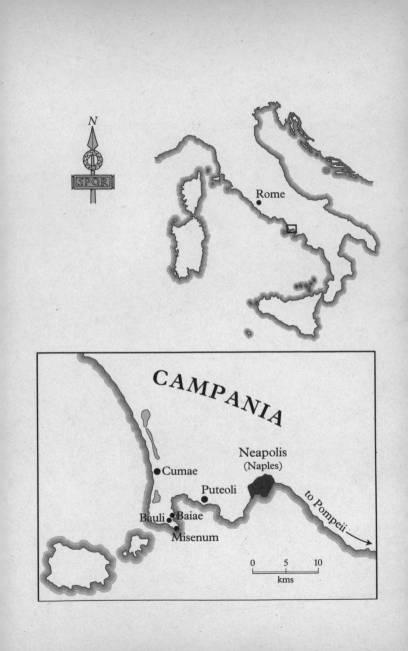

I

Baiae may be the jewel of the Campanian coast and the playground of the beautiful rich, but like any other place it's got its good points too. You have to look hard to find them, mind, and Zethus's wineshop had taken me three days. Zethus's was just a glorified shack, tucked away just above the beach on the Misenum side of town, right on the edge and well off the main drag, but the wine was good and although some of the clientele could seriously get up your nose at times they were okay company on the whole: all locals, and definitely not members of the gilded-eyelashes-and-pet-peacock-on-a-lead set who come down from Rome for the summer. Which suited me just fine. Three days' worth of town-centre wineshops patronised by bleating chinless wonders in holiday mood had had me practically climbing walls. Mind you, since the alternative was spending quality time in the company of Mother and Priscus I couldn't be too fussy.

Currently, the said punters were whiling away the evening by indulging in the quaint old wineshop custom of winding up the drunk.

Me, I wasn't getting involved. No way. Drunk-baiting in general's a purely local sport, restricted to regulars, and any outsider stupid enough to shove his nose in is likely to get it punched; although Baiae may be the playground of bright young things with full purses and fluff where their brains should be, outside the luxury coastal villas belt a Roman purple-striper's there on sufferance. If he wants to stay welcome he learns fast to sit and drink his wine without giving no offence to no one. Besides, baiting drunks just isn't my bag.

This one was a beaut, mind; the drunk's drunk, a real dedicatee: small, seedy, puffy-faced and with a nose on him you could've used to guide ships through fog. He'd been propping up the bar for two solid hours to my certain knowledge, getting silently smashed on Zethus's cheapest house wine which he'd been pouring down his throat like his legs were hollow. By this time it was the bar that was doing the propping, he'd gone through the muttering-to-himself stage and out the other end, and the punters were feeding him free cups just to see how long it'd be before he ended up a sodden lump on the sawdust. Call it a spirit of scientific enquiry if you like, or just morbid fascination. Me, I'd say it was pure simple bloody-mindedness, which was par for the course: wineshop punters, especially places like Zethus's, have a pretty basic sense of humour, and they tend to make their own amusements.

The guy lifted his cup for the umpteenth time, found his mouth at the third try, took another swallow and glared at them. 'Fifteen years,' he said. 'Fifteen years I been in that place, right? Am I right?'

The punter next to him at the bar – the elected straight man – was nodding like a sympathetic owl while his mates behind chuckled into their drinks. 'Yeah. Yeah, right,' he said. 'It's a crying shame, no mistake.'

'Old Juventius, he'd never've done it, never. Juventius was a proper gentleman. Not like that bastard. We had a deal, the old man and me.' He belched. ' "Trebbio, boy," he says, "I'm not greedy. You drop me a lobster or two when you can spare them and we'll call the rent quits." Bastard!'

'He is that.' The punter took a pull at his own wine, reached for the jug and topped up the drunk's. 'No question.'

'Him and his fancy fish-farm, raking it in hand over fist. Fifteen years. Fifteen bloody years.' He belched again and wiped a trickle of wine off his chin. 'Hotel. Man like him, money to burn, what does he want to build a bloody hotel for anyway? Go on, you tell me. You tell me that, right? 'S not his business, hotels.'

'Some people's never satisfied with what they got, sure enough.'

'You're right there. He's a bastard. A *greedy* bastard.' He took another swig. 'We've enough of the sods already.'

'Bastards?' one of the other punters at the back asked innocently. The rest sniggered.

The drunk turned, one elbow on the bar for support, and fixed him with a poached-egg stare. 'Tourists. Tourists, boy, that's what I mean. Come down from Rome, swan about like they own the place . . .'

'Yeah, that's 'cos they bleeding do, most of it,' the punter said. His pals sniggered again, and he shot me a wink. 'Isn't that so, Corvinus?'

But I wasn't going to be dragged in; no *way* was I going to be dragged in, not even by invitation. I sipped my wine: Zethus's does a fair Campanian that his partner gets from a friend in Neapolis. His male partner: both of them are Greek, like most of the natives around Baiae, and the Greeks tend to be pretty open-minded about that sort of thing.

'Don't look at me, pal,' I said easily. 'I'm just staying with family, and they borrowed the villa, they don't own it.'

The drunk took a firm grip of the bar and turned to give me a slow pop-eyed stare, taking in my mantle and purple stripe.

'Got nothing against Romans, me,' he said finally. 'Notassuch. Notassuch.' He picked up his cup and raised it to me. Wine slopped. 'Didn't mean to cause off – . . . off – . . .' He drained the cup and belched. 'Offence.'

'None taken.' I raised my own cup. 'Cheers, friend.'

'Only some of them. Like that bastard. Some people, though, they'd be better off dead, know what I mean?'

'Yeah,' I said. 'Yeah, I know.'

'Just happens he's a Roman too, right? Pure coinc—' He hiccuped. 'Coincidence. Could be anyone, but he's a Roman. No offence, though.' He blinked, staggered, grabbed the bar again and stood swaying. 'Fuck! I'm plastered!'

Zethus was washing cups. He glanced up. 'Maybe you'd best be getting home, Trebbio,' he said quietly.

'Nah, there's still plenty of wine in the jug.' The straight-man punter – his name was Alcis – slapped him on the shoulder and steadied him with his other hand. 'Come on, Trebbio, I'm buying. Okay, lads?'

The other punters grinned. One of them said, 'Sure.'

'No. Zethus is right. I've had enough.' The drunk straightened. 'Anyway, 's a full moon tonight. Best be going. Got to check my lines.' He rocked back and forward on his feet and made a lurch for the door. ' 'Night, all.'

The door closed behind him. Yeah, well; maybe he was smarter than he seemed, even if he was pissed as a newt. He'd come out a winner, anyway, at least a jug of free booze ahead and still mobile. If you could call it mobile. Certainly the punters were looking disappointed as hell, like cats left watching an empty mousehole. Not that I'd much sympathy there. I tapped my own empty half jug and Zethus came round the bar.

'He be all right?' I said quietly.

'Oh, yeah. He's only going half a mile or so along the

beach.' Zethus took the jug. 'Mind you, he's had a bigger skinful than usual.' He turned round to the punters. 'That wasn't nice of you, lads. Not nice at all.'

Alcis gave him a cheerful finger and turned back to chat with his mates.

'Who was this bastard he was on about?' I said.

'That's Murena. Licinius Murena. He owns the big fish-farm and villa just down the coast from here.'

I chuckled. 'Murena, right? Good name for a fish-farmer.' A murena's a moray eel. Sure, it's a regular surname in the pukkah branch of the Licinius family, too, so the coincidence isn't as remarkable as it looks, but then Cicero didn't raise chickpeas for a living, did he? Not that one of *the* Licinii would be exactly strapped for a copper piece or two.

'His grandfather started it a century or so back. It's the oldest and biggest on the bay.' Zethus nodded at the jug. 'Same again?'

'Uh-uh. Make it a cup. I'll have to be getting back soon.' If I came rolling in at one in the morning tripping over the furniture there'd be Looks from Mother at breakfast. Perilla wouldn't be too happy, either. 'What's this business about a hotel?'

'Murena's bought the old Juventius estate between here and town. That's where Trebbio has his cottage. Guy's plan-ning to build a hotel, a big one, for the top end of the market, and Trebbio got the boot this morning. He isn't too pleased about it.'

Yeah, that was putting it mildly; I'd go for homicidal myself. While Zethus went to fetch my wine I sat back and finished what was left in the cup. A hotel, eh? Unusual. You got the things, sure: there was a big one in Ostia, not that long built, and as a location Baiae made even more sense in a way, but something targeting the luxury end of the temporary

accommodation market wasn't all that common. Or a very
safe bet, either. Boarding-houses and inns, right, there've
always been boarding-houses and inns, especially in places
that have a big shifting population or a regular through trade.
Rome and Ostia are full of them, and so is every other city in
the empire. Flats and houses for short-term let aren't rare,
either: there're plenty of entrepreneurs around who'll buy
property they don't intend to use themselves and offer it for
rent by the month or even less. Really top-notch, purpose-
built temporary accommodation though is another matter.
The people it's aimed at and who could afford the prices just
don't need it, on the whole, because when they travel, for
business or pleasure, they make an arrangement with friends,
or more usually friends of friends. Like we'd done: Mother's
society pal Lucia Domitilla and her husband were currently
in Pergamum, and their Baian villa had been standing empty.
You need a house, we've got a house; no problem, deal made.
The next time it's the other way round, and if the second
party can't help direct they probably know someone who can.
On the other hand, given the choice between sweating it out
in Rome for the summer and staying in rented rooms, in
Baiae or anywhere else, Mother would've taken the heat every
time. And the same would go for most of the other people of
her class. Actually *renting* a room – or even a house – is something that anyone with any social pretensions just doesn't do,
unless for some reason they're really desperate. Especially in
Baiae, where the villa prices and the lifted noses keep the riff-
raff out.

   Still, this Murena wasn't totally out of his tree. The
scheme would need serious investment, sure, and it might be
risky as hell, but if it worked he'd be sitting on a gold-mine.
Mother's class wasn't the only money around these days.
There were a lot of very rich plain-mantles – and some even

richer freedmen – in Rome who'd give their eye-teeth to be able to tell their friends they were off down to Baiae for the summer.

Zethus came back with a jug and filled the empty cup.

'So how long has this Murena been here, then?' I said. 'If his grandfather laid down the original ponds the family must be almost local.'

'Search me. Longer than I have, though, and I've been here eighteen years.'

'He come back and forward from Rome, or is he here full-time?'

'Oh, he's a permanent fixture. Goes up to Rome on business now and again as far as I know, but that's all. You don't know him?'

'Uh-uh. Not at all. He a bastard, like Trebbio said?'

Zethus grinned. 'Close enough, by repute. Tight-fisted, mind of his own and a nasty temper if he's crossed, so they say. All the same, I've never met him myself, and Trebbio has his own axe to grind.' He raised a delicately shaved eyebrow. 'You have a reason for asking?'

'Uh-uh. Just curiosity.'

'So ask about his wife, Corvinus.' Alcis had been listening in. Now he half turned in our direction. A few of the other punters sniggered and one gave a soft wolf-whistle into his wine cup. 'There's a lady to be very curious about.'

'That so, friend?' I said easily. Alcis was one of the draw-backs to Zethus's. The guy put my back up in spades.

'Murena's pushing seventy, his wife's a little stunner half his age. Knows what she's about, too.' Alcis took a swallow of his wine and smacked his lips 'I reckon you could be in there if you played your cards right, a rich young purple-striper like you.'

'Cut it out, Alcis,' Zethus murmured.

The guy smiled at him, showing far too many teeth. 'Yeah, well, it's a subject that wouldn't interest you, isn't it, Zethus?' he said. 'Not quite up your street, as it were.' He turned back to me. 'Mind you, you'd have to watch for that tame doctor of hers. Doctors can be nasty, and by all accounts this one's definitely got his feet under the table.'

'She's ill?'

'Oh, no.' He chuckled. 'She isn't, although she might be sickening for something. The doctor's for hubby. Practically full-time, they say. Back and forward to the villa like nobody's business, although the old man looks healthy enough. Nice work if you can get it, eh?'

'Yeah.' Well, I'd had about enough of Toothy Alcis for one evening, and a cup of wine lost was a small price to pay for dispensing with the bugger's company. I stood up, took a single swallow, set the cup down and pulled a reasonable amount of coins out of my belt-purse to cover things. 'Okay, gentlemen, that's about me for the night. Enjoy yourselves.'

'You just remember who it was put you on to her,' Alcis shouted at my back.

'Sure,' I said. 'I'll do that.'

I went down on to the beach. The villa we were staying at was about a mile away on the other side of town, and walking there directly, cutting up to the main road before the first of the townside villas then through the town itself, was the quickest route. Also the pleasantest. It was a beautiful evening for walking. The moon was up and shining over the sea, round and bright as a gold piece, and the water was lapping gently against the pebbles at the edge.

Only there was something else on the beach besides pebbles, something that hadn't been there earlier. An irregularly shaped dark hump, about the size of a body. The hairs rose on my neck.

I went closer. Body was right: I could see the head and limbs clear now in the moonlight. It wasn't moving, either. Oh, shit!

I'd got within five yards when the corpse suddenly turned over on its back and gave an almighty snore. Trebbio, flat out and pissed to the gills. I relaxed.

'Uh . . . you okay, pal?' I said.

No answer, just another snore and a belch. Out for chips. Well, lines or not, full moon or not, I couldn't see Endymion here shifting himself this side of sunrise. I looked back at the wineshop, no more than a hundred yards away. Yeah, I could let Zethus know, which might be a good idea, but that would mean letting Alcis and the rest know as well, and with those buggers' robust sense of humour that was not something I wanted to do, because six got you ten it'd only lead to trouble. It was a warm night, the guy seemed happy enough where he was, so far as drunk and incapable can be counted happy, and if he wanted to sleep on the beach and wake up in the morning with multiple pebble bruises added to his hangover then it was no business of mine.

Forget it, Corvinus. I left him to his dreams and set off home.

Mistake.

2

Me, I'm an early riser by nature, at least when I haven't been out on a binge. My wife Perilla's different, and as for Mother dawn's something she might just know about in theory but as far as first-hand experience goes you can forget it. Add to that that in pleasure-loving Baiae Rome's holidaymaking crème de la crème snore in their socks until the crack of noon and you'll understand that breakfast tends to happen pretty late.

We'd been here five days now and I'd settled into a routine: up just after first light, a walk to the harbour through the practically empty town – the villa was on the far edge, on the Puteoli side, but Baiae isn't a big place – or along the beach, then back in time for the rolls and honey. Early morning's the best time for walking in this part of the world. It's cooler, for a start, and like I say there's no one around barring the slaves clearing up after the parties of the night before and the local fishermen who keep the restaurants along the bay supplied with the huge amount of seafood they get through every evening. Plus the fact that later in the day the place – especially down by the prom, where Rome's gilded beauties go to see and be seen – is heaving with cut-glass accents and primped exquisites of all sexes taking their pet sparrows for walkies. There're plenty of secluded wineshops around to duck into, sure, and I'd tried a few the first couple of days, but they just set my teeth

on edge: overpriced wine, pretentious decor and a conversational background that would've disgraced a
self-respecting parrot. Zethus's might have its faults – Alcis
was one of them – but at least there you didn't get powdered
and perfumed darlings seriously discussing the chicest
colour for litter curtains or sniggering over their previous
night's host's oh-so-last-month choice of dinner menu. And
that was just the males.

For anyone who was anyone, Baiae in July might be the
place to be, sure, but I was tired of it already.

Perilla and Mother were out on the terrace and started when
I arrived back. Perilla can really pack it away at breakfast-
time, especially when she's on holiday, and she was tucking
into a plateful of cheese, eggs and olives. Mother had her
usual gunk in front of her: currently, a bowl of goat's milk
curds flavoured with fruit juice and honey. Jupiter knows why
she hasn't poisoned herself years ago, but she looks fit
enough. And for someone who must be pushing sixty a face
and a body like that shouldn't be allowed, so maybe she has
something after all.

'Good morning, Marcus,' Perilla said. 'Did you have a
nice walk?'

'Yeah. It was okay.' I slid on to the couch next to her and
planted a smacker on her cheek as she reached for another
olive. 'Stepfather not around yet?'

'No, he isn't,' Mother said tartly. 'He's indisposed. Good
morning, dear.'

I glanced at her. Uh-oh; with Mother you didn't get that
tone very often, but when you did it meant trouble.

Bathyllus shimmered over. We'd done a deal, Mother and
me. If the two families were going on holiday together –
and it wasn't my idea, believe me – we'd trade off in the

bought help department. Two sets of domestics in the same house was a recipe for disaster: the clash of interests and personalities would've put more blood on the walls inside of five minutes than you'd get in half a dozen of Euripides's best, and nerves scraped to screaming rawness ain't exactly conducive to a quiet time by the seaside. I got to bring our major-domo Bathyllus while she had her chef Phormio. Not that the arrangement was perfect, mind, because Phormio is to cooking what an asp in a basket of figs is to a lucky dip, but before we clinched the deal I'd got the bastard alone by the pickled onions and promised him there'd be hell to pay at the first wobbler. Disguising food to look like something it isn't may be good Roman culinary practice, but lamb chops made of turnip I can do without.

'Hot roll, sir?' Bathyllus proffered a plate. Yeah, well; that was one thing. The little bald-head is an arch-snob, and the combination of buttling for Mother and being here in Baiae at the hub of the social universe had done wonders for his style. I took one and reached for the honey.

'He isn't well?' I said. 'Priscus, I mean?'

Mother sniffed. 'He has a headache.'

I glanced at Perilla, but the lady was studiously cutting the rind off her cheese. There was something more than slightly screwy here. Mother's husband Titus Helvius Priscus might be pushing seventy-five and look twice that on a good day, but he was a spry old bugger, and ill was something he didn't get. Also, Mother fussed over him like a hen with a day-old chick, and the way she'd said 'headache' didn't exactly ooze sympathy.

'Self-induced,' she added.

I nearly dropped the honey dish in pure shock. *'What?'*

'Seemingly he came rolling in at one in the morning tripping over the furniture, Marcus,' Perilla said, still busy with the cheese and not looking at me. 'Naturally, Vipsania thought it was you—'

'Oh, thanks a bunch!'

'. . . until she realised Priscus's side of the bed was empty. Then, of course, he came upstairs and there was no doubt.'

Bacchus on a seesaw! I didn't believe this! *'Priscus?'* I said. 'You're kidding!'

'Marcus, dear, I do not' – Mother sniffed again – 'kid. Ever. You're at the back of the house; you wouldn't have heard him.'

'But Priscus doesn't even drink! At least, no more than a cup in an evening.'

'Evidently he does now. And it took considerably more than a cup to get him into that state'.

'Fried as a newt,' Perilla murmured.

I glanced suspiciously at her ears. They were bright red, and she was keeping her head well down over the cheese. Yeah, well, I suppose it was funny, but all the same for Priscus to come home drunk was about as likely as a cray-fish tap-dancing the length of the Baian seafront.

'Did he say anything?' I said.

'Not at the time.' Mother set down her spoon. 'Or nothing very intelligible. Bar the singing. *That* was intelligible enough for me, or most of it was, unfortunately. After the fourth verse he climbed into bed fully clothed and went straight to sleep.'

'Uh . . . what about this morning? When he woke up?'

'We exchanged a few words.' Ouch! 'Then he said he had a headache and I came down to breakfast.'

'Ah. Uh . . . fine. Fine.' I picked up the roll and honeyed it in the sudden ensuing silence. 'So you don't know where—'

'No, I don't!' Mother snapped. 'The only thing I know is

that he went into town after dinner, ostensibly to see an anti-quarian friend of his whom I do *not* know. A man called Leonides. They were planning, I think, to discuss Siculan oil-lamps.'

'Right.' Yeah, that sounded more like Priscus: put the old bugger in the sin capital of the empire and spend the evening discussing Siculan oil-lamps is just what he'd do. Only evidently this time he hadn't. No one gets fried as a newt discussing Siculan oil-lamps, not even in Baiae. 'You've, uh . . . Priscus has been to Baiae before. This the first time it's happened?' That got me a wordless glare that would've fricasséed a squid. 'Yeah. Yeah, okay. So maybe he wasn't drunk. Maybe it was just . . . ah . . . over-excitement.'

'About the Siculan oil-lamps,' Perilla murmured.

I shot her a look.

'Marcus, I'm not a fool,' Mother said. 'Of course he was drunk. I could smell the wine halfway across the room.'

'So, uh, what are you going to do about it? I mean, the guy's—'

'*I* am not going to do anything. Personally, I don't trust myself. *You* are going to talk to him. When he's fully sober and compos mentis, that is.'

Oh, shit. The first part, fine, but where Priscus was concerned the second would take until the Greek kalends. 'Look, Mother—'

'This is your department, dear. You're male and the wine-drinker in the family. You have experience of these things. You can tell Titus that I'll accept any reasonable explanation so long as it is accompanied by a grovelling apology and an assurance that it will not happen again.' She stood up. 'Now. *When* he has recovered from his hangover sufficiently to behave in a civilised fashion, and when you've had your little talk, he'll find me in the library. Possibly.'

She left.

I looked sideways at Perilla. She was still paring bits off her piece of cheese, even though the rind was long gone, and her ears hadn't lightened any in colour.

'You, uh, think we could make it as far as Puteoli and get a boat east before she misses us, lady?' I said.

'I wish I'd seen—' She stopped and turned towards me, her shoulders shaking. Two seconds later, we were hugging each other and helpless.

'It's not funny,' I gasped eventually.

'No.' Perilla hiccuped, reached for her napkin and dried her eyes. 'No, it isn't. Vipsania's very upset. What do you think got into him?'

'About three pints of wine, by the sound of things.'

She giggled. 'Don't start me off again! I've been trying not to laugh ever since she told me. But *Priscus*? Marcus, it doesn't make sense.'

'Yeah, right.' I glanced up at the first-floor window where Mother and Priscus's bedroom was. The shutters were still closed, but he'd had his long lie. Ah, well, no point in putting things off: I'd have to do it some time. And Priscus with a hangover headache couldn't be all that much woolier than the old bugger was normally. Which reminded me. 'Hey, Bathyllus!' I yelled.

He soft-shoed over: Bathyllus has the major-domo's trick of always being in call but never being obvious. Me, I think the process has something to do with Democritus's theory of shifting atoms, but that's only a theory.

'That hangover cure you put together,' I said. 'Could you whip one up for me?'

'Yes, sir. Of course, sir.'

Not a blink: we were still getting the perfect butler act. Still, I'd back the Bathyllus Bombshell against any hangover in existence. I'd never asked him what was in it – some things it's better not to know, especially when you're going to be drinking the stuff – but it worked like a charm.

What it tasted like, mind, was something else again.

I knocked on the door, waited for an answer that didn't come, and opened it. With the shutters closed the room was in total darkness. Careful not to spill the Bombshell – what it'd do to the floor tiles was anyone's guess – I went over to where the fine lines of sunlight showed and unlatched the bar. Light streamed in.

'Hey, Priscus,' I said to the lump on the bed. 'Wakey wakey!'

'Mmmaaa!'

Well, at least he was alive and bleating. 'Come on, pal! Show a leg.' I thought again. 'Or maybe don't show a leg. Just sit up, okay?'

For a wonder, he did. The old Egyptian embalmers might've appreciated the next bit, but it scared the willies off me.

'Mmmaaa! That you, Marcus?'

'Yeah.' I shoved the Bombshell into his unprotesting hand. Get them to drink it while they're suggestible and before their nose gets into gear. 'Put that down you.'

He sank the full cupful without a murmur. I felt my scrotum contract in sympathy as I waited for the inevitable reaction.

It never came.

'Quite good, my boy. Thank you.'

I stared at him. 'You liked it?' This wasn't the way things were supposed to go.

'Shouldn't I have? It was very refreshing. Certainly tastier than Phormio's usual breakfast drink. What was it?'

'Uh . . . how's your headache?'

'Headache? What headache?'

'Mother said you had a headache.'

He blinked back at me numbly. I've never quite been able to work old Priscus out. On the one hand, he's got about the same mental grasp of what's going on around him as a codfish has of fretwork, but on the other under normal circumstances he can twist my mother round his little finger. And Mother, for all her society ways, is a seriously sharp cookie.

'Mmmaaa! Not so's you'd notice, Marcus.'

'Fine. Fine.' Leave it. There was a stool by the wall. I pulled it up. 'Okay. Business. You like to tell me what exactly happened yesterday evening?'

That got me another blink. 'I . . . mmmaaa! . . . went to Leonides's.'

'Yeah, right. So I gather. Who's Leonides?'

'An old friend. We've corresponded for years. He . . . mmmaaa! . . . collects Siculan oil-lamps.'

'Uh-huh.' I shifted on my stool. Check; so far, so good, but we weren't there yet. 'How about Baian wine jars?'

'I . . . mmmaaa! . . . don't quite catch your meaning, my boy.'

I sighed. 'Look, Priscus, no one gets smashed out of their skull discussing Siculan oil-lamps. Okay, so maybe it was the guy's birthday and he invited you to split a jug or two. It happens. You're not used to the stuff, it'd be natural for you to—'

'Oh, but Leonides doesn't drink! It brings on his trouble.'

'Fine.' Scratch that one, then, without further amplification. It seemed we were in for an uphill struggle here, and I'd need all my patience. 'So let's skip the oil-lamps. What happened then?'

'He has a fascinating collection, Marcus. Quite unique. Do you realise that the number of early Siculan oil-lamps still extant is only in the region of . . . mmmaaa!—?'

'Forget the fu—' I caught myself. 'Forget the oil-lamps, Priscus. I'm trying to save your guts here. So you left Leonides's hundred per cent sober. What happened next?'

'I . . . mmmaaa! . . . dropped in somewhere on the way home.'

Now we were getting to it. 'Uh-huh. What kind of somewhere?'

'A little place by the baths. Serving drinks and . . . other things. It sounded quite jolly in passing and I thought I'd stop for a quick cup of . . . mmmaaa! . . . warm milk and wormwood.'

'Warm milk and, uh, wormwood.'

'Yes. After all, my boy, I am on holiday. Only they didn't seem to have that, so to be polite I had a cup of wine instead.' He grinned at me like a louche tortoise. 'I've never been inside one of these places before. It was quite . . . mmmaaa! . . . fascinating. Then I got into conversation with a very charming girl from Alexandria –'

Oh, shit.

'– who, would you believe it, Marcus had never . . . mmmaaa! . . . been inside the library *in her life*! Mind you, she'd been lots of other places. Talking to her was quite . . . mmmaaa! . . . an eye-opener.'

Yeah, I'd bet it was. Jupiter in a handcart! 'And, uh, she kept you drinking, right? After that first cup?'

'Oh, I had to keep her company.' There was the louche tortoise look again. 'Fortunately I'd just been to our bankers. Wine is very expensive here, isn't it? Then before I knew it it was . . . mmmaaa! . . . closing time and we all had to go home. She offered me a bed for the night but I thought Vipsania might worry, so I declined.'

I looked at him and he smiled blandly back. I had my suspicions of Priscus. No one could be that dumb and live. Yeah, well, it was none of my business, really. If the old bugger wanted to kick over the traces, so far as it was possible at his age, then fine. He'd been lucky, though: they'd just skinned him, not rolled him and dumped what was left in an alley. 'Well, so long as you're really sorry it happened,' I said. 'Mother's—'

'Oh, but I'm not, my boy!' The smile became a beam. 'What gave you that idea? I had . . . mmmaaa! . . . a marvellous evening! Very entertaining!'

'Uh . . . Priscus . . .'

'I really should get out more often. You must join me next time. You'd be amazed.'

'Yeah, I probably would at that.' *Next time.* Gods! What had we unleashed here? I hesitated, weighing possibilities. 'Priscus, listen to me, pal. Perhaps where Mother's concerned we should stick with the Leonides's birthday idea, okay? And maybe play down the enjoyment factor? Plus I wouldn't . . . ah . . . mention the other place at all.'

'Or the girl? She really was quite . . . mmmaaa! . . .'

'*Especially* the girl.' I stood up. 'You with me?' It was always just as well to check on these things. Priscus's chain of reasoning skipped a few links at the best of times.

'Of course. If you think it's best.' He frowned. 'Only—'

'Trust me,' I said. 'This way you might escape with surface burns. Mention the cathouse and the girl and you're cooked. Mother's expecting you in the library for an explanation. Once there, you're on your own. You want me to send Bathyllus up with some breakfast first?'

'Mmmaaa! I think I could manage an egg this morning. Lightly boiled.'

Lightly boiled. Yeah, that'd make two of them.

I went downstairs.

That afternoon we took the carriage to Cumae. Priscus and Mother were pretty quiet, then and at dinner later, but whatever the old bugger had said he seemed to have smoothed the thing over. After dinner I went along the beach to Zethus's. There was only one topic of conversation, but that was a show-stopper.

Licinius Murena had been murdered.

3

'They found him this morning,' Zethus said, filling my cup. 'Or what was left of him. In one of the eel tanks.'

I winced. Eels are carnivorous, and they ain't fussy feeders. There're black stories about gourmets feeding their morays on human flesh because they think the fish tastes better that way. Sometimes it's dead human flesh, but not always.

'Who's "they", pal?' I said.

'Ligurius. He's Murena's manager.'

'Was,' Alcis, along the bar, sniggered. 'When he got to him he only had half a boss left. Hardly enough for a decent funeral.'

'Ill of the dead, Alcis,' Zethus murmured. 'Let's have some respect.'

Alcis opened his eyes wide. 'I'd nothing against the old bastard, me.' He sipped his wine. 'Unlike some.'

There was a thoughtful silence. Zethus's wasn't crowded, but the regulars were all there. They were all ears, as well.

'He'd never.' Zethus put the jug he'd poured from back on the shelf.

'Want to bet?' said Alcis. There was a murmur of agreement from the surrounding punters, and a low comment or two.

I took a mouthful of wine. 'Uh . . . who are we talking about here?'

Alcis turned to face me. 'Trebbio, of course,' he said. 'Who else'd've done it?'

'Come on, boy,' Zethus said. 'Trebbio wouldn't hurt a fly.'

'Flies maybe. Licinius Murena, now' – Alcis grinned back at his circle of mates – 'well, he's another matter, isn't he?' One or two of the punters chuckled. 'In here the night it happens, damning the bugger blue, then he goes out to check his lines not a hundred yards from Murena's place. Pull the other one, Zethus, it's got bells. Trebbio's for the chop, you mark my words.'

'Trebbio checks his lines every night,' Zethus said. 'And he may have a mouth on him but he's no killer.'

Maybe it was time I stepped in here. 'Trebbio didn't do it, pal,' I said to Alcis.

That got me the wide-eyed stare. 'Yeah? How do you know?'

'When I left myself I found him on the beach pissed as a newt and snoring. He wasn't capable of walking five yards, let alone murdering anyone at the end of them. Besides, it doesn't necessarily sound like murder to me. What's wrong with the guy just falling in in the dark and drowning?'

Alcis laughed. 'Oh, yeah! Murena knew these tanks like the back of his hand. And what'd he be doing up there that time of night?'

'Talking to the fish,' Zethus said. 'The villa's only a couple of hundred yards away. He always goes down there last thing for an hour or so. You know that, boy. Everybody knows that.'

Alcis scowled. 'Yeah, well. Then that includes Trebbio, doesn't it? The bastard only had to wait his chance.' He turned round again. 'Lucius. You walked back to town along the beach last night at closing time. You see anything of Trebbio?'

'Uh-uh.' One of the other punters shook his head. 'Wasn't there then.'

'And that was – what? – an hour after you left, Corvinus?' Alcis turned back to face me. 'Anyway, what makes you the expert? Trebbio's got a head on him like a block of oak. He could've done it, easy.'

'Anyone could've done it.' Zethus topped up a punter's cup. 'Or like Corvinus says it could've been an accident.'

'Accident to hell.' Alcis chuckled. 'Got to hand it to the bugger, though. He's paid Murena out nicely. Poetic justice. Pity he won't get away with it for long.' He drew his finger across his throat. 'Psssst!'

Well, I couldn't fault him there, anyway. If it was murder, and the family took it up – which they definitely would – then as the only suspect Trebbio's neck was on the line, sure enough. And if he was found guilty then it meant a quick appointment with the public strangler.

I sipped my wine.

If . . .

That was what stuck in my throat. There were too many ifs. It could've been an accident, sure, whatever Alcis said. The guy made a habit of visiting his tanks after dark, these things weren't fenced in and the walkways were pretty narrow. Slippery, too, maybe. And even if he had been murdered, the proof against Trebbio amounted to zilch. At best, he was in the wrong place at the wrong time, but there again like Zethus said that wasn't unusual, he was out that way every night. And he might not have been there yesterday evening at all. I'd seen Trebbio myself, and I'd've said barring a short stagger home he was out of things for the duration. Suggesting that in his condition he'd walked half a mile up the beach, got into a fish-farm that probably had a serious wall around it, negotiated a set of fish tanks and pushed a man into somewhere he didn't want to go just didn't add up.

'So where is he now?' I said.

'No idea.' Alcis grinned. 'If the bugger's got any sense, he's halfway to Neapolis. The town officer can't tell his arse from his elbow, sure, but even he'll see letting a prime murder suspect run around loose is—'

He stopped. The door opened. A dozen pairs of eyes zeroed in on it and the only sound was a single cup being laid down on the bar.

'Evening lads,' Trebbio said. 'How's it going?' He hesitated when he saw the expressions. 'Uh . . . lads?'

The frozen tableau broke up.

'Grab him!' That was Alcis, naturally, but the two punters nearest the door were off their stools before the words were out of his mouth. Not that it needed more than one. Trebbio wasn't big, and with the physical condition he was in a seven-year-old kid could've taken him one-handed, easy. They slammed him back against the closed door with a beefy shoulder either side pinning him to the boards, and he hung there gasping.

Okay, that was it. I stood up. 'That's enough,' I said. 'Let him down.'

'Corvinus, you just—' Alcis began.

'You want to lose a couple of your shiny teeth, pal?' I said quietly, without looking at him. Then to the two punters: 'Let him down. You want to ask him questions, fine, go ahead, but to answer them he has to breathe. Door's closed, he's got nowhere to run. Let him down.'

They did, a bit sheepishly. One of them even pulled up a stool and got him on it while another uninvolved punter handed him a cup of wine. They weren't bad lads in Zethus's, most of them, and he was one of their own, after all.

Trebbio drank the wine in a oner and passed the back of his hand across his mouth. He was shaking.

'What the hell's going on?' he said.

'You killed Murena,' Alcis said.

The guy's jaw dropped. 'I did *what*?'

'Pushed him into a tank full of morays last night.'

Trebbio shook his head numbly. 'I never! 'Course I never!' He frowned. 'Murena's dead?'

Alcis grinned. 'Come on, Trebbio! You know he's fucking dead! By this time half Baiae knows.'

'Not me. I been out in the boat. Fishing.' Trebbio jerked his head in the direction of the beach. ' 'S down on the shore now. Been out all day, since first light, and just got back.' He raised a pair of eyes like blood-cracked poached eggs. 'Zethus, you tell them to cut this out! They're having me on, right? A joke's a joke, but this isn't funny!'

Zethus said nothing. I noticed, though, that when the rumpus started he'd reached under the bar for the heavy stick all bartenders keep there in case a customer needs placating. He was still holding it. A nice guy, Zethus.

'You go and check your lines last night, Trebbio?' Alcis said.

'Sure I checked my lines! I do it every night! You know that!'

Alcis shot me a triumphant look. Shit. Well, if he'd managed that in the state I'd left him in a head like a block of oak was right. Still, he'd admitted it straight off, and taking the rest into account that impressed me. If it was acting then he was wasted as a beach bum.

Zethus's silence must've registered. Suddenly, without warning, Trebbio slumped. If one of the guys standing behind him hadn't caught him in time he'd've been off the stool. 'You're not having me on?' he mumbled. 'Murena's dead?'

'Pork-dead.' Alcis grinned again. 'So when you went—'

'You see anything, Trebbio?' I cut in. 'Last night, when you checked your lines? Over by the fish-farm?' He goggled at me. 'Valerius Corvinus. The Roman. You remember me?'

'Yeah. Right.' He pulled his hand across his mouth again and shuddered. 'Someone give me another drink. Oh, bugger!'

One of the punters handed him a full cup and he drank it down, holding the cup in both hands. Even then he spilled half of it.

'Answer the man, Trebbio,' Zethus said quietly.

'Yeah. I saw a light. Maybe two,' he muttered. ' 'S not unusual. The old man goes down nights to talk to the fish, and he takes a lamp. They come up to the light. Or maybe I'm wrong, maybe that was another night.' He raised his eyes. 'It could've been.' He drank the last dregs of the wine, tipping the cup back to get the last trickle, then licked his wine-soaked hand. 'I can't . . . fucking . . . *remember*, okay?'

'So you checked your lines,' I said. 'Then?'

'I went home and went to bed. What else would I do?'

'You didn't see anyone? On the beach, by the fish-farm?'

'Who'd be out there at that time of night? Nah, I didn't see a soul.' He looked, suddenly, frightened. 'I didn't kill him, right? Never laid a finger on him. I wouldn't, not ever. I just went home.'

Alcis glanced at me. 'You finished, Corvinus?' he said sourly.

I shrugged. 'Yeah. More or less.'

'Right. Then we'll get this bugger down to the town officer's. Lucius! Philo!'

The two guys behind Trebbio leaned forward and took his arms. They were gentle enough this time, sure, but they weren't having any arguments. Trebbio didn't even struggle.

At the door, he turned and looked directly at me. The two cups of wine seemed to have settled him, if anything, because his eyes were steady and he didn't mumble. 'I never done nothing, Corvinus,' he said. 'I swear it. You'll help me, right? You're a Roman purple-striper, they'll listen to you. Whoever killed the bastard it wasn't me.'

'Come on, Trebbio,' Alcis said. 'You can tell that to the town officer.'

The three of them hustled him out.

After they'd gone the bar was pretty quiet. There was plenty of conversation, sure, but it wasn't loud, and the punters kept their backs to me. Maybe they felt a bit ashamed. I hoped so, anyway: even if Trebbio had committed a murder the guy was obviously in a total funk. It'd been like kicking a puppy.

I finished my wine, dropped a handful of coins on the counter, and turned to leave.

''Night all,' I said. 'Somebody look after his boat.'

Jupiter!

Perilla was still up and around when I got back, sitting out on the terrace overlooking the sea. There was no sign of Mother or Priscus. I just hoped the old bugger wasn't out on his own somewhere painting the town red.

'You're back early, Marcus,' she said.

'Yeah.' I kissed her and lay down on the next couch. Bathyllus oozed over with the homecoming cup of wine.

'Nice evening?'

'Interesting.'

'Oh?'

I told her. About halfway through, her lips set in a line and stayed set. The rest of her wasn't exactly radiating joy and delight, either.

'Corvinus, we're on holiday,' she said when I'd finished. 'You are *not* getting involved.'

'Ah . . . who said anything about—'

'And *don't* try to tell me you're not thinking about it, because I won't believe you. Not unless I spot a few flying pigs first.'

'Yeah, well.' I cleared my throat. 'Actually there is the patron-client aspect of things to consider, lady.'

'*What* patron-client aspect? Come off it, Marcus! This man Trebbio is *not* your client! You don't know him and have no connection with or obligation to him whatsoever!'

I sighed. Oh, yes I did. I wasn't flannelling there; I'd thought the thing out on the way back, and there was no getting round it: I was clean-gaffed, caught by the obligatories. Not that I was too upset about that, mind, but then the lady didn't have to know everything. 'Look, Perilla,' I said. 'If the punters in Zethus's represent local opinion, which I suspect they do, then Trebbio's a dead man walking, and I'd swear he didn't murder anyone. And he asked me directly to help him. I can't buck that.'

'Help him how?'

'I don't know. But for a start I thought I might go and see the town officer. Explain the situation. According to Alcis at Zethus's, the guy isn't altogether on top of his job. If I can get him to see the potential problem here and how it might affect him then maybe we can exert a little pressure.'

Perilla was staring at me. 'What potential problem?' she said. 'And what kind of pressure? Corvinus, if you're intending to—'

'No big deal, lady,' I said. 'And at the end of the day it's in everyone's interests. I was just going to point out to the guy that, *pace* Toothy Alcis, there's about as much proof at present that Trebbio murdered Murena as wouldn't fill a salt spoon, that I was aware of the fact, and that if he let things go as they were going and the result was that Trebbio got himself bowstringed I would be having serious words with my very good friend in the praetor's office at Rome. After which the bugger would be lucky if he ended up running the urine collection service from the public latrines. Little truths like that.'

'What friend? Marcus, you don't have any friends in—'

'Sure I do. Caelius Crispus.'

'*Crispus*? He wouldn't do you that size of a favour!'

'Yeah, I know that and you know that. But the town officer doesn't know that, does he? And I'm betting that he'll be too shit-scared to check.'

'Corvinus, this is ridiculous! It's also pure naked black-mail, and totally unjustified! Why should you—'

'It's the easiest, quickest way.'

'To do what? You *are* going to interfere, aren't you? *Really* interfere.'

I said nothing.

'Marcus, I wish for once you'd just—'

'Look, lady. Believe me, if I don't get involved here then Trebbio's dead meat, and I know that whoever killed Murena — if anyone did kill him — it wasn't that poor sod. Only I could be wrong, and that'd be okay too, because then I'd know for sure I *was* wrong. You see? Now. All I need is the authority to gather evidence, right? One way or another, for or against, it doesn't matter so long as it's hard proof.' She was still frowning. 'You want me to forget the whole thing and spend the time instead strolling along the front looking at the yachts and ogling the girls, or can we just save a man's life here?'

She was quiet for a long time. Finally, she said, 'All right,

Marcus. You win. Not that I had any doubt you would, mind. But I still don't like it.'

'Yeah, well . . .'

'Anyway, why are you so sure that this Trebbio *isn't* the killer? Just because he claims not to be and has the cheek or perspicacity to ask you for help doesn't mean he isn't guilty after all.'

I grinned to myself: the fingers of her left hand had gone absently to the curl of hair at her temple, just above the hair band, and she was twisting it. She only does that when she's sleepy or interested in something and thinking. Perilla may pretend she's got no time for sleuthing, but she likes a puzzle as much as I do. She's just ashamed to admit it to herself, that's all. 'Trebbio, didn't know a thing about the murder until Alcis told him,' I said. 'Unless he's the best actor since Roscius I'd swear to that. Second, he didn't make any bones about admitting he'd gone to check his lines near the fish-farm last night, and if he had killed Murena then that'd be crucial. Third, I gave him an out and he didn't take it. It would've been easy enough for him to say he saw someone skulking along the beach the time of the murder. He didn't. Fourth . . .' I paused.

'Fourth?'

'He said he'd seen – or thought he'd seen – two lights at the fish-farm. One, fair enough: that would've been Murena himself. But no one carries two lamps. Sure, the guy was confused and he said himself he could be wrong, but two lamps means two people. And you don't show a light if you're planning to sneak up behind someone and push them into an eel tank.'

'So?'

'So if there were two lamps then it had to be murder. Or at least there had to be two people involved. And if the second guy was carrying a light he couldn't've minded being seen and recognised, not by Murena at least. Which meant that he had to be someone Murena knew.'

Long silence.

'Ah,' Perilla said.

I'd got her. Well, holidays in Baiae were boring anyway.

4

It worked like a dream. I had to compromise, sure – Trebbio was kept locked up in Baiae's tiny holding-cell off the market square – but after a fifteen-minute interview with an increasingly worried town officer I walked out with a letter empowering me to investigate Licinius Murena's death.

That day was the funeral, butting in would've been crass, and besides we were booked for a visit and dinner to one of Mother's friends who had a villa further down the coast, near Misenum. Pals of my mother's can be hit or miss, but this one and her husband were okay, even if they did bring the conversation round pretty smartly to their new yacht and keep it there. Priscus, I noticed, was unPriscusly quiet throughout; he has a tendency to assume that everyone he comes in contact with has a deep and abiding interest in recherché topics like Umbrian marriage customs and Phoenician silver mines in Spain. This time we hardly got a single bleat out of him the whole visit. I had the distinct impression that the old guy was sulking.

We stayed over. The next day as soon as we got back I sent Bathyllus round – equipped with the town officer's letter – to arrange a meeting the following afternoon with Licinius Murena's widow.

Okay; so we were in business. First stop was the fish-farm itself, half an hour before the scheduled meeting, to check out the basic facts. Zethus had said that Murena had been found by his manager. I couldn't remember the guy's name, if I'd ever heard it, but obviously he was the one to talk to.

Fish-farms are common everywhere along this part of the Campanian coast. Some of them – the ones belonging to ordinary private villas – are pretty small-time and hardly worth the name: a couple at best of simple concrete tanks formed by projecting berms closed off at the far end and with a coarse-meshed gate on the sea side that lets the small fry in so the captive fish can feed but can't get back to the open sea. Basically, they're just larders for keeping shellfish or the finned variety alive until it's wanted. Others – the commercial ones and the ones belonging to Baiae's richer punters – are a lot more complex: anything from a dozen to fifty huge tanks, subdivided to make finding and lifting the fish easier and prevent the more vicious buggers from snacking on their less aggressive pals. Some places even have tanks that're closed off from the sea altogether and kept supplied with fresh water from wells and springs inland: freshwater fish like barbels fetch prices you wouldn't believe, even here in the seafood gourmet's paradise where there's plenty of the other sort. Fish-fanciers can be pretty obsessive, too. The story goes that old Lucullus – a gourmet if there ever was one – had an underground channel cut through the mountain between his estate and the sea, just so he could keep his dinner fresh and swimming. Digging the channel cost more than the estate.

Mind you, the returns are pretty hefty. Fish costs an arm and a leg in Rome, especially in winter. Prawns and sea-urchins can be literally worth their weight in gold pieces, and a decent-sized tuna'll set you back the price of a slave. Serious stuff.

Murena's fish-farm was very definitely in the second category: a network of concrete tanks projecting out into the bay beyond the stretch of rocks at the far end of the beach where Trebbio must've had his lines, and for a good hundred yards along the coast the other way. There was a flanking wall cutting the place off from the shore and running up to a gate further inland, but it'd collapsed at the sea end to an easily climbable height and been left unrebuilt. Either Murena had been slovenly over repairs or he hadn't viewed theft as a serious danger. Whichever the reason was, for anyone who didn't want their presence officially known informal access to the farm from the sea side would be easy-peasy. One for the prosecution, although even with his head for booze I doubt if Trebbio could've managed it in the state he was in when he left the wineshop.

Under normal circumstances I'd've shinned over the wall to check out the practicalities, but this first time things had to be done formal. Besides, for the purposes of the interview I was wearing a decent mantle, and these things aren't designed for a scramble over brickwork. I followed the wall up the beach to the gate.

There was a slave on duty, naturally: places like that, you don't just wander in as the mood takes you. A young guy with a prominent Adam's apple. He stood up when he saw me coming.

'Yes, sir?'

'Marcus Valerius Corvinus,' I said. 'I've got an appointment with the Lady Gellia.'

'Villa entrance is further on, sir.'

'Yeah, I know. I wanted to have a word with the farm manager first. What's his name?'

'Ligurius, sir. No problem.' He unlatched the gate. 'He's probably in his office. Straight ahead and to the left as you go in. If he's not then any of the boys'll tell you where to find him.'

'Thanks, pal.' I paused. 'You on here nights as well, by the way?'

'No, sir. No one is. The gate's locked at sunset.'

'Keys?'

He hesitated, then said carefully, 'Uh . . . could I ask your reason for asking, sir?'

I took out the letter I'd brought with me. Not that the guy could read it – literacy isn't part of a gate-slave's job description – but it looked official and had the town officer's signature at the bottom.

He glanced at it, swallowed – investigations into a master's death always make the bought help uneasy, for obvious reasons – and nodded. 'Ligurius has one. He's responsible for locking the gate at sunset and opening up in the morning. Decimus Tattius. And the master himself, of course.'

'Who's Tattius?'

'The master's partner, sir.'

'Uh-huh.' I filed the name for future reference. 'Ligurius live on site?'

'No, sir. In the town.'

'There isn't a night-watchman?'

'Not necessary, sir. There's one up at the villa, but we've never had no trouble, and the villa being so close the place is safe enough.'

'Fine. Thanks, friend.'

I went in. It was more or less what I'd expected. To the right – between me and the sea – were most of the tanks, with here and there a slave walking along the berms with a long netted pole. As I watched, one of them slipped the net end of the pole carefully into the water then lifted it with a kicking fish trapped in the mesh. He laid the fish on the ground, checked the side of its head, measured it against a length of cord he kept round his waist, then put it gently back into the water.

Ahead and to the left, the gate-slave had said. Sure enough, set against the high boxwood hedge that probably screened the farm off from the villa gardens behind was what had to be the office building, open-fronted and with a stretch of stone counter, a bit like a free-standing shop. There were two guys inside, a tunic and a mantle, with their backs to me, talking. The mantle was wearing mourning. I went over, and when they heard me coming they turned round.

'Ah . . . I was looking for the manager,' I said. 'Guy called Ligurius?'

The tunic gave me a very careful once-over. 'I'm Ligurius,' he said quietly. Which, by the look of him, was his normal tone of voice. 'How can I help you?'

'The name's Marcus Valerius Corvinus,' I said. 'I've got an appointment with the Lady Gellia.'

The mantle – mid-forties, long-jowled and po-faced – had been giving me a once-over of his own, not a very friendly one, either. 'Oh, yes,' he said. He stretched out a reluctant hand. 'Titus Licinius Chlorus. Murena was my father, and I'm also the business's accountant.'

I shook. The hand was thin and parchment-dry with fingers like leather-wrapped bones. 'I'm, uh, sorry about the circumstances,' I said.

'So are we all.' That came out dry too, but there was something in the tone that jarred. Sarcasm, maybe. A cold bugger, this, and he was watching me closely, like I was a specimen. 'You asked for Ligurius. No doubt you wanted to know the background details to my father's death before you talked to us.' I didn't answer, but that didn't matter because he'd already turned to the manager. 'You won't need me for that. Apua, bring Valerius Corvinus up to the house when he's finished, will you?'

'Certainly,' Ligurius said. I glanced at him. Interesting: the voice had been quiet like before, but there was no forelock-tugging tone to it, and no 'sir' tacked on the end. The guy wasn't wearing a freedman's cap, either. Freeborn, then, and careful that people knew it. And what was this 'Apua'? I doubted if someone like Ligurius merited the three names, and in any case Apua was one I hadn't heard before. The word meant 'anchovy'. Maybe it was a nickname.

'We'll see you later, Corvinus,' Chlorus said.

'Sure.'

He left. Ligurius and I stood looking at each other. He was about the same age as Chlorus, but a good head shorter: no more than five four, spindly as a hazel stick and balding. Not the sort of guy who stood out in a crowd.

'Now,' he said. 'You'll want to see where it happened. Follow me.'

We walked towards the top line of tanks, then for twenty or thirty yards along the curve of the first row. Finally, Ligurius stopped.

'This is it,' he said.

I looked down into the water, and the hairs rose on my neck . . .

There must've been dozens of the brutes, five feet long if they were an inch and the thickness of my thigh, stacked under the water to within a foot of the surface like rolls of cloth in a draper's shop. As I watched, the one nearest me moved, sliding his long belly across the tops of his pals like he and they were greased. I caught the glint of a wicked eye and a flash of teeth bigger than belonged by rights on any fish.

'Almost fully grown,' Ligurius said. 'Another month or so and they'll be ready.'

My gut turned. 'You're still going to sell them?'

He shrugged. 'It's not my decision, but why not? There's a lot of money tied up in these beauties.'

Yeah, and I'd bet that the fact they'd breakfasted on their erstwhile owner wouldn't harm the sale price, either. You'd think covering that up would be the natural thing to do, but you'd be wrong: like I say, where morays that've eaten human flesh are concerned there's always some weirdo who's prepared to pay extra for quality.

Ligurius moved so he was standing beside me, looking down; like we were next to a grave, which in a way I suppose we were. 'I found him in the tank when I did my morning check,' he said. 'Or what was left of him. I wouldn't've known at all but for the mantle.'

Jupiter, the guy was calm enough! That might just be how he was made, sure, but I had the distinct impression that losing his boss even under these circumstances hadn't cracked him up unduly. Which was interesting.

'What time do you pack in for the day?' I asked.

'Sunset. I lock the gate behind me when I go. The farm's still accessible from the villa, though, of course. The perimeter wall goes round both.'

'I understand Murena made a habit of coming down here alone of an evening.'

'That's right. With a bag of scraps from dinner. He liked to watch them feed.'

Gods! I shut that image out of my mind. 'Could it have been an accident?'

He sucked on a tooth for a long time before replying. 'It's possible. Never mind the fish, once he was in the tank it would've been difficult for him to get out. He couldn't swim, and there was no one around that time of the evening to hear him shouting. If he shouted at all.'

'Why shouldn't he?'

'He'd been getting fainting fits recently. He could've been unconscious when he hit the water.'

I felt my eyebrows rise. 'Fainting fits?'

'So I believe, although I can't vouch for it personally. He always looked healthy enough to me. You'd have to ask his doctor.'

Was I wrong, or was there a certain woodenness of expression there? More than usual, that is. And Toothy Alcis had mentioned a doctor. . .

'Who would that be, now?' I said.

'His name's Diodotus. He has a practice in town.'

'Okay.' I very carefully didn't look at him. 'So what about . . . not an accident?'

Pause; *long* pause. 'That I wouldn't care to comment on,' he said at last. 'Perhaps you'd better talk to the family.'

Yeah; right. And the woodenness was still there, with bells on. There were things the guy was obviously not saying, even by implication, and I was beginning to get a prickle at the top of my spine. 'They would be who, exactly, now?' I said. 'I've got names for the Lady Gellia and the son who just left, Titus Chlorus. Who else is there?'

'The younger son's Nerva. Aulus Nerva. Then there's a daughter. Real name's Licinia, naturally, but she's always been called Penelope.'

'Any of them Gellia's kids?'

He almost smiled, but not quite; no more than a twitch of the lips. 'No. Gellia's younger than any of them. The boss married her after his first wife died.'

Had there been just a smidgeon of hesitation before the last word? I wouldn't've put serious money on it, mind, but that's how it came across. And I was still getting the poker face.

'How about the partner?' I said. 'What was his name? Tattius?'

But Ligurius had already turned and was walking back towards the office. 'I'm just the hired help, Corvinus,' he said over his shoulder. 'If you want any more information you'll have to get it from the family. If you're done with me – and I can't really tell you anything else – then I'll take you up there now.'

I followed him, thinking hard.

Yeah, well: accident it may still have been, but I'd met one of the sons and the manager so far, and if they were anything to go by I reckoned that as far as real, genuine grief at Murena's death was concerned the fish had the edge.

Things were shaping up very nicely.

5

*T*hem. *The family. We.*

    I'd been given enough hints and I ought to've realised, sure. My appointment was with the widow Gellia, not with the whole boiling, but there they all were, reclining or sitting in the villa's main atrium, stiff-faced as ancestral death masks. And watching each other closely out of the corners of their eyes, as if any moment one of them might jump up and decamp with the family silver.

I couldn't be wrong, no way; the body language and the general atmosphere made that clear from practically the moment I walked into the room. I knew, absolutely and irrevocably, that whatever the cause or causes of it might be all the members of the Murena family hated one another like poison.

No wonder they were all sitting here; not one of them trusted any of the rest further than they could spit.

Not that I suspected I was flavour of the month either, mind.

'Ah, Corvinus, so you've arrived.' That was the one I *had* met, Titus Chlorus. Stupid bloody observation, sure: the fish-farm was only two hundred yards away the other side of the gardens, and Ligurius had taken me to the door, but I could see the reason for it. The guy was seriously nervous. He wasn't the only one, either, by any means. Which was interesting.

'Yeah,' I said.

'Let me introduce you. My father's widow, Gellia . . .'

A hard-faced, brassy woman in a blonde wig and black eyebrows, early- to mid-thirties, sitting on a chair and sporting a mourning mantle that practically knocked my eyes out. She gave me a frozen nod.

'. . . sister Penelope . . .'

In another chair to one side, slightly out of the circle. Odd. Early forties, probably, small and dumpy, 'matron' written all over her. Her white mantle wasn't a patch on Gellia's, and although she didn't look exactly slovenly she clearly didn't take much trouble over her appearance. She was the only one of the four, though, who was composed. Small, neat hands with only one ring on the engagement finger, resting motionless on the chair arms.

'. . . and my brother, Aulus Nerva.'

The youngest of the three siblings, probably mid-thirties. Like Chlorus, he was reclining on a couch. His mourning mantle and stubble didn't go well with the podgy lad-about-town face, overneat haircut and flashy signet ring. He was the only one of the four to be drinking. He raised his cup and, like Gellia, gave me the briefest of nods.

'Take a seat, Corvinus,' Chlorus said. 'Some wine?' He motioned to a slave standing by one of the side tables. I went over to the remaining couch and lay down. 'Now. Apua' – he corrected himself – 'forgive me, Ligurius, rather, will have told you about how he found my father, so we can skip that part if you don't mind, yes?'

' "Apua"?' I said.

Chlorus smiled. 'I'm sorry. It's a family nickname, one of my father's coining. Father was fond of nicknames.'

Murena the eel boss and Apua the anchovy manager. Right. Quite a sense of humour the old bugger must've had.

No doubt it creased them up when fish-farm owners got together and swapped anecdotes. I reached out and took the cup of wine the slave handed me.

'I understood the town officer already had someone in custody for killing my husband,' Gellia said. Nice enough voice, but there was a nasal twang to it that I reckoned could get wearing after a while. Five minutes would do me.

I couldn't complain about the actual comment, mind: straight to the point, no messing. The strange thing was that every eye in the room had zeroed in on her, and not with approval, either.

'Gaius Trebbio. Right,' I said. 'Only I have personal reasons for thinking he couldn't've done it.' Was it my imagination, or was there a general sharpening of interest? 'Besides, why should it be murder, lady? Why not an accident? I was told Licinius Murena had fainting fits.'

Gellia sat bolt upright in her chair. 'Who told you that?' she snapped.

Queer: me, if our positions had been reversed, I'd say an accidental death would've been better news than murder, and so, I'd bet, would ninety-nine per cent of the world's population. Gellia, though, seemed to take the suggestion as a personal insult. The strange thing was I had the impression that at least two of the other three weren't exactly taken with the suggestion either. With Penelope I couldn't tell. She just stared at Gellia with what looked like distaste and terminal boredom.

'Ligurius,' I said.

'Did he, now?' Chlorus said softly. I glanced at him. His eyes were on Gellia. 'Well, well. Bravo, Anchovy!'

Gellia ignored him. 'My husband,' she said, 'had several fancies about his health. That was all they were: fancies. For his age he was as strong as an ox.'

'That's not what Diodotus says,' Chlorus said mildly. 'Or, for that matter, I'm afraid, what you – I use the plural, note – have been telling us for the past few months.'

She went brick red, and for a moment her composure cracked. 'Just what do you mean by that, Titus?' she snapped.

'In fact, I can remember you yourself saying only four days ago—'

'*How dare you!*' Looking at her, I'd've said that Gellia was within a copper piece's-worth of throwing herself at Chlorus's throat. 'I never—'

'Oh, yes you did.' Chlorus was completely at his ease. 'I remember it distinctly. You told me four days ago, when I called round about the cost of repairs to Number Three Tank, that Father had taken a giddy turn after breakfast, and you were quite concerned. There's no point in denying it now, Gellia. That will do no good at all.'

'Hear, hear, Titus,' Nerva murmured. 'Don't you believe her, Corvinus. She always was a little liar, and now she's got Dad safely dead—'

Gellia whirled round. '*Aulus, you complete—*'

I held up a hand. 'Lady? Gentlemen?' Shit; what was I into here? Revelations were one thing, but at this galloping rate there'd be blood on the tiles before we'd even started. 'Maybe we could keep this reasonably amicable, okay?'

Gellia subsided. Fancy wig or not, made up to the eyeballs or not, she was no looker in herself, and a complexion that currently would've given a beetroot a run for its money didn't help things much, either. She took a deep breath. 'I'm sorry, Valerius Corvinus,' she said, cut-glass tones back in spades. 'What must you think of us?'

'In your case that should be pretty obvious, I'd imagine,' Nerva said. 'And he'd probably be right.'

Gellia ignored him, but her colour heightened. 'You have some questions,' she said stiffly to me. 'Perhaps you could ask them.'

'Ah . . . okay.' I cleared my throat. Maybe we'd better do this formal at that: it was probably safer. I felt like a kid poking at the workings of a military catapult: the slightest mis-prod and the thing would go off. 'The night your husband died. I understand he took a bag of scraps down to the farm to feed the fish.'

'Yes. He did that every evening. He was quite fond of the brutes, the gods know why.'

'Right. What time would that be?'

'An hour or so after sunset, after we'd finished dinner. That was when he usually went.'

'He was pretty well normal at the time? Nothing unusual?'

'Not at all. He was rather upset, as it happens. By events earlier in the day.' She smiled unpleasantly, and her eyes rested on Nerva. I glanced at him. He was glaring at her with complete loathing.

'Ah . . . what events would these be, now?' I said.

'Perhaps you'd do better to ask Aulus.'

I looked at Nerva and got a stare blank as a marble statue's. I waited. Nothing. Well, we'd get there eventually, no doubt. I turned back to Gellia. 'And you didn't realise he hadn't come in again?' I said.

'No. I went off to be bed shortly afterwards. We have separate bedrooms.'

'What about the house slaves?'

'Lucius was a late owl. He enjoyed the dark. Sometimes he'd take a walk along the beach before he went to bed, and the slaves were ordered not to wait up. He was very considerate that way.'

'No one else missed him?' I looked at Chlorus.

'None of us lives here Corvinus,' he said. 'We didn't know Father was dead until Gellia' – he smiled at her – 'sent to tell us the next day. She was the only one present at the time of Father's death.' He paused, and then said carefully, 'Of the family, that is.'

Gellia shot him a vicious look but said nothing.

'There was someone else in the house?' I said.

'No, of course there wasn't,' Gellia said tightly, her eyes still on Chlorus. 'Barring the slaves.'

'You're sure?' Nerva muttered. 'No doctors, for instance?'

The lady's glare flashed back to him, but this time she didn't speak.

We were on sensitive ground here. The reason was obvious: Chlorus and company, or he and his brother at least, because it would seem that Penelope was staying out of things, suspected that their stepmother was having an affair with this doctor and that the pair of them were responsible for Murena's death. Not all that likely, on the face of it, not from what I'd heard so far, anyway: common sense said Gellia would hardly invite a lover round for a nightcap with her husband at home, especially if she intended to stiff Murena before they turned in for the night. On the other hand, this was Baiae, and morals were looser in the fleshpots of the south. Common sense, in Baiae, didn't always feature. The murder aside, it was a big villa. I wondered how far apart their separate bedrooms were and what were the chances of interruption.

There again, there was a lot of mud-slinging going on here. Far too much for on-the-spot assessment.

'Fine,' I said. Let's get back to something we knew about. Or at least something there didn't seem to be much argument over. I'd given Nerva his chance, and if he didn't want to take it then that was up to him. 'So Murena was, ah, "upset" when he went down to the fish-farm? By events earlier in the day?'

Silence; *long* silence. Chlorus coughed and glanced sideways at Nerva. If looks could kill then the one Nerva was giving Gellia would've fried the lady to a crisp.

'Yes,' she said. She looked back at Nerva and smiled. Then she said slowly, 'He had had a terrible argument with Aulus, you see. Just before dinner. Isn't that so, Aulus?'

Nerva sat up straight on his couch and tried a smile of his own. It didn't work. 'It wasn't an argument,' he said. 'I was just—'

'It sounded like an argument to me. I could hear the raised voices all the way from the study,' Gellia said. 'Gambling debts again, was it? Or one of your business schemes? Lucius wouldn't tell me.'

Nerva had coloured up. 'What we talked about – *talked* about – had nothing to do with my father's death!'

'Possibly not.' Gellia's eyes came back to me, and she smiled again. 'However, the fact remains that you were closeted with him for a good half-hour and you parted on *most* unpleasant terms. That's quite enough for me.'

'I was gone long before he was killed!'

'Of course you were.' Gellia sniffed. 'In such a temper, too. I was almost frightened.'

Nerva turned away. I heard him murmur 'Bitch!' into his wine cup.

'Of course, Corvinus,' Gellia carried on sweetly, ignoring him, 'Aulus isn't the only one in the family to have money problems. Titus here has a daughter getting married in three months' time, little Hebe, quite a society affair, and now with poor Lucius dead as the eldest son he can easily afford to—'

'That's enough!' Chlorus was on his feet. Cold fish or not,

he was as angry as his brother. 'Gellia, you'll stop this . . . this *ridiculous*—'

'There's no need to get excited, dear. I'm just apprising Valerius Corvinus of the facts.'

'True enough, Titus,' Nerva said. 'Dowries come pretty expensive. Especially in Hebe's case.'

I looked from one to the other. Gods. Forget a three-way ball-game; I felt like I was watching one of those free-for-alls in the arena where the aim is to end up still breathing when everyone else is a bloodied corpse on the sand. We'd got way beyond ordinary family sniping and backbiting here, and in nothing flat, what was more. It was almost as if the three of them had had their knives ready-whetted, and just been waiting for the chance to plant them. The accusations might be veiled, sure, for the most part, but they were accusations none the less, made deliberately with one eye on me and with a cool viciousness that had nothing to do with simple point-scoring. This was for real.

The only member of the group who didn't seem to be playing the game was dumpy Penelope. She hadn't spoken or even moved since Chlorus had introduced her, and she'd been watching the proceedings from her chair on the side-lines with an expression of complete contempt. Now she turned to me.

'As you can see, Corvinus,' she said mildly, 'we're a very close, loving family. We all thought the world of Father, and his death has come as a terrible shock to all of us.'

That stopped the other three in mid-flow, and they all turned to glare at her. Nerva set down his cup.

'You hated his guts,' he said brutally.

'Yes.' She nodded. Her tone didn't change. It was completely matter-of-fact. 'Yes, you're quite right. I hated him and I always will. In that I'm no different from the rest of you, but at least I admit it. Whoever killed Father, he only got what he deserved. I'm glad he's dead and I hope he rots in hell.'

'Penelope!' Gellia snapped. 'You'll take that back!'

'No I won't.' She stood up. 'Now if you'll excuse me I'll be getting off home. A pleasure to have met you, Valerius Corvinus.'

She left. We stared at each other in silence. Finally, Chlorus cleared his throat. 'You'll have to forgive my sister,' he said. 'She's . . . naturally, she's upset, very upset by Father's death, as we all are. And I hope I don't need to tell you that there's absolutely no truth in—'

'Right.' I stood up too. The hell with more questions; my brain was whirling, I felt faintly nauseated, and all I wanted to do was get away and think. 'Well, maybe I should be going myself. Unless there's anything else you can tell me?' I hoped not; I *really* hoped not: I'd had enough of this vicious shower to last me until the Winter Festival, and then some.

Their relief was palpable; obviously, after Penelope's little outburst, a truce was in progress.

Nerva grunted, picked up his wine cup and took a hefty swig. 'That's all, Corvinus,' he said.

'Yes. I'm sorry.' Gellia gave me a brittle, company-manners smile, as if the four-way spat had never been. 'I'm afraid we know little more about Lucius's death than you do. If we can help in any way in future, of course, then please don't hesitate to ask.'

Nerva grunted again.

'I'll show you out,' Chlorus said.

6

Bathyllus was outside the door when I got back, doing something to the knocker involving a small brush and the contents of a pottery jar. He turned round, brush poised.

'Good afternoon, sir,' he said. 'Did you have a pleasant morning?'

'It was interesting.' I climbed the steps. 'Any chance of a cup of wine?'

'Certainly, sir. I'll bring it out at once.' He laid the brush and jar down. The jar was half-full of a thick honey-coloured gunk that even at that range was playing hell with my sinuses. Not normal brass polish, that was sure. And you didn't paint doorknockers.

'Just out of curiosity, Bathyllus,' I said. 'What're you doing here, exactly?'

'Painting the doorknocker, sir.'

'Ah . . . right. Right.'

'It's in the nature of an experiment. A mixture for preserving the shine on outside brasswork involving naphtha, pine resin, gum arabic and various other substances.'

'That so, now?'

'Indeed. Did you realise that brass exposed to the elements will only retain its full shine for seven or eight hours after polishing?'

'No, I can't . . . say that I did.'

'Most unsatisfactory. And that's not taking actual physical contact into consideration. On the other hand, applying a protective coating of this mixture once a month will extend that to a whole day, probably more. In theory, at least.'

'Really?' Jupiter on a bloody tea-tray! I wished I hadn't asked now. Meton's obsession was food, which was bad enough but understandable. Cleaning substances were something else. Only Bathyllus could get orgasmic over metal polish. 'That's . . . that's pretty good, Bathyllus.'

'Mind you, there are problems. I'm not completely sure about the proportions of terebinth oil to resin, and the drying rate is not all that I'd wish. Perhaps—'

'Fine, fine,' I said. Bathyllus doesn't go on these jags often, but when he does encouraging him is not a good idea. 'I'll take your word for it, little guy. Just go and fetch that cup of wine, okay?'

'Very well, sir.' He was looking definitely unchuffed.

'Is Perilla around?'

'She's in the garden, sir. With your mother.'

'Great.' I reached past him for the doorhandle. 'In that case I'll . . .'

. . . at which point my brain caught up with the rest of me.

Slowly, I relaxed my grip. Nothing happened; I was still holding the knob like my fingers were glued to it. Which, in fact, they were.

'This is, uh, one you prepared earlier, right?' I said.

Bathyllus cleared his throat. 'I did just tell you, sir. About the drying rate.'

Bastard. I unprised my fingers, which wasn't easy. 'Bathyllus . . .'

'Yes, sir?'

'Watch my lips. Experiment over. The rest of that gunk goes out now.'

'Very well, sir. If that's how you feel.' He sniffed. 'I'll fetch a cloth and some hot water.'

'You do that. And if I don't have my right hand back as was within the next ten minutes then you, sunshine, are hamburger. Clear?'

That got me another sniff as he exited. Bugger; a threat like that from any other slave-owner would've had the bought help pissing in their sandals. Maybe I should re-read the manual.

The garden was quite a feature of the villa: Lucia D, who owned the place, was a sucker for flowers and greenery in general, and there must've been a dozen big beds, easy, laid out in a diamond shape round a central pergola with a trellised vine growing up it.

'So, Marcus, how did your meeting go?' Perilla asked.

'Like a refight of Cannae. The house slaves're probably still mopping the blood off the floor.' I kissed her, pulled up the third of the pergola's wicker chairs and set the wine cup Bathyllus had filled for me on the ground. 'Afternoon, Mother. Where's Priscus?'

'I haven't the slightest idea.' Mother twitched a fold of her impeccable mantle irritably into place. 'He *said* he was off to visit that oil-lamp friend of his, but that was hours ago. He's been acting very strangely of late: "shifty" is the word I'd use. Personally I wouldn't put too much credence in the statement.'

'Ah . . . right. Right.' Hell; what was the mad old buffer playing at? Still, it wasn't my concern. Or I hoped it wasn't. I'd got enough problems of my own at present.

'How do you mean, "a refight of Cannae"?' Perilla said.

'They were at each other's throats from the moment I walked in. Serious stuff, too. They all think it was murder

and they were all trying like hell to persuade me that one of
the others had done it. Me, I wouldn't be surprised if one of
them wasn't right. If we want suspects apart from Trebbio
we've got them by the bucketful. With relatives like that the
poor bugger was lucky to last as long as he did, and
the eels're pussy-cats in comparison.'

'But that's terrible!'

'Yeah.' I took a swig of the wine. 'Look, Mother, I'm going
to need your help, okay?'

'With what, dear?'

'Background information. I've got four names.' I ticked
them off on my fingers. 'The widow, Gellia. Elder son Titus
Chlorus. Younger, Aulus Nerva. Plus the daughter. She goes
by the name of Penelope. They'll do for starters. You know
anything about them? In the dirty linen way, I mean.'

Mother drew herself up. 'Marcus, dear, I do *not* listen to
gossip! And I certainly do not repeat it.'

I grinned; sure, and I was Tiberius Julius Caesar
Augustus. Mother might be a very sharp lady, but she'd been
holidaying in Baiae on and off for years and she'd taken to
the town like a fish to water. Baian society is all about gossip.
After all, if you can't amuse yourself by tearing a friend's
reputation to shreds over the canapés and honey wine then
what's the point in coming to the place?

'Steel yourself,' I said.

'Well, if you think it really will help.' She ducked her head
to hide a smile. Like I say, my mother's a smart cookie.
Token protests are one thing, but hypocrisy's another, and
she's a natural Baian through and through. 'The daughter I
know nothing whatsoever about; she obviously doesn't mix
in society. Chlorus is some sort of financial lawyer.' Yeah,
that made sense: he'd told me himself that he was the farm's
accountant, and he'd got 'lawyer' written all over him.

'Rather a dry stick, I understand. Unlike his wife, who is' – she hesitated – 'completely the opposite.'

Uh-huh. 'Yeah? Who's she?'

'Her name's Catia. I've met her several times. *Not* the world's greatest brain, but with her looks and interests she doesn't have to be.' Miaow. 'I gather their daughter is marrying young Manlius Torquatus in the autumn. Quite a coup, although the Manlii Torquati aren't what they were these days, financially speaking.'

I sipped my wine. Right; that fitted in with what I knew, too. Although the Licinii were a good family, as far as pedigree went they weren't by any means in the Manlii Torquati bracket; at least, Chlorus's branch wasn't. Gellia had mentioned (mentioned, hell: she'd thrown it in my face!) that he was strapped for cash. He would be: an engagement like that would mean a heavy dowry, and I'd bet under the circumstances the Torquati, being short of a copper piece or two themselves, would drive a hard bargain.

'Go on,' I said.

'The second brother, Aulus Nerva, has quite a reputation locally.' Mother was frowning; she was enjoying this, I could tell, despite the protest. When she and my father were married he might've been the career politician of the family, but where marshalling facts and arguing from them was concerned Mother could run rings round him any day of the month. Nowadays she rarely got the chance to practise. 'Or two reputations, rather. He thinks of himself as a shrewd businessman, and he's partly right. Certainly, where business is concerned he's no fool. On the other hand, he *is* a compulsive risk-taker, and not particularly concerned with the moral aspects of a deal either. "Flashy" is a good term.' She paused. 'He's also very much the society playboy, especially where gambling and women are concerned. And – which may interest you, Marcus, with your fascination for soiled laundry – he's rumoured to have more than a brother-in-law's fondness for Catia, which she reciprocates.'

I leaned back. 'Is that right, now?'

'I don't know about "right", dear. You asked for gossip and gossip is what you are getting.'

'Fair enough. What about Gellia?' This was the big one. If we were talking *cui bono* here then Murena's widow was right at the front of the queue.

Mother was obviously aware of that as well, because she took her time before answering. 'Gellia is . . . quite sad, in a way,' she said slowly.

My eyebrows rose. 'Sad' wasn't the word I would've chosen for that lady; not even in the top hundred. But then Mother didn't use words lightly. 'Yeah?' I said. 'You care to amplify?'

'Certainly. You get women like her often in Baiae; men sometimes, but these are rarer. She's common – I'm speaking in Baian social terms, you understand – she has no style, which would go a long way towards making up for her poor looks, she has a vindictive streak a yard wide, and, worst of all, she's aware of none of this. She thinks she's a *femme fatale* but isn't, nowhere near it, despite the fact that she is breaking her neck to be one. Which is why she's so friendly with Catia, who is.'

'Uh-huh.' Well, I'd just have to take that assessment on trust. Not that I doubted it was valid: I'd a lot of respect for Mother's opinion, especially where people were concerned. 'How did she get on with her husband?'

'Reasonably well, under the circumstances. As far as I know, at any rate.' She straightened a fold in her mantle again. 'Of course, she's much younger than he was, and in Baiae that leads to the obvious result.'

'Lovers?'

'She is very careful; slightly surprising, given her character, but then Murena had a certain reputation of his own for holding old-fashioned values, and seemingly he controlled the purse-strings. Kept quite a tight grip on them, what's more. Matters may not have gone beyond simple flirting, but I have heard that she's rather involved at present with a man by the name of Aquillius Florus. He's a friend of Aulus Nerva's, and out of much the same mould. If you're interested.'

A friend of Nerva's, eh? Well, that explained why that particular handful of mud hadn't been thrown, by one of the brothers anyway. I filed the name for future reference. 'Not this doctor guy? Diodotus?'

'Diodotus is another name I've heard mentioned, yes,' Mother said cautiously. 'Although not so often, and not with much . . . authority. Certainly he's a good-looking young man, and of course an intimate of the family. Very popular with the better class of patient. He has quite a successful practice near the town baths.'

Right. And if we were picking and choosing with an eye to a murder accusation then the doctor/wife combination would score every time. Presumably both Chlorus and Nerva – or Nerva, at least – would've known about this Florus character, but as an accomplice the doctor had the better mileage. No wonder his was the name that'd been dropped. I'd have to find out more on Florus, though.

'What about Murena himself?' I said. 'You know anything about him?'

'Not a lot, dear. Apart from in connection with Gellia. He didn't go into society much; as I said, in many ways he was quite strait-laced, a businessman rather than a *bon viveur*. Not a spender, either. *Quite* the wrong type to be the subject of gossip.'

'He, uh, was planning to build a hotel. On the edge of town, on what was the Juventius estate.'

'Was he, indeed? How unusual. Well, there I'm afraid I can't help you.'

'What about his partner? A guy called Tattius?'

'Not a name I'm familiar with either, Marcus. I'm sorry. I know nothing about the business side of things.' She stood up. 'Now, if you've finished with me I'm afraid I must be going. Titus promised to take me to one of the jewellers in Fountain Street this afternoon, then on for a chat with Cornelia Gemella, but since he seems to have forgotten all about it I shall go by myself. You really will have to have another word with him. He's been behaving most peculiarly.'

'Ah . . . right,' I said. Bugger. 'Yeah, I'll do that. When I see him.'

She sniffed. '*That* may not be for some time, on present showing. Goodness knows what he and that friend of his have to talk about all day. I'd've thought that even Siculan oil-lamps had a very limited conversational value.'

We watched her go. Perilla was looking thoughtful.

'It is strange,' she said. 'About Priscus. Vipsania's right; he's scarcely ever around at the moment. She's right about the shiftiness, too, when he is here.'

'Yeah, well.' I grinned. 'Me, I'd bet the old guy's finally hit his teens head-on sixty years down the line. Only for the gods' sake don't tell Mother.'

She whipped round and stared at me open-mouthed. 'He has *what*?'

'Priscus has discovered the joys of booze and loose company. My guess is that he's only using his oil-lamp pal as an excuse for bunking off to a wineshop somewhere. Or maybe something worse.' I told her about the chat in Priscus and Mother's bedroom.

'Marcus, you are not serious!' She was looking at me like I'd just told her the guy was screwing ducks. 'You *are* serious! Holy Juno! *Priscus?*'

'Call it a midlife crisis if you like, lady. Or in his case maybe even that's pushing things. The gods know what triggered it, but there we are.'

'What are you going to do about it?'

Now it was my turn to stare. '*Me?* Why the hell should I do anything?'

'You're head of household. It's your duty.'

'Jupiter on bloody wheels, Perilla! The guy's twice my age and in possession of all his marbles.' I stopped; be fair, Corvinus. 'Well, some of his marbles. If he wants to spend a little quality time in wineshops and so on then that's his affair. Besides, I don't know for sure that that's what he's doing. He may be round at his friend's house discussing—'

'Siculan oil-lamps. That's nonsense and you know it.'

I sighed. 'Yeah. Maybe I do. Okay, I'll talk to the old bugger. But if there's any grounding to be done or strips to be torn off that's Mother's job. Leave it for now. What about my suspects list?'

'What about your suspects list?'

'Come on, Perilla! This is important!'

'All right. Go ahead if you must.'

Not exactly bouncing with enthusiasm, but you had to take what you got. And, as I say, the lady had a reputation for disinterest to keep up. I settled back. 'Okay. My count to date is five. Which, coincidentally, is the number of people I've talked to today and doesn't include the doctor. Call it six. With an option on this Florus guy. Seven.'

'Marcus—'

I ignored her. 'Take Gellia first. The motive's obvious, the oldest in the world. She's half her husband's age, she's got an eye for the men and she's on a reasonably tight leash financially. She could sit and wait for the old guy to pop his clogs, but she isn't getting any younger and Baiae isn't exactly a place that's conducive to nurturing the old-fashioned wifely virtues.'

'Your vocabulary is improving.'

'Shut up lady. She also has the means – that's her doctor pal – and the opportunity.'

'How is the doctor the means? That's assuming, of course, that he'd have anything to do with it, which is a moot point in itself.'

'Ligurius – that's the manager – told me that Murena had been suffering from fainting fits recently. Gellia was pretty upset when I mentioned them and she tried to deny it, but Titus Chlorus confirmed. Okay; so let's say Murena's tame doctor, at Gellia's suggestion, had been feeding him something that made him black out at times. All it'd take would be for one of the pair, Gellia or the doctor, to wait their opportunity to push him into the eel tank and blame it on an accident. Or maybe even simpler. The guy wasn't subject to fits at all, they were a complete invention. Neither Ligurius nor Murena's sons've ever seen him taking one of them, so the only proof would come from Gellia or the doctor. But they would provide a pretty good excuse subsequently for an unfortunate accident, wouldn't they?'

'Yes, but, Marcus, you said yourself that Gellia denied her husband had the fits. Surely if she had killed him she would've confirmed it.'

'That's fine so long as there's no suspicion of murder, lady. Only by the time I spoke to Gellia and company there was, and it was a whole new ball-game. Trebbio had been arrested for a start, and I'd sent round my letter from the town officer authorising me to investigate the death. Chlorus is a smart cookie, and he doesn't like Gellia at all. As things were, her story about the fits, the way Murena died and the rumours linking her and the doctor would all combine to point the finger pretty convincingly. Gellia may've started out nurturing an "accident" verdict, but now she has to discount it for her own good; it wouldn't be safe for her to do otherwise, not with her step-family out to see her nailed. And, naturally, if she did come down on the side of murder she'd have to finger someone else in her turn. Which brings me to Chlorus and Nerva.'

'Hmm.' Perilla was twisting a lock of hair. 'Go on.'

'Nerva's the most likely prospect, barring Gellia. The evidence is circumstantial, sure, but he had a row with his father over money the day he died. At least, Gellia suggested it was over money, and he didn't deny it. Chlorus's motive's the same. Gellia mentioned his daughter's marriage too, and he's obviously hard up for cash to meet the dowry. With Murena dead they'll inherit a packet when they most need it; it's as simple as that. As far as opportunity's concerned either of them could've climbed over the wall at the beach end and killed the guy without anyone being any the wiser.'

'Marcus, dear, I'm sorry, but this is all very thin.'

She was telling *me*? 'Yeah, I know that. We're just on the nursery slopes here. Still, it's a start. And you weren't over at the villa, lady, you didn't see that crowd. There was a lot of nervousness about, and a lot of hatred. Murena wasn't liked, not by his family, anyway. Don't knock that for a motive, either.'

'What about the daughter? Penelope, did you say?' She frowned. 'Why Penelope, incidentally?'

'I didn't ask. Maybe she just doesn't like being called Licinia. That wouldn't surprise me; she hated her father like poison.'

Perilla glanced at me sharply. 'How on *earth* do you know that?'

'She told me straight out. Made quite a thing of it. It could've been a double bluff, sure, but it still puts her on the list.'

'All right, Marcus. That makes four. Five counting the doctor, and presumably you'd lump the phantom Florus in with Gellia. Who's the seventh?'

'Ligurius. He found the body.'

'Oh, terrific! Motive? Means? Opportunity?'

I shrugged. 'None of them as yet. Apart, maybe, from a silly nickname Murena gave him. He seems to've had a quirk that way, the old man. Still, Ligurius is the fish-farm manager, and Murena was killed at the fish-farm. And he didn't seem too cut up about losing his boss, either. I've got the rest down so why not Ligurius? Make it a full bag.'

'That is *not* a reason to suspect him.'

'Yeah, well, you can't—' I stopped. Bathyllus was bringing a man up the path: a tall guy in a Greek mantle. 'Who's that?'

'I've no idea. One of Vipsania's friends, perhaps.'

'Mother's in town. Bathyllus would've sent him away.' Now the man was nearer I could see he was in his late twenties, maybe early thirties. Tall, well-built, olive skin, jet-black curly hair and a nose with a bridge so straight you could use it to draw lines. Greek, for sure; real Greek, not south-Italian-local, and good-looking enough to've modelled for a temple pediment Apollo.

'Good afternoon, Valerius Corvinus,' he said, holding out his hand. 'I'm sorry to disturb you. My name's Diodotus. I was Licinius Murena's doctor.'

7

Well, for someone who'd just lost a patient Diodotus seemed pretty relaxed about things. Mind you, the responsibilities of the modern doctor stop short at dosing the customer against a sudden attack of moray eels, so giving him the benefit of the doubt for the present where murder was concerned I supposed that was fair enough.

We shook.

'Pull up a chair,' I said. 'This is my wife Perilla.'

'A pleasure to meet you, madam.' Soft-spoken, serious, not much of a smile – from the looks of him I didn't think he'd smile very often – but perfectly friendly and completely at his ease. Good vowels, too; we were speaking Latin, and by his accent he could've passed in Rome for one of the top Five Hundred, easy. Mother had said he had a successful social practice in Baiae, and I wasn't surprised. With these looks, that voice and that manner he'd have the wealthy matrons queuing up and panting. No wonder Gellia had been smitten.

Bathyllus was still hovering. 'You care for some wine?' I said.

'No, thank you. I scarcely touch it, and certainly not before sundown.' He sat. 'Please don't let me stop you, though.'

'Just the half jug, then, Bathyllus,' I said. The little guy bowed and moved off. 'Now.'

'I thought you might like to talk to me, Valerius Corvinus.'

'News travels fast.'

'In Baiae, certainly.' He shrugged; an elegant raising of the shoulder. 'In any case, I was paying a professional call in the neighbourhood and it'll save you a journey.'

'You have a lot of patients? Besides Licinius Murena, I mean?'

'Enough. Mostly minor digestive problems caused by an over-rich diet. Life in Baiae isn't exactly conducive to a healthy regimen, so much of my work is correcting the effects of over-indulgence. Or trying to correct it. Frequently the task is an uphill struggle.'

'I was told Murena suffered from fainting fits.'

I'd asked the question without signalling it just to see how he reacted. He didn't blink, but he did lean back in his chair and take his time answering.

'That's so,' he said cautiously.

'How severe?'

'Nothing to give serious cause for concern, and he was responding well to treatment, but all the same—'

'What was the treatment exactly?' Perilla said.

He turned to her politely. 'You have a knowledge of medicine, madam?'

'No. Just an interest in it.'

'I see.' The slight flaring of the nostrils suggested that taking an interest in medicine wasn't something the guy wholly approved of. Not where a layman was concerned, anyway. Laywoman, rather. I was glad it'd been Perilla who'd asked the question, not me. 'Well, then. The problem arises, as does every illness, from a systemic imbalance; in this case, a superfluity of blood rushing into the brain at times and driving out the vital spirit, what we call the *pneuma*, which is the source of consciousness. A mild programme of regular bleeding is the most effective treatment, together with gentle exercise and a light diet of seafood and vegetables plus an avoidance of red meat and the heavier wines. That was what I prescribed.'

'I see,' Perilla said. 'Thank you.'

'You're very welcome.'

Jupiter on skates! 'Would it have been possible for Murena to have had one of these fits the night he died?' I said.

The grey eyes came back to me. 'Yes. Of course. Perfectly possible. But as I said the fits were not serious; hardly more than a slight dizziness which would disappear after a few minutes' rest. Murena would have had ample warning of an attack, certainly enough for him to find somewhere to sit or lie down in safety until the *pneuma* was restored.'

'That's not what Titus Chlorus said. Or implied, rather.'

That got me a level stare, and the grey eyes had turned frosty. 'Perhaps not, Corvinus,' he said. 'But there again, I'm not responsible for Chlorus's opinions, or indeed those of any of the Murena family. They are not doctors, and they may have . . . other reasons for saying what they do. I'm simply giving you the medical facts which you can accept or not just as you please.'

'Right. Right.' I shifted on the chair. 'And apart from the fits Murena was generally healthy, was he? For a man of his age?'

'Moderately so. He had a slight tendency towards dyspepsia, but not a developed one. And as I say that complaint is endemic to Baiae.'

'His widow said he was concerned about his health. More than usual, that is. Were you treating him for anything else?'

The frostiness was still there. 'Valerius Corvinus, I've already told you. I can't answer for any statements except my own. And there is such a thing as patient confidentiality, even when the patient is dead.' I waited. 'In any case, the practical answer to your question is no, apart from a simple standard dyspepsia mixture to be taken as required. I don't believe in treatment for treatment's sake, even when the patient or one of his relatives suggests it. Barring administering the regimen I've already described I took no other action.'

One of his relatives. Interesting expansion there. Maybe it meant nothing, but still . . .

Bathyllus had arrived with the wine. 'How about your relationship with the widow herself?' I said as he poured. 'Gellia?'

'How do you mean, "relationship"?' Forget frosty; the look he was giving me was straight off an Alp.

'You get on with her okay?'

Pause; *long* pause. Well, he was a smart guy; he must've heard the rumours, even if there was nothing in them. 'Gellia is . . . was . . . my patient's wife,' he said.

'And?'

I'd seriously annoyed him, I could see that. The eyes narrowed to slits and the nose lifted a good two inches. It was like being glared at down a ruler. Even so, he took his time answering. 'And nothing,' he snapped. 'Let me make one thing very clear, Valerius Corvinus. A doctor – any doctor who merits the name – ascribes voluntarily to a code of conduct. This includes an oath not to procure poison or an abortion, to work solely for the good of his patient and to abstain from the seduction of anyone, slave or free, in his patient's household. I am a doctor. Please remember the fact.'

Well, that was me told. But at least it was out in the open, whatever the truth of the matter was. It was time to smooth down a few ruffled feathers. 'Fair enough,' I said. 'Okay. Let's leave the medical side of things. What about Murena himself?'

'Again I have to ask you what you mean.' His voice was still icily polite. 'And to remind you what I said about confidentiality.'

'Understood. But you're local, I'm not, and you know the family. He was a businessman, right?'

'He was.'

'You know anything about the business side of things?'

'No. I'm not a businessman myself, in the general sense of the word. Licinius Murena never discussed anything with me except for his health. And if you expect me to—'

'No hassle, pal. I'm only interested in generalities. I could get them elsewhere, sure, but since you're here maybe you can help fill in a few details. That be okay?'

He gave a guarded nod. 'Possibly.'

'Great. Thanks.' Jupiter! We'd a real touchy bugger here! 'Murena had a partner, Tattius.'

'Decimus Tattius, yes.'

'He live locally?'

'I think he has a villa on the main road, about a quarter-mile inland from Murena's.'

'It's a long-established partnership?'

'Yes. As far as I know. I understand they were colleagues in Rome before Murena moved to Baiae permanently twenty-odd years ago. Political colleagues.' He was relaxing. Or at least the urbane politeness was back. I doubted if the guy ever let himself relax altogether; he had that uptight, preoccupied feel to him that you get with people who don't look past their jobs. 'He doesn't take a very active part in the business, though. That's largely a family concern.'

'Did Licinius Murena have a nickname for him?' That

was Perilla. Odd question, but then I'd told her about Ligurius and the lady's mind sometimes works in strange directions. I glanced at her curiously.

So did Diodotus, and his eyebrows went up. 'He did, as a matter of fact. He called him Oistrus. Why do you ask?'

'No particular reason. It's just that Marcus mentioned he had a habit of giving people nicknames. Thank you.'

Oistrus. 'Gadfly' in Greek. 'While we're on the subject of nicknames,' I said, 'how about the others? His family, I mean?'

'I don't see what relevance—'

'Just filling in background. Come on, pal, it can't do any harm.'

He was frowning. 'Very well. Gellia was the Butterfly. For, ah, obvious reasons. Aulus Nerva was Agyrtes.'

' "Scoundrel"?' Perilla said.

' "Vagabond" is better.' His lips twisted. 'Your Greek vocabulary is excellent, madam.'

'What about Titus Chlorus?'

He hesitated. I had the impression he might've balked if I'd asked the question, but Perilla was good at these things. 'Scythrops.'

Scowler. Good name for Chlorus. I grinned. 'The daughter. Penelope. Was he responsible for that one as well?'

'I couldn't really say.' Diodotus was still frowning. 'I would hardly have thought so, or not in the way you mean. It's not really a nickname as such, is it? But in any case we're verging too much on the personal here, certainly beyond my professional capacity. If you're finished I should be—'

'Murena was thinking of building a hotel,' I said. 'On the Juventius estate. You know anything about that?'

'I told you. We didn't discuss business.'

'Not even in general terms?'

He hesitated. 'He did mention it, once or twice. Just the bare fact, not in any detail.'

'I get the impression the idea isn't too highly thought of locally. Am I right?'

Another hesitation. 'It may cause certain . . . frictions, yes.'

'Who with?'

His brows came down. 'Corvinus, I came here to offer what help and information I could as Murena's doctor. Perhaps we're moving a little far from—'

'Please?' Perilla said.

'Very well.' He cleared his throat. 'Although this is really none of my concern, you understand, and I have patients to attend to this afternoon. Murena . . . it was felt that Murena's business interests should stop at fish-breeding. Tourists and tourism are another matter. There are already several businessmen in the town who operate in that area and who are . . . perhaps one could say a little upset at the prospect of having to compete with someone they view as an outsider.'

'Such as?' I said. 'Oh, come on, pal! I'm not asking you to tell me anything I couldn't find out from elsewhere.'

'The main one is a gentleman by the name of Philippus. Licinius Philippus.' Diodotus stood up suddenly. 'Now I really must be going. If there's anything more I can do for you, within the medical sphere—'

'*Licinius* Philippus?' I said. 'He's Murena's freedman?'

'Oh, yes. Indeed. But he was freed a long time ago, as a very young man. Now he's one of the richest men in Baiae.' He held out his hand. 'I'm delighted to have met you.' He nodded to Perilla. 'Madam.'

We watched him go.

'So, lady,' I said, when he'd disappeared back through the portico. 'What do you think?'

Perilla was twisting her hair. 'He's a very cold, precise person, isn't he? Very . . . serious-minded.'

'Yeah.' I sipped the wine. 'That was the impression I got. Probably a whizz at his job because he can't see far outside it. Which doesn't argue for a relationship with Gellia, does it?'

'Not very well. Or not on his side, rather, even without his disclaimer. I can see, though, how she'd find him attractive.'

I grinned. 'Is that so, now?'

'Oh, yes. Most women would. But, well, as far as any conspiracy to murder is concerned – if you're thinking along those lines – I suspect the influence would have to go the other way, with him being the motivating force. He'd be too . . . selfish to have it otherwise. And that isn't likely, is it? Why would Diodotus – Diodotus, not Gellia – want rid of Murena?' She tugged a stray fold of her mantle into place. 'Besides, he was quite correct: doctors have to be terribly careful to avoid any suspicion of scandal, especially in places like Baiae. Young good-looking ones above all. He certainly struck me as sincere and anxious to be helpful as far as he could.'

'Right.' Bugger. Still, what she'd said about him being no cat's-paw was a fair point; me, having seen the guy I'd tend to agree. And what little evidence we had that Diodotus and Gellia were an item hadn't exactly come from an unbiased source. Chlorus and Nerva had their own axes to grind. Apropos of which: 'These nicknames. What made you ask about them?'

'I don't know. Just a feeling. But I'm glad I did.' She was still twisting her hair. 'Licinius Murena doesn't seem to have been a very . . . *pleasant* person, does he, Marcus? Not in himself.'

'Uh-uh.' Not pleasant was putting it mildly; *bastard* – the general consensus so far – summed up the guy pretty well. 'He had Chlorus pinned, though, didn't he? And Nerva as well, from what I've seen of him. Vagabond's a good name. Whatever his faults, I'd bet Murena knew people.'

'What kind of man gives his sons nicknames like Scowler and Vagabond, Marcus? Not to mention calling his wife Butterfly?'

'All three fit, lady. From what I've seen of the trio, anyway. And they're not exactly a close family.'

'No, they aren't, are they?' She was still looking thoughtful. 'Quite horrendous, really. What about Gadfly? For the partner? What's his name, Tattius?'

I shrugged. 'Pass. I haven't met him yet.'

'Do you know anything about him at all?'

'Only what Diodotus told us.'

'That he was a former colleague of Murena's and wasn't directly concerned with the business. Yes. So why Gadfly? What's gadfly-ish about him?'

'Gods, Perilla, I don't know! There could be a dozen reasons for calling him that. And like I say I've never met the guy.'

'Perhaps you should, then.' She smiled. 'It's probably nothing, dear. Just a fancy. But it is curious.'

Yeah, now she came to mention it it was: I could see how the other names worked, after all. And the whole business angle was definitely one we still had to go into. This freedman of Murena's, Philippus, was certainly an oddity. Slaves freed young aren't all that common, to put it mildly; slaves're valuable commodities, part of their owner's capital, and it either takes them years to save enough to buy themselves out or they get their freedom as a reward for a lifetime of service, usually in the master's will when he personally has had everything out of them he's going to get and doesn't have a vested interest any more. And from what I'd heard of Licinius Murena I doubted if he'd been the kind of woolly philanthropist who'd do things any different. So how had this Philippus got his slap on the ear? Not to mention the nest-egg he'd need to bankroll a career in business? That was a question that needed answering, too.

'Right,' I said. 'First thing in the morning I'll—'

'Mmmaaa! Marcus, my boy! How are you today? Perilla, you're looking radiant.'

I glanced round. The wanderer had returned. Priscus was coming up through the garden from the direction of the side gate.

8

He was looking pretty radiant himself, in a snazzy new mantle. That would've been unusual enough – snazzy mantles and Priscus just didn't get on, or not past the first meal, anyway – but he'd also been freshly barbered. Scented, too: I could smell him even over the flowers in Lucia Domitilla's flower garden.

'Ah . . . hi, Priscus,' I said. 'How's it going?'

'Not bad. Not bad at all, thank you.' He sat down on the chair Diodotus had vacated.

'You, uh, have a nice chat with your friend? What's-his-name, the oil-lamp man?'

'Leonides? No, I'm afraid he was – mmmaaa! – out for the day. Some unexpected business in Puteoli. Still, it was a pity to waste the journey so I had a wander round the town instead.' He beamed at us like a louche myopic monkey. 'Fascinating. Quite fascinating. Especially that quaint little district behind the market square. Do you know, Marcus, Vipsania and I have been coming here for years and I never knew it existed?'

Yeah. Right; I could see how that might be, with Mother in charge. Baiae may be the playground of the idle rich, but even in that bracket tastes vary considerably and the old town behind the forum caters for most of them, legal and otherwise. Mostly after sunset, but the entrepreneurial locals being what they are some places stay open all day. 'Ah, is that so, now?' I said cautiously.

'Speaking of Vipsania, Priscus,' Perilla said, 'you know you were supposed to take her shopping this afternoon then on to Cornelia Gemella's?'

He blinked at her. 'Mmmaaa?'

'She went on her own. She was quite upset.'

'But that was tomorrow, surely.'

'Today,' I said. 'And upset's an understatement. You may live to see another sunrise, pal, but I wouldn't give odds.'

'How very unfortunate.' The old bugger was still blinking away like a stunned owl. 'I was certain it was tomorrow. She's already gone, you say? In the carriage, no doubt? Oh, tut!' He sighed. 'Well, there isn't much that I can do about it now, is there?'

'You could take the litter,' Perilla said.

'Oh, I don't think so. Gemella's place is well out in the country. It'd take hours. But to get back to the quaint little district I was telling you about, Marcus . . .'

Perilla stood up suddenly. 'I have things to do, dear,' she said. 'Perhaps you'd like to chat to Priscus on your own for a while. In private.'

Oh, shit. 'Uh . . . right. Right,' I said. 'Catch you later.' As she walked towards the house I reached for the jug Bathyllus had left, poured myself a belter and downed half of it at a gulp. I had a feeling I was going to need it here. 'Okay, Priscus,' I said. 'Confession time. Let's have the gory details.'

That got me the shell-shocked owl look again. 'I beg your pardon?'

'Look, cut it out. It's just us now, I'm no fool and you've

got beans to spill, so level. First off, you didn't get your dates mixed up, did you? You knew damn well you were supposed to take Mother jewellery-shopping today. And I'd bet a gold piece to a corn plaster you never went near your pal Leonides's.'

'Ah . . .'

'Now, personally I couldn't care less whether you worked your way through every wineshop and cathouse in Baiae' – Jupiter! – 'but after Mother's had your guts for bootlaces she'll rip out mine for an encore, and that's something I have a definite vested interest in. Understand?'

'Marcus, my boy, I assure you I didn't . . . I would never . . . mmmaaa! . . .'

'So let's just have it straight, right? No flannelling.'

He blinked at me for a good half-minute; seventy-plus or not, the image of a sulky teenager. Finally, he cleared his throat and said stiffly, 'I simply felt the urge this morning to have a shave and a haircut in one of the barber shops off the market square. Also to purchase a – mmmaaa! – new mantle at a draper's emporium which I had noticed yesterday and indulge in a short stroll. There was nothing wrong in any of these actions, I trust?'

'Priscus, a shave and haircut take an hour, max. Say the same for buying the mantle. That leaves several hours unaccounted for. Don't faff around.'

'I must say I – mmmaaa! – resent your tone. If I want to—'

'Resent it all you like, pal, but very shortly Mother's going to be back spitting blood, and this time as far as I'm concerned she can haul your liver out through your gizzard while I stand back and applaud. So give. What else happened?'

He fizzed for a bit. Then he said, 'If you must know, while I was having my – mmmaaa! – haircut I got into conversation

with a most charming gentleman in the next chair. A local
businessman. We had a very interesting chat about . . .
various things.'

'Such as?'

'It transpired that he had connections in the – mmmaaa! –
entertainment field.' Priscus blinked at me. 'Did you realise,
Marcus, that gambling halls are quite legal in Baiae?'

Uh-huh. Well, we were getting somewhere at last.
Gambling – proper gambling, as opposed to private wagers –
isn't strictly legal anywhere, barring at the Winter Festival,
but it's one of these things the authorities turn a very
substantial blind eye to, especially when kickbacks are
involved, which they usually are. And Baiae, being a holiday
place where the punters aren't short of a gold piece or two,
is a real hotspot. 'So this "charming gentleman" took you
somewhere and you lost your shirt, right?' I said. Well, it
could've been worse.

'Oh, no. Nothing like that. Although we did on his suggestion visit one of the establishments concerned in which he
happened to have a controlling interest. Located in, as I said,
that rather quaint old district behind the market square. It
was quite an eye-opener. *Quite* an eye-opener. There were –
mmmaaa! – these girls – young ladies, rather – with, if you'll
believe it, hardly a—'

'Priscus,' I said, 'Mother is going to kill you.'

He grinned his louche innocent's grin. 'Oh, I've no intention of telling Vipsania. She wouldn't understand at all. This
is – mmmaaa! – just between you and me, my boy. Our little
secret.'

Gods! 'Uh . . .'

'After all, where's the harm? And as I say I didn't lose a
copper piece. If anything I made a slight profit. And I
enjoyed myself enormously.'

I groaned. 'Priscus, that was what's called a come-on. The next time it'll be for real and you'll get creamed.'

'Nonsense. Philippus may be a freedman but he is also – mmmaaa! – a complete gentleman. I'm quite convinced he would no more—'

'*Who* did you say?'

He blinked at me. 'Philippus. The owner of the—'

'Licinius Philippus?'

'That I don't know, Marcus. Possibly. He only gave me the one name.' He paused, and I could almost see the delayed trickle-feed process happening. 'Wasn't your dead man a Licinius?'

'Yeah,' I said. 'Yeah, he was. If it's the same Philippus then he used to be a slave of his.'

'Really? How coincidental. And it explains, I suppose, why he was so interested in you.'

I stared at him. '*He* was interested in *me*? When the hell did my name come up?'

'Oh, very early on. At the haircut stage. He'd – mmmaaa! – asked whether I was alone in Baiae and naturally I said no. Then in the course of the ensuing conversation, I happened to mention that you were investigating a suspicious death for the authorities here and he was *most* intrigued. Asked me all sorts of questions which of course – mmmaaa! – I couldn't answer.' He grinned and chuckled. 'Really, my boy, I almost felt at times that I was being interrogated. It was quite exhilarating.'

I sat back, brain buzzing. Shit! Maybe it had been simple curiosity at that, but I wasn't laying any bets. Diodotus had said that this Philippus had been seriously unchuffed with Murena's hotel idea, and if he wasn't exactly in the prime suspects' bag already that was only because he was an unknown quantity. And if someone like Priscus had spotted a deliberate grilling then it must've been as obvious as a hippo in a bird-bath.

'Uh . . . you make any sort of arrangement to go back to this place?' I asked.

'Oh, yes. Nothing definite, though. Philippus said it gets – mmmaaa! – quite lively of an evening, and he suggested I might like to drop in after dinner some night to see it at its best.' He beamed. 'I must say the offer is most tempting. *Most* tempting. And if you would care to come with me, Marcus, I'm sure Philippus would make you very welcome.'

Hmm. 'Listen, Priscus,' I said. 'This is important, pal, so take your time and think before you answer. Did Philippus himself say that or is this you talking here?'

'Oh, it was his idea. Completely. He was most insistent that you be included in the invitation; not that I – mmmaaa! – wouldn't be delighted to have you along for my own sake, of course.'

Interesting. If Philippus's prime concern was to get his hooks into a patsy then inviting me to tag along was the last thing he'd do. So either the guy was genuine, which I doubted, or he had an ulterior motive; and what *that* could be was pretty obvious. If he was keen to find out what lines I was chasing in the Murena case then he wouldn't've got very far picking Priscus's brains; he'd need to talk to me direct.

The big question was, *why* was he keen? Scrub simple curiosity: Philippus, I knew, had his own business-related reasons for wishing Murena into an urn, and even if I didn't know yet how strong these were the guy was right up there on the suspects list. And coincidence was something I didn't believe in. I'd like a quiet talk with Philippus myself.

On my own terms, though. When I had it I didn't want to be nursemaiding Priscus. Just the thought of having to explain to Mother when she found out – and she *would* find out – why I'd allowed him to persuade me into taking him to a gambling hall gave me goosebumps. Especially if, while I was chatting to the boss, he lost what back teeth he still had in some dice game or other. Which, given his current kicking-over-the-traces track record, was what the daft old bugger would almost certainly do . . .

Uh-uh. I couldn't risk it. No *way* could I risk it, because Mother would kill me. She'd kill both of us. Still, there was no point in hurting the guy's feelings in the process.

'Ah . . . there's just one major snag, Priscus,' I said.

'Oh, I'm sure you can think of something to tell Vipsania.'

This time I was the one to blink. Yeah. Right. Sometimes I wonder if Priscus isn't sharper than he looks. I had the distinct feeling here that I was being hustled.

'Look,' I said. 'Let's just, uh, put this on hold for a bit, eh, pal? A few more days won't matter. Leave it with me and I'll get back to you.'

His face fell, like a kid's when he's told that a birthday treat has had to be cancelled. 'If you insist, Marcus,' he said. 'Although I must admit I was rather looking forward to it. Couldn't we just—'

'No. Watch my lips.'

'Very well. If that's how you feel . . .'

He got up and wandered off. Shit. Well, sometimes you had to be cruel to be kind. And if he did knot the bedsheets together now and do a runner off his own bat then my conscience was clear.

Still, that little conversation had given me a lot to think about. Priscus had been got at, no question, and not just as a gambling hall owner's mark. The fact that he hadn't been able to provide any information worth the name was irrelevant: he'd still been soaked.

So why?

Licinius Philippus was one guy I just had to see.

9

The next morning I rode out to see Murena's partner, Decimus Tattius.

Diodotus had said the guy had a villa on the main drag, inland of Murena's. Out the other way, towards Puteoli and Neapolis, the countryside gets pretty rugged, especially when you come to what the locals call the Burning Fields, but in the Misenum direction the whole peninsula's taken up with luxury villas whose owners can afford to give nature a helping hand. Sure, you occasionally do get flocks of sheep and goats lifting their heads to give you evil-eyed stares from the bosky shade while quaint shepherds, straight out of the blunt end of a pastoral, blow their oaten pipes at you from under an arbutus. But the general impression is of scenery that's been civilised to within an inch of its life, often involving topiaried hedges, architectural features that wouldn't be out of place in one of these snappy modern *trompe-l'oeil* frescos and the periodic scream of an ostrich from some rich bugger's private zoo.

The road was busy, busier than you'd expect from a dead-end direction, but there's a fairly constant stream of traffic to and from the naval base at Misenum itself on the peninsula's tip. When I reckoned I must be getting close I asked a slave on duty outside one of the villas for final directions and he pointed me towards a set of iron gates further up the drag.

Tattius's place wasn't big – not by the neighbours'

standards, anyway – but it was still pretty impressive. At first glance, at least: the gates were fancy expensive ironwork, fixed to marble pillars, but they could've done with painting and the gilded fish that topped them had a bad case of scale-rot; while the slave sitting outside them had on a tunic that was darned in places and looked like it'd been washed half a dozen times too many.

'The master at home this morning, sunshine?' I said.

'Yes, sir.' The slave got up and opened the gates. 'Just go in.'

I walked the mare up a paved carriage-drive towards a porticoed entrance with a line of statues in front of it. At least, there were a line of statue pedestals, but two or three of them were empty. A slave in a tunic that was hardly better than the gate-slave's was sweeping the marble steps. He set his broom against a pillar and came towards me.

'I was looking for the master,' I said.

'He's at breakfast, sir. What was it about?'

I dismounted. 'The name's Valerius Corvinus. I was wondering if he could spare a few minutes to talk to me about his partner. Licinius Murena.'

'Oh, yes, sir.' The guy's voice took on a hushed, reverent quality that indicated he knew the partner in question had recently been stiffed. Not that that was surprising, mind: the slave grapevine is second to none, and Murena's death would be old news by now. 'If you'd care to wait I'll tell him you're here.'

He went inside. While the mare nuzzled the grass at the edge of the driveway I looked around me. Yeah, right; initial impressions confirmed. The place wasn't falling apart – far from it – but it had a slight air of seediness that suggested Tattius was having difficulties living up to the manner to which he'd evidently become accustomed. The box hedges round the ornamental fountain were just that little bit over-grown, and the fountain itself could've done with a scrub out. There were these missing statues, and the second slave's tunic: one could've been chance, but not two. Some of the trellising that supported the roses was—

'Valerius Corvinus? The master will see you, sir. Follow me, please.'

I did. They were eating al fresco, in a small enclosed peri-style garden off the atrium. 'They', plural. The woman was Penelope.

I pulled up short. 'Uh . . . I'm sorry,' I said. 'I didn't know—'

She got up. 'Good morning, Valerius Corvinus. You wanted to talk to my husband, I understand. If you'll excuse me I'll leave you in peace while you do so.'

Decimus Tattius rose and watched her go inside. They hadn't exchanged a word. Then he turned to me, smiled and held out a hand.

'Pleased to meet you, Corvinus,' he said. We shook. 'You've breakfasted?'

'Yeah, yeah, that's okay.' I was still looking after Penelope, vaguely fazed. 'I'm sorry, sir. When I met your wife yesterday she didn't mention—'

'So I see.' Tattius motioned me to a chair. His face was expressionless. 'It doesn't matter. Now. How can I help you? I understand you're investigating the death of my partner.'

He'd've had to be about Murena's age, late sixties or early seventies, but he looked fit enough, if more than a little over-weight and with a pouting, pendulous look to his lips, more like a sulky kid than a senior citizen. His grip, though, had been firm and hard.

'Yeah.' I sat down. 'Don't let me disturb your breakfast.'

'Oh, I'd finished.' He laid himself back on the couch. 'This is a dreadful affair. Although I did hear they've caught the man they think did it.'

Despite the sentiments I'd met crocodiles who sounded sorrier than Tattius. Still, the murder had been five days ago now, so maybe the shock had worn off. 'Gaius Trebbio,' I said. 'There's . . . an element of doubt over that.'

'Is there, indeed?' He raised an eyebrow. 'I'm surprised. Lucius mentioned Trebbio to me several times, and seemingly the man had made direct and specific threats. Also I was told he was wandering drunk in the neighbourhood of the fish-farm at the time it happened. Personally I'd've thought – if poor Lucius's death wasn't natural, which seems to be the general opinion, although I'm not convinced, myself – that the evidence was fairly conclusive.'

'There's some,' I admitted. 'But I wouldn't call it all that conclusive. They quarrelled over Trebbio's eviction, didn't they?'

'I'd hardly call it quarrelling. Lucius had bought the Juventius estate, which included the man's cottage.'

'Trebbio had had the place for fifteen years. That's a long time.'

'You haven't seen it yourself?'

I shook my head.

'Then take my word, "cottage" is dignifying it: it's no more than a hovel, a shack, hardly more than a ruin. Trebbio was simply camping out there.'

'None the less . . .'

'I'm saying that to describe the place as a property and this Trebbio as an evicted tenant is overstating things. If Lucius chose to terminate the lease he had a perfect right, legally and morally, to do so. It was a purely business matter. He'd no quarrel with the fellow personally – why should he? – and Trebbio had no right to complain.'

'Ah . . . you say "Lucius" and "he". It wasn't a partnership decision to buy the estate, then?'

Tattius frowned. 'Oh, I suppose it was. Technically, at least.'

' "Technically"?'

'I don't really involve myself much in the business side of things, Corvinus. I know nothing about fish or fish-farming, and care less. All that was Lucius's concern, and increasingly over the years his sons'. Plus Ligurius's naturally. The Anchovy's a real tower of strength.'

There was a certain something in his voice I couldn't place. Smugness? A touch of contempt, maybe? I didn't know, but it was there, and I didn't like it above half. I wasn't sure I took to Decimus Tattius: the guy had a greasy feel about him that was simultaneously as flash and as run-down as his property.

' "Anchovy",' I said. 'That was Murena's name for him, wasn't it?'

Tattius looked at me in surprise. 'Yes, it was, as a matter of fact. Lucius had a habit of giving people around him nick-names. He did it all the time, and it was, I'm afraid, one of his less endearing traits, especially since he had no compunction about using them to the person's face. But then, that was Lucius for you. He never did have much respect for people's feelings. Ligurius, as it happens, didn't and doesn't mind. We – the family – call him Anchovy now as a matter of course; there's no opprobrium involved.'

'He called you Oistrus,' I said. ' "Gadfly".'

Tattius's eyes narrowed. 'Yes, he did,' he said slowly. 'Where did you hear that, Corvinus?'

'Care to tell me why? Just out of interest?'

'To tell you the truth, I can't remember now; we've known each other practically since boyhood. In any case,

I've grown quite used to it over the years and it certainly doesn't offend me. If it ever did.'

Yeah, well, from his initial reaction that was something I wouldn't risk too hefty a bet on. He hadn't liked me using the name; he hadn't liked it at all. Still, I let that go. 'The partnership. When did it start?'

'Oh, that's ancient history, too. As I said, we were very old friends, did our junior magistracies together. Then – well – we both independently decided that politics and public life weren't for us. Lucius's family have always had interests down this way, fish-farming especially through his grandfather, and when he made the decision to move permanently from Rome and develop the farm commercially I took up his suggestion to go into partnership. We've been here ever since. That's all there was to it.'

'But you've never really involved yourself in the business?'

Tattius smiled. 'To be frank, that suited both of us. I'm no businessman and never have been; Lucius was, very much so, as were – are – his sons. I don't interfere. I leave things to them and let them get on with it.'

'What about this hotel idea? I understand it's a new venture.'

'Yes.' Tattius looked down briefly and plucked a stray thread from his tunic. 'Yes, it is.'

'You didn't approve?'

He hesitated. 'As I said, Corvinus, I'm no businessman. I leave – left – decisions like that to my partner. However, again – to be frank – I did think that it was a little . . . misguided.'

'In that way?'

'I'm not criticising Lucius – how could I? – but the capital outlay was considerable and the returns doubtful at best, certainly in all but the very long term. The farm is doing reasonably well and always has done, although the profits aren't as large as you might think after the costs have been deducted. Also, there was . . . a certain amount of local opposition to contend with which Lucius, being Lucius, refused to take into account.'

'His freedman Philippus?'

Tattius shot me a sharp look and took his time answering. 'Yes indeed,' he said finally. 'Forgive me, but you really are remarkably well-informed, especially in so short a time. How on earth did you find out about Philippus?'

'Murena gave him his freedom when he was quite young, didn't he?'

Another hesitation. 'He did.'

'You know why?'

'No. Lucius may have been my partner, but his private life was none of my concern. No doubt he had his reasons.'

'Or where he got the money from originally to start him up in business?'

'I don't follow.'

Odd. There was something definitely defensive about the guy now, and that was interesting. 'I've been told that Philippus is one of the richest locals in Baiae. Granted he may be a good businessman, but he must've got his original stake from somewhere. On the other hand – by all accounts – there wasn't much love lost between him and his ex-master. So I was just wondering . . .'

'I'm afraid I can't help you over Philippus, Corvinus.' Tattius's face was closed now. 'You'd have to ask the man himself.'

'Yeah,' I said. 'Yeah, I'll do that.'

'Not that I suspect you'll get a civil answer. Philippus is not what you'd call a civil person. Once a slave, always a slave.'

I shifted on my chair. 'Uh . . . to change the subject. Murena's family. What can you tell me about them?'

It might've been my imagination, but I thought Tattius looked relieved. 'In the business sense?' he said. 'His elder son Titus is the lawyer of the family. Also he oversees the company's accounts. Aulus is more like his father, the practical businessman and decision-taker. Although' – he smiled – 'he's rather more adventurous than Lucius ever was, which can be both good and bad. He's a natural gambler, and although Lucius did have a gambling streak it wasn't particularly developed.'

'They, uh, didn't get on very well. Or so I understand.'

The cautious look was back. 'There was a certain amount of friction, yes. But no more so than in most families.'

Yeah, right. And I was a baboon. Still, I couldn't expect too much from that direction. After all, he was a relation by marriage. 'What about Gellia?' I said.

'Again I have to ask you what you mean. Gellia isn't involved on the business side of things.'

'They were a happy couple?'

'As far as I know. They were as close as couples from the upper bracket usually are, particularly in Baiae.'

Which wasn't saying much, but then again of course I couldn't expect more. 'She have money of her own?'

I thought he wasn't going to answer, which considering the question he'd be within his rights not to do, but finally he did. 'Her father was an oil-shipper in a small way, in Puteoli. She's not rich, but she has a competence.'

'When did they get married?'

'About five or six years ago.'

'Murena was a widower, wasn't he? I mean, his first wife died, he didn't divorce her.'

'That's right.'

'She been dead for long?'

'Almost thirty years now.'

Strange: I could swear he'd tightened up again for some reason. 'She couldn't've been very old.'

'No. She was a long-term invalid, never strong.'

'What about your wife? Penelope? From the way she spoke the last time I saw her she didn't get on all that well with her father. Or with the rest of the family, for that matter.'

He stood up suddenly. 'Corvinus, I'm sorry. I know you have a job to do, and I'm happy to help you all I can, but your questions are becoming a little personal. Could we stop now, please?'

Yeah, well; I'd been wondering myself how far I could push it, and I wasn't really surprised he'd choked me off. I stood up too. 'Sure,' I said. 'My apologies. And thanks for your time.'

He smiled – with his mouth, at least – and held out a hand. 'You're very welcome. I wish you luck. Although, it has to be said, personally I think Lucius's death was either a tragic accident or the man responsible is in custody already. I'll see you out.'

There was no sign of Penelope. I collected the mare – the sweeper-slave had tied her to a hitching-post further along the portico – and rode back to Baiae. Thoughtfully.

10

I took my time riding back.

So what had we got out of that little conversation? Several things, and all of them puzzling.

First of all – and this was the biggie – the simple fact of the partnership itself. Friendship's one thing, but business is another, and especially considering what I knew of Murena's character he'd been no softie. Even in the most easy-going of partnerships there has to be a certain quid pro quo, and in the Murena/Tattius *ménage* I couldn't see what that'd been. Scratch expertise: Tattius had admitted he wasn't a businessman and that he'd no knowledge of or interest in fish-farming, and that side of things seemed to have been Murena's province completely. The same went for money. I might be missing my bet, but unless he was a real eccentric I doubted if Tattius was exactly rolling; not judging by the state of his villa, anyway. Of course, the cash might've gone into the business right at the beginning and drained away, but then he hadn't given that impression either. Me, if that'd been the case I'd've expected more complaints and a lot more bitterness. He'd seemed, if anything, satisfied with arrangements. No, all things considered, I'd reckon Murena had paid the lion's share of the bills as well. Plus the fact that the farm had been his to begin with. So if neither expertise nor money was the basis for their partnership then what was left?

The marriage tie between Tattius and Penelope was a third possibility, and on the face of it the most likely. I didn't know exactly when Tattius and Murena had gone into business together – barring Diodotus's mention of the fact that Murena had moved down from Rome some twenty-odd years back, so presumably it'd been about then – but if the wedding had come first then taking your son-in-law into the family business is a good old-fashioned Roman custom. Only that scenario posed serious problems of its own, didn't it? From what he'd said Tattius had never been a junior in any way: he and Murena had been equals from the start. So as far as the partnership per se went, any existing marriage was an irrelevance and we were back again to the simple question of Tattius's contribution to the original arrangement. Friendship – even if the guy was already his son-in-law – wouldn't't've been enough, not for a full partnership, not for a businessman like Murena. That idea was out.

If, on the other hand, the partnership had *preceded* the marriage then there were problems there too: it raised the question of why, if Murena was already making all the running financially and otherwise, he'd given Tattius his daughter at all. Oh, sure, again it's an old Roman custom to cement a business alliance with a wedding, but Tattius and Penelope weren't an obvious couple. They were thirty years apart in age, for a start; also, like I say, friendship and business are two different things. A marriage alliance, in families like Murena's, is definitely part of the business side and if Tattius didn't have all that much going for him in himself then, partnership or not, someone like Murena would've thought twice about signing his only daughter away in a marriage contract. Or should've, rather, because he obviously hadn't.

Plus that scenario still left us with the original problem of why the partnership in the first case . . .

Shit; I was going round in circles here, and my brain was beginning to overheat. Leave it. There was an answer somewhere, sure, but at present finding it was in the flying pigs category.

The same applied to the question of Tattius's nickname. I'd met Tattius now and it still didn't make sense. Whatever the guy was, he was no gadfly: I'd reckon he had about as much get-up-and-go as a flatfish. Not that he was soft; he just didn't show any signs of stirring himself, let alone spurring anyone else on. Oh, he was pushing it now and boyhood nicknames don't have much relevance at that age, but it was still odd. Why Gadfly? You'd think there ought to be some signs there, but there weren't.

What else? Just his general manner. By Tattius's own admission the two had known each other practically since they were kids, both as friends and business partners. Yet when he'd talked about Murena he could've been talking about a comparative stranger. Certainly there'd been no real grief. He hardly even seemed to care all that much that the guy was dead. Again, it was nothing definite, and if he had it would've left him in a minority of one, but somehow it just didn't fit.

Last, there was the business of the wife. Murena's first one, the one who died . . .

That'd been screwy, because it was unexpected. Yet I couldn't be wrong: there had been a . . . *reticence* there: Tattius had been reluctant to talk about her. And why the hell should he be? After all, like he'd said, the woman had been dead for almost thirty years. So why?

Bugger. Questions, sure; after that talk with Tattius I had them in spades. As far as answers were concerned, though, everything added up to one big zilch.

Puzzling was putting it mildly.

*

To get to the villa where we were staying I had to go through the town centre. Baiae isn't as crowded as Rome, sure, nowhere near it, but by mid-morning – which it was now – there were a fair number of people around. Not the gilded-wonder set, mind. That time of day, in Baiae, most of them are still sleeping off the night before or being variously prinked, painted and clipped for the strenuous evening ahead. Plus the fact that too-direct sunlight and fresh air are so bad for the complexion, and what's the point in going out when there's no one to see you, darling? There were just the ordinary working punters, the sort you'd see in any small town: old biddies with string bags full of vegetables, slaves doing the household shopping and guys driving laden donkeys and/or carrying an assortment of hardware or chickens on poles. Real people, in other words.

Under these circumstances, riding's not a good idea, not when the streets are narrow, the poles are at groin height and most of the guys who are carrying them are selectively blind to pushy buggers on horseback. I dismounted and led the mare by the bridle.

I was passing through the market square – nice marble statues of Augustus and old Julius, if you're interested, which I wasn't – when I thought of Priscus's gambling hall. He hadn't told me exactly where it was, of course, but these places aren't common, even in Baiae, and I knew the rough direction. I might as well check it out – and check out its owner Philippus – while I was in the area. That was one guy I *really* wanted to talk to.

I left the mare at a handy water-trough outside the baths and headed down the most likely looking side street. This close to the centre, most of the buildings have shops of various kinds on their ground floors while the owners live above. Or, of course, use the whole place for business: the girls on two out of three of the balconies I passed obviously weren't there to hang up the family washing, and like I say in that part of town the entrepreneurial ethos is alive, well and ready to give anyone a good time at any hour.

I stopped by a vegetable-seller's, waited politely until the old biddy in front of me had bought her leeks and had a long conversation with the shopkeeper about her martyrdom to Feet, and asked for Philippus's place.

'It's over by the baths,' the vegetable-seller said. 'You can't miss it.'

'You mean the baths by the square?'

'Nah. The ones in that direction.' She pointed.

If Baiae has a lot of anything for its size, it's baths. The locals might cater for the worst excesses Rome's gilded holidaymakers can ask of them, but at least they do it clean. 'Got you,' I said. 'Thanks, Grandma.'

I hadn't gone far wrong: another street down, one to the left, then back up a hundred yards or so the way I'd come. I found the place no bother, largely because of the door-slave out front: a huge German with braided hair and moustache and a gut on him so big that pedestrians were having to take a detour to get round it. It wasn't all beer and sausage, mind: the guy was seriously muscled, and he had a mean look in his eye. Evidently Philippus didn't take any nonsense from unwanted customers. I'd reckon that if Big Hermann here bounced you you'd stay bounced for a month.

I checked with him that it actually was Philippus's, getting a slow stare and a final supercilious nod in answer, and went in.

The place was impressive. Like I say, gambling in public's technically illegal most of the time, and although as long as the owner pays his taxes and adds a generous sweetener there isn't much chance of the local authorities closing him down, that doesn't mean he can be too obvious about things. Most gambling dens are pretty basic, no more than a back room in a wineshop with two or three tables set aside for bones or dice, or if they cater for the more sophisticated punter a couple of Twelve Lines or Robbers boards that the landlord keeps behind the bar until they're asked for. Definitely, in other words, a low-key business, and one where – if need be, and the law comes knocking – the owner can hide the evidence of his nefarious practices pretty smartly.

How Philippus had swung it I didn't know, but we were in a totally different league here. Forget the wineshop back room: barring the furnishings and fittings, the place could've been a top-of-the-range private house or a high-class brothel, with frescoed walls and inlaid marble flooring. The central atrium was twice the size of mine at home, easy, and the pool had a Venus-and-her-nymphs fountain that could've graced a Janiculan villa. That wasn't all, either. A staircase in polished cedar led up to a mezzanine level under a dome painted with assorted watching gods and goddesses, and at the far end of the room a set of pillars gave out on to a porticoed garden, while two or three side doors showed that there was a lot more that I hadn't seen yet.

The place wasn't crowded – it wouldn't be, this early in the day – but it wasn't empty, either. Atriums're pretty sparsely furnished, as a rule, but besides a fair sprinkling of statues and bronze candelabra this one had at least a dozen tables, each with its full complement of chairs or couches. About half of them were occupied, and there was a sort of busy hum that you get when you're somewhere that people are taking what they're doing seriously. No one looked up.

A girl came over – probably African, from one of the

nomad tribes that worked the territories inland of the Roman-run coastal strip – and I could see why Priscus had been dribbling down his mantle. Sure, she wasn't exactly showing the family jewels completely upfront, but you could see where they were all the same, and they weren't fakes, either. Dark skin but not too dark, eyes like a deer's and a body under the tight filmy tunic that was all curves in the right places.

'Good morning, sir,' she said. 'You're alone? You'd like to play?'

'Ah . . . no,' I said. 'Not today, thanks. I was just looking.'

She smiled – perfect, regular teeth, white as ivory – and ducked her head. 'That's quite all right, sir. Perhaps another time. Would you care for some wine? The house Rhodian is excellent.'

'Yeah. Yeah, that'd be great.' She turned to go. 'Uh . . . the boss isn't around, is he? Licinius Philippus?'

'I'm afraid not, sir, although he'll probably be in soon. You wanted to talk to him?'

'If he can spare me a minute or two, sure.'

'Corvinus! Valerius Corvinus!'

I looked round. Two guys had just come through one of the side doors. I didn't recognize the first, but the one behind was Aulus Nerva. He was out of his mourning clothes – well, that hadn't lasted long, had it? – clean-shaven and wearing a sharp mantle with the folds impeccably draped over a pricily embroidered tunic.

'How's the sleuthing going?' he said, holding out a hand and beaming.

'Okay.' I shook, cautiously; when I'd seen Brother Aulus the day before he hadn't exactly rolled out the welcome mat, and I couldn't see why the situation should've changed much, let alone reached the bosom-buddies stage.

Still, you take things as they come. 'I'm plugging along.'

'This is a friend of mine, Sextus Aquillius Florus.'

Uh-huh; Mother had mentioned him in connection with Gellia. Very much in connection. I could see why she'd be attracted. Florus was mid-thirties – about her age – tall, well-built with chiselled aristocratic features and crisply curling dark hair glistening with scented oil that must've cost half a gold piece a squirt. A typical rich Baian playboy, in other words, and a bored matron like Gellia's wet dream. Priapic rabbits came to mind.

He looked like he'd have about as much brain-power as a rabbit, too.

'All right, are you, Corvinus?' he said. 'How's the boy?'

'Not bad,' I said.

Meanwhile Nerva was still beaming at me, but there was tightness to his smile and his eyes were slightly wary. 'How did you find out about this place?' he said.

I shrugged; if he wanted to pretend that neither of us knew about Philippus's connection with his father, then that was fine with me. For now, anyway. 'My stepfather dropped in for a while yesterday. I was just checking it out for myself.'

'That so, now? We were here yesterday ourselves. What was his name?'

'Priscus. Helvius Priscus.'

Nerva gave a chuckle that I didn't quite like. 'Ah, yes. An elderly chap, isn't he? Scholar. We had a bit of a chat. I didn't know he was a relative of yours, though.' He glanced round the room. 'What do you think?'

'I'm impressed.'

'Not bad, is it? Better than you'd find anywhere in Rome, or even Alexandria.' The girl arrived with a goblet of wine on a tray. 'Bring another two of these for Sextus and me,

Marta. Or – hang on! – bring us the half jug.' He turned back to me. 'Care to join us, Corvinus?'

'Yeah, sure. Why not?' I took the goblet – it was silver, and heavy – and followed them over to a table. 'You come here often, then?'

'Often enough. I'm not playing this morning, though. Sextus and I have business later and we just stopped in for a drink on the way.'

'Seeing a man about a grain barge.' Florus laughed too loudly. Nerva shot him a look.

'That so, now?' I took a sip of the wine – it was pretty good, and cooled to perfection – put the goblet down on the table and stretched out on one of the couches. 'How does it work? The set-up here, I mean?'

Nerva took the couch opposite. 'You can play privately, in which case the house takes its cut from the winner. A tenth of his winnings, which believe me at Philippus's amounts to a lot more than peanuts. Or of course Marta or any of the other girls'll be glad to take you on, in which case it's just straight win or lose. They're good, though, so if you choose that way you have to watch yourself, and there're no limits.' He grinned. 'On the other hand, you get the pleasure of their company for the duration. Either way, the booze is free. It's first-rate booze, too.'

'Sounds pretty good,' I said. 'Uh . . . it's all above board, is it?'

'Sure,' Florus said. 'No loaded dice here, Corvinus. And the girls – well, they'll play for something else than money if you ask them nicely.' He chuckled and winked. 'Pay on the nail if they lose, too.'

I glanced around the room. There were a couple of tables with girls at them – real lookers, good as Marta – but most of the punters were obviously taking the private option. And from what I could overhear of the conversation Nerva was right: Philippus's clientele were no pikers. A ten per cent cream-off would be serious gravy, even if wine was included.

Priscus – if he hadn't been lying to me, which was always a possibility – had been lucky to get out still wearing his shirt right enough. Maybe the old guy had hidden talents after all.

Marta came back with the wine order. Nerva raised his goblet to me.

'Cheers, Corvinus,' he said. 'Success in your investigations.'

'Yeah. Right.' I sipped.

'So. How are they coming on?'

I know when I'm being pumped. 'Like I said, I'm plugging along. It's early days.'

'No suspects yet?'

I shrugged.

Nerva was turning the goblet in his hands. He frowned into the wine. Then he looked up. 'If I were you I'd think about my brother Titus,' he said.

Jupiter! The bugger didn't believe in the subtle approach, did he? Even Florus looked taken aback, and I reckoned that guy had all the subtlety of a sock in the jaw.

'Uh . . . why's that, now?' I said carefully.

'Gellia told you. He's strapped for cash at the moment; seriously strapped. His daughter's marrying young Manlius Torquatus in a few months and he has to find a dowry of a cool half-million which I know for a fact he hasn't got. Dad's death is . . . very convenient.'

'I understood you weren't too solvent yourself, pal,' I said. 'If we're talking money.'

'True.' Nerva smiled. 'But then I know I didn't kill him. Where Titus is concerned I know nothing of the kind. And he's always shown . . . shall we say violent propensities.'

'Such as?' I said.

'A few years ago he had one of his slaves flogged to death for breaking a fluorspar wine-dipper.' He glanced at Florus, who was looking nervous. 'You'll confirm that, Sextus?' Florus grunted. 'The slave was well past his best, naturally, or Titus wouldn't have wasted him. All the same, it might be relevant. And I was told – although I can't vouch for the truth of it – that if his major-domo hadn't talked him out of it he would have carried out the flogging himself. As it was, he insisted it be done in his presence. He'd've enjoyed that very much, knowing Titus.'

I was staring at him. Lack of family loyalty was one thing – I wouldn't't've expected it from him, no more than I would have from any of that bunch – but this was something else: a gratuitous planting of the knife. Obviously the reason for inviting me over, plus the false matiness. Nerva was shaping up to be a really unpleasant bugger, one of the most unpleasant I'd ever come across, which was saying something. I put down my goblet. 'I think I'll be going,' I said.

'No, don't hurry off.' Nerva smiled. 'It's just a suggestion, and if it doesn't fit with your own thoughts then forget I mentioned it. However, do give Titus your consideration, won't you? He's not a very nice person, believe me, and certainly not the moral, upright soul he pretends to be.'

'The last time I saw you, pal,' I said evenly, 'you were siding with him against your stepmother. You can't have it both ways.'

His smile disappeared, and he glanced at Florus to see whether that had registered. It had: the other guy was scowling. 'Oh, well, I've thought again, haven't I?' he said quickly. 'But perhaps you're right, perhaps we should drop the subject.'

The hell with that; he'd started it and if he wanted to play footsie with hobnailed boots on it was fine with me. 'So where were you yourself, friend, the night it happened?' I said. 'Just so's we can get rid of that possibility and clear the ground?'

He blinked; that he hadn't been expecting and I wouldn't't've asked the question so directly if the bastard hadn't changed the rules himself. Still, there it was, and he couldn't avoid it. There was a long silence; over at one of the other tables someone threw Venus and his opponent swore.

Finally, he said, 'I was here, as it happens. All night, or until the early hours, at least.'

There wasn't a trace of friendliness in his voice now.

'Oh, no you weren't, Aulus,' Florus said. 'Not that night. Remember you said—'

Nerva rounded on him. He had coloured up like a beetroot. 'You keep your—' he began. Then he froze.

'Valerius Corvinus?' someone said behind me. 'Marta says you were asking for me.'

I turned. Yeah; this would be Philippus.

I I

For one of the richest men in Baiae he didn't look much. Five foot nothing in his sandals, face like a squashed over-ripe plum, wearing a battered freedman's cap and a tunic that looked like he'd used it to dust the floor with and then slept in it. Plus military-grade halitosis which was already making my eyes water and a set of vowels that would've disgraced an adenoidal parrot.

On the other hand, either of the two heavies who were standing behind him could've ripped my arms off and beaten me senseless with them without breaking sweat. Little details like that tend to stifle criticism.

'Ah . . . right,' I said. 'Right.'

He grunted. 'If it's about what I think it is then we'd best go up to my office.'

Without another word or having acknowledged Nerva and Florus in any way, he moved off in the direction of the stairs. On top of everything else, I noticed he had a bad limp. All in all, not an odds-on contender for the Charismatic Freedman of the Year title.

I took a hefty swig from my goblet, almost emptying it – I reckoned I was going to need all the fortification I could get here – and stood up. Nerva was staring at me like any moment I'd do a Democritus in reverse and disappear in a scattering cloud of atoms.

'Uh . . . see you later, lads,' I said.

The heavies fell in behind as I followed Philippus towards
the stairs and up them to the mezzanine. Presumably they
opened this part up when things got busy in the evenings,
because there were more tables and couches. Philippus
carried on past them down a short corridor to a door at the
end. He took a key from his belt, opened the door and went
in. All this without a glance back to see if I was following.
Mind you, with the heavies in tow I didn't have much of a
choice.

I'd expected – seeing the state of Philippus – that the office
would be a mess. It wasn't; quite the opposite. The big desk
was clear apart from an inkwell and a clutch of pens in a
rough unglazed clay holder. One long wall of the room was
lined, side to side and floor to ceiling, with cubby-holes, each
with two or three docketed tablets poking out; the other was
the same, only with half the cubbies empty. The wall
opposite the door had a barred window in it, probably – from
the lack of traffic noise – overlooking the porticoed garden
below. There was a chair behind the desk and another two
facing it: plain wood, with no cushions. That was it. No
ornaments, no decoration, nothing. The place would've
shocked a Spartan.

'Sit down,' Philippus growled. 'You two' – to the heavies
– 'push off downstairs. I'll call if I need you.' He parked
himself behind the desk. 'All right, Corvinus. Never mind
the formalities because I'm busy enough without this. Let's
get down to brass tacks. It's about Licinius Murena being
eaten by his namesakes, yes?'

'Yeah,' I said. 'More or less.'

'So talk. And spit it out, I'm not interested in pussyfooting
around.'

Gods! *This* was Priscus's 'charming gentleman'? Either
the dozy old bugger had been coming the uncooked

Minturnan again for unfathomable reasons of his own or his ability to sum up character would've disgraced a brick. Or, of course – and I didn't discount this explanation – Philippus had been putting on charm with Priscus that he wasn't bothering to waste on me.

Not that I had to take it lying down, mind.

'Fair enough, pal,' I said. 'Very laudable. Although I'm just a bit curious to know how you square that attitude with bushwhacking my stepfather.'

He looked at me. Just . . . *looked*. I had the distinct feeling that making that little comment had not been a wise move. Finally, he said, 'You want to talk to me or not?'

'Uh . . . sure.'

'Go ahead, then. I'm all ears. And remember what I said about the pussyfooting.'

Shit! We'd a real touchy bugger here, didn't we? Unfortunately, he was a touchy bugger with a pair of attendant trolls downstairs who'd come when he whistled, so maybe I'd better make a few allowances. 'You, ah, didn't see eye to eye with Murena over his plans to build a hotel, I understand?' I said.

'Damn right I didn't. Hotels were none of his business.'

'Why not? It's a free country.'

He leaned forward and I got the full benefit of his ongoing breath problems. I sat back quickly. 'Listen. Baiae's a small place and you don't get far in it by poaching on another man's preserve. Me, my niche is accommodation, girls and gambling, full stop. I don't touch restaurants, cookshops and wineshops – that's Publius Callion's patch – and I don't own carriage or boat-hire outlets either, because that's Mamma Gylippe. The same goes for a dozen other types of enterprise that're big here and getting bigger year by year. I could, sure, I've got the money to invest, but I don't because that's the way things work locally. I've got to live in this town like everybody else and in business one hand washes the other. There're unwritten rules and we all know them. Murena's bag was fish-farming. He was doing okay, and if he'd wanted to expand in that direction I'd've had no quarrel with him. As it was, when he bought the Juventius estate to build a hotel it was war to the knife. Now have I made myself clear?'

'Yeah. Yeah, more or less.'

'Good.' He sat back again. 'Then we talk on that basis. If you expect me to shed any tears for Lucius Licinius Murena, boy, then you'll wait until hell freezes.'

'Not even as your patron?'

That got me another long look that could've been pickled for a year in acid. Then he said, 'I'll only tell you this once, Corvinus, so I suggest you listen very, very carefully. Murena owned me when I was a kid, sure, I don't deny it. But that bastard was never my patron. Not ever.'

'Why not? It's the usual arrangement, isn't it?'

'Maybe so, but it wasn't in my case, boy. I made my own way, pulled myself up by my own fucking bootstraps, with no help from him. He didn't offer it, I didn't want it. I don't owe him nothing, and never have. Clear?'

'Uh-huh.' Point taken. 'So why did he free you in the first place? You mind telling me that?'

'He didn't. I bought myself off him, fair and square.'

'You *what*?'

His eyes challenged me. 'Sure. For hard cash, paid upfront. All Murena did was agree to take the money.'

I must've been goggling. Jupiter alive, this didn't add up, no way! Slaves, even the bargain-basement type, which Philippus wouldn't't've been, don't come cheap. And no slave, the age he must've been then, could've had anywhere near what it'd cost to buy himself out, not even if he was moonlighting behind the master's back, which is the usual slave trick to build up a nest-egg.

'Uh . . . how did you manage that, pal?' I said.

'That's my business. But it's the plain truth, I'm telling you to your face, and you just remember it. Where Murena and me was concerned the account was cleared long ago.'

'Fine.' It wasn't, not by a long chalk. Still, I wasn't going to argue the point. Not with this venomous dwarf ready to jump down my throat and rip my liver out at the first objection. 'Ah . . . care to tell me how you got your original stake?'

The glare hadn't shifted. 'Sure. Gladly. I found a fucking pixie's hat and got my three wishes. And you might as well believe me, Corvinus, because that's all I'm saying.'

'Okay, okay!' No change out of that one either, then, and the topic not so much closed as nailed shut, barred and padlocked and with a warning notice pinned on it. Well, on present showing I hadn't really expected anything else. Touchy wasn't the word. Time to back off. 'So let's change the subject,' I said. 'You know the family? Murena's family? I mean currently, as it were?'

I could feel him relax slightly, but he still looked about as friendly as a rhino with piles. 'No. Except by reputation and report. Barring Aulus Nerva, of course.'

The way he said it suggested he didn't have much time for them, Nerva included. 'You mind giving me a thumbnail sketch? Just for the record?'

'Of Nerva? The bastard's got some business sense, more than you'd think to look at him. He's more of a nose for it than his father, anyway. He'd do better if he'd cut down on the gambling, but that's his affair, and I'm not crying.'

Yeah. Gellia had mentioned Nerva's gambling debts. Apropos of which: 'He comes in here pretty often, doesn't he?'

'He's a regular customer of mine, sure.'

'He play privately or against the house?'

Philippus shifted in his chair. 'A bit of both,' he said. 'Most of the punters do. But then I'd say that was none of your concern either.'

'Was he here five nights ago? The night of the murder?'

He frowned. 'Think he did it, do you?'

I didn't answer.

'Well, it wouldn't surprise me. Either him or that cold bugger of a brother of his. They're both bastards and always were. But that I can't tell you, not from personal knowledge because I wasn't in that night myself.' His eyes challenged me to make something of it, but I kept my mouth shut. 'He claim he was?'

'There, uh, seems to be a bit of disagreement on that score,' I said.

'It's easy to check. Ask any of the girls on your way out. They'll remember. They know all the regular customers.'

'Yeah. Thanks. I'll do that.' I shifted ground again. 'With Murena dead he'd take over on the business side of things, would he?'

Philippus was suddenly tense again. 'Him and Titus Chlorus, sure,' he said. 'Plus the partner, Tattius.'

'Equal shares, three ways? I don't mean money, I mean deciding policy.'

He shrugged. 'That's their concern. They'd have to work it out among them.'

The guy was obfuscating; that was plain as the nose on his face. Still, he hadn't told me to piss off yet, so I pushed things. 'I've met Tattius already. He's not the policy-deciding type.'

'Fine. Then it'd be just the two of them.'

'How about Chlorus? I know he takes care of the finances – the formal accounts, at least – but how involved is he with the planning?'

Philippus shrugged again. 'Don't ask me. Like I say, I keep to my own side of the fence, I don't know nothing about other people's arrangements.'

'But you know Chlorus?'

'I told you. By reputation. Just by reputation. I haven't set eyes on him for years. He doesn't gamble, but he's a good lawyer and good with figures.'

'I get the impression the two of them don't exactly hit it off. As brothers, I mean. And I understand Nerva's a bit too fond of Chlorus's wife. That'd spill over on to the business side, wouldn't it?'

The acid look was back. 'I don't deal in smut, Corvinus,' Philippus said slowly. 'And like I say I'm not involved with the family, either. Not any more, not personally. You want to talk about the business side of things, where it affects me, that's fine, but nothing else.'

'Okay. So with Murena gone what happens to his hotel plans? You think his sons'll go ahead?'

Pause; *long* pause.

'That's up to them,' he said at last. 'They know my opinion on that score, at least Nerva does. And you know it yourself now. If you want anything more you'll have to ask them.'

Another door slammed. Well, that was to be expected, although it raised a few interesting questions. Like just how far Philippus was prepared to go to discourage them if they did carry on. And how far he'd gone already. 'Nerva's pretty thick with Aquillius Florus, isn't he?'

The eyes narrowed. 'What's that supposed to mean?'

I shrugged. 'I don't know. Maybe nothing. But I got the impression that they were in business together on their own account as well as being gambling pals. That so?'

'It's possible.' He was cautious. 'What exactly makes you think that?'

'Just something Florus said when we were talking downstairs. Something about a grain barge.' I wouldn't have mentioned it if I hadn't caught the look that Nerva had given his less-than-up-to-speed sidekick when he'd dropped the information, but it was worth a passing question. 'You know anything about that?'

Philippus didn't answer at once. He sat back, his left hand – I noticed the fingernails were broken and chewed – resting on the desk top. The fingers drummed briefly.

'No,' he said carefully. 'No, I can't say that I do, boy. I'm obliged to you. They mention any details?'

'Uh-uh. Just that.'

'Is that so, now?' He sucked on a tooth. Then, suddenly, he got up. 'Okay, Corvinus. I've given you all the time I can spare, and I've important business to see to. It was nice talking to you. Oh, and if you're a gambling man yourself you'll be very welcome any time you care to drop in. I owe you one.'

'That go for my stepfather as well?'

'Naturally. Always glad to see someone whose credit's good. And Helvius Priscus seemed to take to the place.' He must've noticed my expression, because he chuckled. 'Don't worry on that score, boy. We run an honest house here, and I've a reputation to keep up. My girls'll cover any bet a customer cares to make if he has the money to back it, sure, but they play fair and they don't use loaded dice. Or if they do they're out on their backsides quicker than you can spit, and they know it. Now I'll see you to the door.'

When we got back downstairs Nerva and Florus had gone. Maybe I was imagining things, but I reckoned Philippus didn't look too pleased.

I asked the African girl privately whether Nerva had been in the evening of the murder, and she gave me a categorical no. Florus got an equally categorical yes: he'd played a few games of dice with one of the other girls, but he hadn't arrived until later, well after sunset. So that was one set of questions answered, anyway.

Which left me with the rest.

Time for a think, and a spot of lunch. There're plenty of cookshops in the market square area. I chose one with tables outside that looked reasonably full, checked what was on offer from the board – seafood dumplings with green beans in a coriander sauce: this is Baiae, remember – gave the order to the waiter and settled back with a half jug to be going on with.

So. Not a bad morning's work. The biggie latterly, of course, was the mystery about how Philippus had got his freedom and his start in business. Oh, sure, on the face of it that could have nothing directly to do with Murena's death, but just the fact that he'd clammed up so spectacularly was more than curious.

Added to which, the events that all seemed to have taken place around the same time, - twenty to thirty years back – were piling up. I laid them out. First, Murena's move from Rome and his partnership with Tattius. Second, Tattius's marriage to Penelope. Third, the death of Murena's first wife. Fourth, Philippus's manumission . . .

Not the smidgeon of an explanation or a reason for any of them. Oh, I could theorise, but—

'May I join you, Corvinus?'

I refocused and looked up. Jupiter, we were doing well for members of the Murena family today. First Nerva, now Chlorus.

'Yeah,' I said. 'Yeah, sure. Help yourself.'

Things were moving.

12

I caught the waiter's eye and made a tipping motion with my right hand as if I was holding a wine cup. He nodded and disappeared inside.

'I hope you don't mind the intrusion.' Chlorus pulled up the chair opposite: the cookshop was one of these chichi places heavy on the Gallic wickerwork. 'I can't stay long in any case; I'm on my way to an appointment with my banker in the square.' Matey as hell, just like his brother. No prizes, though, for guessing why Corvinus was suddenly flavour of the month, not where these bastards were concerned; I waited for the inevitable question, and it came. 'How are things going? Any progress?'

I gave him what I'd given Nerva. 'I'm plugging along.'

'Good. Good.' There was a pause. Then when I didn't amplify: 'My apologies for the scene you witnessed yesterday, by the way. Father's death came as a great shock to us all. We were all rather . . . overwrought.'

'Yeah,' I said. 'So I noticed.'

Silence again; maybe he'd caught my tone. I hoped so, because mutual family backstabbing was one thing, but fake tears I could do without. At least Penelope had been upfront.

The waiter came back with my dumplings and a second cup.

'You like some lunch?' I said.

'No. No, I don't eat at all at mid-day, and as I said I have an appointment. A little wine would be welcome, though.'

I poured. It was good stuff, better than I'd expected in a tourist trap like this: Campanian, sure, but not the mass-produced rotgut from the big estates that you get in Rome. 'Cheers.'

'Cheers.' He raised the cup. 'Incidentally, I hear you had a talk with Diodotus.'

'Oh? And where did you hear that?'

He ignored the question. 'Did you ask him about the fainting fits?'

'Yeah. He said they weren't as sudden – or as violent – as all that.'

'Really? I'm surprised.'

'That the fits weren't serious? Or that Diodotus told me they weren't?'

He let that one go past him as well. All I got was a bland smile. 'You . . . ah . . . formed an opinion of him? Diodotus, I mean?'

'Yeah. He struck me as straight enough.'

'Indeed.' He cleared his throat. 'Well, you're entitled to your view.'

'Right.' I picked up the spoon and started in on the dumplings. If the guy wanted any dirt spreading re the doctor, he'd have to do it himself.

Which was just what he proceeded to do.

'You know that he owns a half-share in the bathhouse round the corner from here? On the edge of Market Square?'

I put the spoon down. 'No, I didn't.'

'The co-owner is Lucius Philippus.'

Shit. 'Is that so, now?' I said.

'It isn't generally known, but yes.' He took a sip of his wine. 'Interesting, isn't it?'

Interesting was right: my brain was buzzing. Philippus had

mentioned accommodation as one of his areas of investment, sure, but a bathhouse didn't exactly fit into that
category, or into any of the others. And I hadn't known that
he and the doctor had any connection at all. Of course, Oily
Chlorus here could be shooting me a line, but things like that
are easily checked and I doubted if he'd take the risk. I
wondered what other little nuggets I was missing where
Philippus was concerned. He hadn't liked Murena, that was
certain. And by his own admission he hadn't been at the
gambling hall the night of the murder.

'Then there was the Drepanum incident,' Chlorus said.
'Something else you should know about him. That's interesting as well.'

'Uh . . . what Drepanum incident would that be?'

'I heard of it quite by chance when I was in the town on
business a few months back. Seemingly Diodotus used to
practise there before he moved to Baiae. There was a' – he
paused and took another sip from his cup – '*another* young
wife with a rich elderly husband. Diodotus was treating him
for the stone. The man died, suddenly and unexpectedly, in
his litter.'

'These things happen, pal.' I picked up my spoon and
kept my tone expressionless. 'Especially if the guy was
getting on in years.'

'Indeed they do, Corvinus. However, the coincidence is
striking, wouldn't you say? And Diodotus left Drepanum
shortly afterwards.'

Yeah, well; no surprises there. I knew enough about
doctors and doctoring to know that if you lost a patient
under these circumstances it didn't do much for your professional street cred. Still, despite the obvious fact – the
painfully obvious fact – that Chlorus was still sharpening his
knife for Diodotus and Gellia, he was right; if true, the story

was interesting. And I hadn't crossed Diodotus off the list, far from it. 'Does Gellia know about this?'

'Of course. That's the point.' He looked at me slyly. 'I told her myself immediately I got back. Perhaps a mistake, in retrospect.'

Uh-huh. 'What about Murena?'

He frowned. 'I beg your pardon? I'm not with you.'

'Did you tell him as well?'

A momentary hesitation. 'Yes, I did, as a matter of fact.'

'And?'

'He . . . paid no attention.'

From Chlorus's slightly poker-up-the-rectum expression the old man had probably laughed in his face. That's not to say, mind, that he'd been right to do it. Only – if the news that the rumour was out had got back to Diodotus through either Murena or Gellia – I would've thought, should his thoughts be tending that way, the knowledge that his current patient knew he'd been under suspicion of murder once already, would've put the brakes on a repeat performance.

'You mind if I ask you about something else?' I said. 'Not connected with Diodotus?'

'Of course not. I'm delighted to help in any way.'

Yeah, right. Sure he was. My grip on the spoon tightened. 'Your brother and Aquillius Florus. They've got some business together involving a grain barge. You know anything about that?'

'Ah.' He looked smug. 'So you've found out about the barge, have you? It's one of Aulus's more extravagant schemes. Extravagant in both senses of the word. He put it to Father a month or so ago and the old man sent him off with a flea in his ear. Quite rightly so, in my opinion, and not on financial grounds alone.'

'Go on.'

'Florus's cousin is something at the naval base in Misenum. Seemingly he heard of a grain barge – one of the big ones, you know, that ply between Egypt and Puteoli – that was being put out of commission. Aulus's idea was – is – that they should buy it and do it up as a floating brothel-cum-gambling hall. Ludicrous, of course – the capital investment, even split two ways, would be huge, the comparative risks enormous – and morally . . . well, personally I find the morality suspect to say the least. So did Father.' He paused and then said, very deliberately, 'You know, Corvinus, although I hate to shed suspicion on my own brother, I do wonder if that barge wasn't the subject of the argument he and my father had in the study the day he died. Certainly Aulus isn't one to take no for an answer. And he'd have to get the money from somewhere, wouldn't he?'

'Yeah,' I said non-commitally. 'Yeah, I suppose he would.' Jupiter, what a pair! I'd already had Aulus Nerva practically accusing his brother of parricide and here was Chlorus reciprocating the favour. Not that the point wasn't well made, though. And if Philippus had been one jump ahead of me when I'd told him about the grain barge – which I'd bet the smart dwarf had been – it explained why he'd been so anxious for further details. Also why he'd been so disappointed to find Nerva and Florus gone. I'd probably unintentionally thrown a major spanner in the works there, because having heard him express his opinion re poaching on other people's business preserves I could see how a plan to open a floating brothel-cum-gambling hall would *really* piss the guy off. Not that that would lose me any sleep, mind. 'Ah . . . one last question, pal, if you'll answer it for me.'

'Yes?'

'How did your mother die?'

He blinked. 'I beg your pardon?'

'It was a natural death, was it?'

'Corvinus, you have no right to—' He stopped; he'd gone bright purple to the roots of his hair. 'Why do you want to know?'

'If you don't want to answer, pal, then that's fine by me. I can always ask someone else.'

'No. In any case, there's nothing that . . . at least—' He stopped again and took a deep breath. 'Mother was a chronic invalid. She also walked in her sleep; the doctor said the habit was connected to the disease. One night she . . . the slave who was supposed to be watching her had dozed off. Mother walked out of her bedroom, fell downstairs and broke her neck.'

I stared at him. Oh, shit. 'This was, what, thirty years back, right?'

'Yes, it was, as a matter of fact. Exactly, twenty-nine.'

'Anyone see it happen?' I could've bitten my tongue off as soon as I asked the question: Chlorus might be oily, but he wasn't stupid.

Not that he seemed unduly put out, although he didn't reply at once. I could've been mistaken but I had the impression he was weighing up two possible answers, which was interesting in itself. Finally, he said, 'Yes. My sister. And my father. They both came out when they heard her moving. My father's room was next door to Mother's and Penelope's was just down the corridor.'

'They couldn't do anything?'

Pause again. Chlorus cleared his throat. 'She'd walked before, of course. The doctor said that waking her would be more dangerous than leaving her alone, so he didn't interfere. Then she . . . her foot must have come out of one of her slippers. She tripped and fell. My father tried to catch her but he was too late. She tumbled all the way down.'

'And your sister?'

'She came out of her room after my father left his. She could do nothing either.' A third pause, longer this time. 'Corvinus, I should not really be telling you this, but Penelope claimed that it was no accident. That Father had pushed her.'

For a second, it didn't register, then it did. 'You're saying Murena killed your mother deliberately?'

'No, of course not. I'm only saying that Penelope *believed* that he killed her. She still does. Complete nonsense, of course, she must have been mistaken – have misinterpreted – but there you are. That's Penelope for you; she always was a strong-minded girl, very stubborn, very sure of herself even when she was obviously in the wrong. It's why she hated Father. Why she's always hated him. I thought perhaps you'd better know that too.' He stood up. 'I'm sorry, I really must be going. Thank you for the wine.'

My brain still felt numb. 'Uh . . . one more thing, pal,' I said. 'No offence, but I asked your brother and I'd better ask you just to balance the books. Where were you the night your father died?'

This time he didn't hesitate. And the smugness was back in spades. 'At Ligurius's house. I'd gone round to warn him about a slow-paying customer in Pompeii.'

I raised my eyebrows. 'That late? After hours? Couldn't you have talked to him during the day?'

'He lives not far from me. It's often more convenient to call round in the evening than to make a daytime trip out to the farm and that's what I usually do. The Anchovy doesn't mind.' Yeah, I'd bet! 'You can confirm it with him if you don't believe me.'

'Right. Right.' Sure I would! 'Thanks.'

'Don't mention it.'

He left. But it wasn't the smug way he'd delivered his alibi that stuck as I watched him go (that'd check out, or the bastard wouldn't've been so happy to give it. Or so quick). Nor was it even the story of his mother's death (dear gods, I didn't even know the woman's *name*!).

It was the look in his eye, when he told me about Penelope hating her father, of complete and utter satisfaction.

Nice family, right? First Gellia slagging Chlorus and Nerva, and vice versa; then Nerva putting the boot in on his brother; now Chlorus doing the same for Diodotus, Nerva and Penelope.

I felt faintly sickened. There wasn't the worth of a copper piece to choose among the lot of them.

I didn't feel like any more of the dumplings, but I poured myself more wine and sat back to think things through. Well, that had been a facer. I didn't doubt the story had been true, in its essentials at least – Chlorus wouldn't've risked making it up from scratch – but the angle he'd given it was a different matter. Gods, what a shower! If I hadn't asked about the mother's death no doubt eventually one of the brothers – and I couldn't see much difference between Chlorus and Nerva there, they were both venomous bastards – would've found some excuse for telling me about it, just to spread the poison. So. Penelope believed that her father had been directly responsible for her mother's death. Whatever the actual facts were – and I'd have to follow that one up before I was much older – it gave her reason in spades to hate him and so, possibly, to have murdered him. Nice one, Chlorus.

What he'd told me about Diodotus was interesting too. Oh, sure, his motives were obvious, but again facts – if you accepted them – were facts. Whatever line Diodotus had shot me about the ethics of the medical profession, that Drepanum business was too coincidental for comfort; too coincidental, certainly, for me to dismiss it as irrelevant out of hand. And the connection with Philippus had been completely unexpected. If the two were partners – or at least shared a business interest – then it wasn't beyond the bounds of possibility that they were in bed together in other ways. That was another angle that I'd have to check.

Add Brother Nerva's projected scam with the grain barge. From what Chlorus had said, that was a factor too. The guy was pressed enough for cash as it was – I knew that – and the grain barge would put the lid on things. If he'd floated the idea past his father and got the dull thud, then he'd be getting pretty desperate. Murena's death would've removed a considerable obstacle: he'd have, if not the money itself yet, at least the guarantee of the money, and, what was just as important, virtual control of the company's policy. Not a clincher by any means – I didn't know how vital he considered his grain barge idea to be – but again something to bear in mind.

Of course, re the grain barge and controlling interest in the company, there was another possibility to consider. Philippus had acted surprised when I'd mentioned the barge, sure, but all the same the guy was a sharp, sharp cookie where business was concerned, and his information network was probably pretty hot stuff. The case for his knowing about it already was at least arguable.

Okay, given that, a second scenario. Let's say that he *did* know about it; that what surprised him – or rather knocked him out of kilter – wasn't the news that Nerva and Florus were planning to set up in competition with him but that the nosey purple-striper looking into Murena's death was in on the secret. Gambling was Philippus's bag. Nerva would know that. He'd also know that if he got into a head-to-head with a hard bastard like Philippus the chances were he'd come off a poor second best. Right. So say instead that he's completely open about things. He approaches Philippus with the barge idea and suggests a three-way partnership rather than the two-way one that he and Florus have got going already.

It would work; sure it would. Nerva would benefit because he'd neutralise a potential future business rival, and probably avoid having his balls stamped on in some alley in the process. Also, he'd be able to tap into a major new source of finance, which was something he was desperate for. Sure, now the profits would have to be split three ways rather than two, but this was Baiae, and once the thing was up and running they'd be pretty considerable. On the plus side, his own capital outlay to get them into that state would be a lot less. In his present circumstances the advantages would outweigh the disadvantages, no question.

So much for Nerva. Philippus, now . . .

This was the crux of the scenario. If that was the sum total of the deal then Philippus would benefit in the usual ways, naturally. On the other hand, the guy could do better: a lot better, especially since he's no milksop and for personal reasons so far undisclosed already hates Licinius Murena's guts. Currently, Murena's in the process of using company funds to finance the building of a hotel, and Philippus may be spitting blood but he's hamstrung. Okay. So then Nerva comes along and makes his pitch re the grain barge scheme. Philippus brings up the subject of the hotel. He doesn't approve and – because Murena has refused to bankroll Nerva on the project's account – he understands that Nerva doesn't approve either. He points out that without Licinius Murena there wouldn't *be* any hotel project and that with his father out of the picture Nerva could invest the family company's money as he liked. Also, that Nerva doesn't have any more love for Murena than Philippus does. That being the case, and to simplify matters, it might be in both their interests to put the old guy into an urn . . .

Of course, there was that argument between Nerva and his father the day of Murena's death to explain. With the Philippus deal up and running, he wouldn't't've had to ask Dad for money again at all. All the same, I only had Chlorus's suggestion that that was what they'd quarrelled over, and Chlorus had his own fish to fry. It could've been about something entirely different – Murena, by all accounts, hadn't been the most easy-going of men – and if so the theory still held

Bugger Chlorus. I didn't like the man, and he was as slippery and self-serving a customer as I'd ever experienced, but intentionally or otherwise he'd put the ends of more strings into my hands in those five minutes than I'd bargained for. Now all I could do was play the game, follow them up and see where they led.

So where did I start? With the most puzzling string, the one I knew the least about, the death of Murena's first wife. How that fitted in I didn't know, but my guts told me that it was important. Or could be important. Another talk with Penelope was in order there, sure, but I couldn't go in there cold. I had to get the background first. So who could I ask? Not Tattius: there was something about the guy that made me uneasy, and he was Penelope's husband, which put him out of court in the first instance. Someone who'd known the Murena family a long time but wasn't directly connected with them.

I swallowed the last of the wine, paid my bill and set out for the fish-farm and another talk with Ligurius.

13

'Fadia. Her name was Fadia.' Ligurius was eyeing me speculatively from the other side of the office counter. He put the set of bills he'd been working on to one side. 'She's been dead almost thirty years. Why would you be interested in her?'

I shrugged. 'I'm interested in everything at the moment, pal. Anything and everything that comes up.'

'Things aren't going too well?'

There it was again. I'd had it with Nerva, then Chlorus, now I was getting it from Ligurius: the too-casual question that hinted at more than just curiosity. I gave him the same answer I'd given the other two: 'I'm plugging along. We'll get there in the end.'

He grunted and flicked one of the abacus beads back to its starting point on the wire. 'Fair enough. What do you want to know?'

'She was an invalid, wasn't she?'

'An invalid?' He looked at me sharply. 'Who told you that?' Then, when I didn't respond: 'Not that it matters, they're all as bad as one another. My bet would be Chlorus. He's always been the mealy-mouthed one of the family.' He waited. I waited longer. 'Well, Corvinus, invalid'd be one description. Fadia was odd when Murena married her. Nothing extreme, just what you'd put down to fancies and obsessions; wouldn't wear anything blue, wouldn't step on the cracks between paving stones. Over time it got worse. Latterly she wasn't exactly insane but she wasn't all that far from it. She hadn't been out of the house for years, never left alone for a minute. She even had a slave watching her at night while she slept in case she did something silly.'

'What sort of silly?'

'Any sort. Burned the house down. Or tried to harm herself. That was always a possibility.'

This was an angle I hadn't thought of. 'You mean she was suicidal?'

'There were a couple of incidents. Like I say, it was possible.'

'You think she did kill herself in the end?'

That got me a long, considering stare. Finally, he looked away. 'No. No, her death was an accident, as far as I know. As far as anyone knows for certain.' He paused, and I had the distinct feeling that he was going to say something more. If so, he changed his mind and turned back to me. 'All the same, it was an accident waiting to happen, and maybe it was for the best. A release for everyone concerned, including her. You heard about the sleep-walking?'

'Yeah. She fell downstairs, didn't she?'

'That's right. Fell and broke her neck on the way down. She was dead before she reached the bottom.'

This was the tricky bit. 'Uh . . . there seems to be a question over whether her husband was involved. As more than a witness, I mean.'

He glanced at me sharply, then looked away again. 'So I've heard,' he said.

'You have any opinions on that score?'

'No. I wasn't there, and me, I can't see that it matters now. Like I say, the death was a release for everyone concerned, including the woman herself. And whatever the truth it was a long time ago. Water under the bridge.'

Yeah, well, maybe. But I couldn't leave it at that, no way. Evidently to get a reaction I had to spell this one out. 'Penelope claims that her father was responsible. She believes she saw him push her. Or that's what I was told.'

His eyes came back to me. 'By Chlorus again?' He turned away as if he was going to spit, but didn't. 'Chlorus is a shit-stirrer, Corvinus, and always has been. And he's never liked his sister. Never liked anyone, much.'

'You mean he's lying?'

'No. At least, not about the believing part. Chlorus doesn't lie if telling the truth – or as much of it as'll suit, anyway – will do his business for him. What actually happened that night's another matter, and like I say I'm not qualified to give an opinion.'

'What happened to the slave? The one who was supposed to be on watch?'

'Murena had her flogged to death.' He must've noticed my expression because his lips twisted. 'Oh, yes. He ordered it there, and then. He was within his rights, of course – technically, at any rate – and he was quite justified over the blame aspect, because if the woman had been doing her job properly the accident would never've happened.'

'Even so, that's what it was. An accident.'

He flicked another bead on the abacus back and forward before he answered. 'You didn't know the man, Corvinus,' he said neutrally. 'That wouldn't matter to him; accident or deliberate, it'd come to the same thing. He could be cruel when he liked, very cruel. If you were wise you didn't cross Licinius Murena, or if you did you learned to regret it.'

'That's a trait he passed on, isn't it?' I said. 'I was told

Chlorus had had one of his slaves beaten to death for breaking a wine-dipper.'

Ligurius nodded. 'That's so. It happened a year or so back, caused quite a stink locally; killing a slave for next to nothing might be acceptable behaviour in some quarters, but not around here. It'll've been Brother Nerva told you this time, no doubt?' I didn't answer, but he grunted and half smiled. 'Right. Oh, they love putting their knives into each other, these two. They're both bastards, Corvinus, and the old man was worse than either.'

Yeah, I'd go along with that. As far as Nerva and Chlorus were concerned, anyway, and I'd take his word for it on Murena.

'So why do you still work for them if you dislike them so much, pal?' I said. 'Just out of interest? You're no slave, not even a freedman, you can do what you like and go where you like. Why not just up sticks and leave?'

Another long, slow look. 'Because I enjoy my job and I'm good at it,' he said quietly. 'Because, bastard or not, the old man knew that and he left me to it. Because my father managed the farm and his father before him. And because I'm not particularly ambitious.'

'You'll stay on? Even now Murena's dead and you'll be working for the sons?'

'Why shouldn't I? I despised him as much as I despise them, more so, but that didn't affect things any. Why should it now? And they've got more sense than to make any changes where they don't need to.'

Fair enough. It was just a question, anyway. Which reminded me: 'Ah . . . one more thing. While we're talking about Chlorus, and while I remember. The night of the murder he said he was round at your house. That right?'

Ligurius's mouth twisted and he nodded again.

'Discussing a slow-paying customer. A retailer in Pompeii we've had trouble with before. Yes, that's right enough, Corvinus. He came round just after the lamps were lit.'

Not so much as a pause for thought, and if he didn't like the guy – which he clearly didn't – he'd have no reason to fib. Shit. 'Was that usual? I mean, he could've seen you during the day anytime.'

'No, he couldn't. Not as easily, anyway. He isn't out here very often, or even up at the villa, and we both live in the same part of town, the other side, near the Neapolis Gate. I'm not married, I don't socialise, and so he's not putting me out much. Not that that aspect of things would worry Chlorus. Yes, it's usual.'

Bugger. It was still possible, sure, but if Chlorus had been discussing business with Ligurius the other side of town at sunset the chances of him having rushed off, covered the distance to the farm and murdered his father in the time available were up in the flying pigs bracket. It let Ligurius out, too. Ah, well. 'To get back to Fadia—' I began.

One of the farm slaves came up behind me. 'Sorry to disturb you, boss,' he said to Ligurius.

'Yes, Nestor, what is it?'

They were speaking Greek, which didn't surprise me much: there's a strong Greek influence in Campania, of course, and most native Campanians – whether they're *echt* Greeks themselves or not, which the slave evidently was – are bilingual. Take a walk down any town street on market day and at times you can almost make yourself believe you're east of the Adriatic.

'The tunny in Tank Five,' the guy said. 'I pulled a couple of them out to see how they were doing and they're crawling with *oistroi*. You want to come and look?'

My guts had gone cold. Ligurius didn't seem to notice

anything. 'All right,' he said. 'Give me five minutes.' He turned back to me and shifted into Latin. 'I'm sorry, Corvinus. You were saying?'

'Uh . . . *oistroi*,' I said. 'That's Greek for "gadflies", right?'

Ligurius smiled. 'Right. But in fish terms an *oistros* is also the name for a sort of parasite. You get them sometimes, on tunny especially. Nasty, persistent little buggers, worse than leeches in a way and more difficult to get rid of once they've got a hold. I'll have to see to it.' The smile died. 'What's wrong? You feeling all right?'

Holy Jupiter best and greatest! 'Yeah,' I said. 'Yeah, I'm fine. It's just . . . ah . . . I thought the word meant gadfly, that's all.'

I must've looked as stupid as I felt, because Ligurius was looking at me peculiarly.

'Of course it does,' he said. 'Nothing wrong with your Greek. But there's no reason why you should know the other meaning. Even a born Greek wouldn't, unless he was in the fish trade himself. Now if you've finished with me for the present and you don't mind I'll just go and check up on those tunny. We've quite a few orders pending and the customers won't be too happy if we send them sick fish.'

'Uh . . . right. Right.'

My brain felt numb. So an oistrus was a kind of parasite, was it?

Shit.

I left Ligurius de-fleaing his tunny, or whatever the hell you did to the brutes under these circumstances, picked up the mare from where I'd left her tethered by the gate, and headed for home. Or rather, in the first instance, in the direction of Zethus's wineshop. I hadn't been there for four days, not since the day after the murder when Alcis and his pals had bagged Trebbio, and I reckoned I owed myself a celebratory cup of wine.

I'd still to work out the details, but it was pretty certain that Murena's partner Tattius was a wrong-'un; more, it was obvious what the guy's game had been. You don't nickname anyone 'Parasite' without a reason, and I'd bet my boots to a mouldy olive that Murena had done it deliberately. Whether Tattius himself appreciated the full implication, though, was a moot point. Sure, on first assumptions he ought to do, but that wasn't necessarily the case: Ligurius had said that unless you were up on fish-trade terminology you'd probably never have heard of that particular meaning and by his own admission Tattius knew next to nothing about the business. My bet – and I'd've risked a pretty hefty one – was that it was Murena's private joke. Certainly calling his partner Oistrus to his face for over twenty years and knowing that the guy didn't understand the insult fitted with what I knew of the old bastard's character. And his nasty sense of humour.

Ligurius must've known, though, and that was interesting because Ligurius, in addition to having been Murena's – and Tattius's – manager from the outset, was a smart, smart cookie. Yet he hadn't batted an eyelid. Curious; but then Murena's farm manager was rather a strange guy. I'd risk another bet that there was more going on inside his head than I knew about. He hadn't liked his boss, either, that was clear enough. But then I'd've been surprised if he had, because on present showing that would've put him in a minority of one.

So, what had we got here? The 'parasite' side of things explained a lot. It explained the unequal partnership, the fact that it had happened in the first place and how it could carry on despite the fact that Murena was pulling far more than his weight. And it explained (I supposed) the fact that Tattius was married to Murena's daughter.

What it didn't explain was why.

Oh, sure, the implication would've been obvious to a congenital idiot; Tattius had – and had had for years – some sort of a hold over Murena and he was bleeding him for it like an oistrus bleeds a tunny: *worse than leeches in a way and more difficult to get rid of once they've got a hold*, Ligurius had said. So what we had was good, honest, old-fashioned blackmail. But what could the hold have been?

Something to do with the death of Murena's first wife.

It had to be that, sure it did, unless the old bugger had other skeletons in the closet that I didn't know about. Which was possible, of course, but Fadia's death was a natural front runner. So. What if Penelope was right? What if Murena *had* pushed the woman downstairs, Tattius knew he had and – which was crucial – could prove it, even after all these years?

That stopped me. Shit: Penelope. If I was right then Penelope knew she was part of the price. And, being married to Tattius, where would that leave her?

Hating her father's guts even harder, and a prime suspect for killing him, that's where.

Only, if Penelope was so convinced that her father had killed her mother, why hadn't she said so, publicly, at the time, as presumably she hadn't? Or had she? And why, knowing as she must've done that she was part of the payoff, did she agree to the marriage?

My head was spinning. We were getting into deep water here. Oh, yeah, I was on to something, I knew that in my bones, but there were far more questions than there were answers. Like what did all this have to do with Murena's murder? Granted, Penelope was shaping up nicely as a suspect, but I couldn't see a middle-aged matron tiptoeing

down to the fish-farm and pushing her father into the eel
tank. Although, on second thoughts, why not? She'd hated
him bad enough, that was clear, and if I was right she'd had
good reason, better than most. But why now? Why not any
other time these twenty-nine years, when she was younger,
slimmer and fitter?

Then again, if Tattius was the killer where was his motive?
Blackmailers don't murder their victims: it happens the other
way about. If the worm suddenly turns things may be
different, sure, but Murena was no worm and if he'd paid up
happily for – again – twenty-odd years why should he
suddenly balk now?

None the less, whoever had done the pushing Murena had
ended up in the tank, and five got you ten the reason
had something to do with his dead wife. If not directly, then
indirectly. It all made sense somewhere along the line, yeah,
no argument; the biggest question of the lot was where?

I got to Zethus's with my tongue hanging out. There was a
fair scattering of punters round the bar but luckily no Alcis;
luckily, because after a hard day's sleuthing I don't think I
could've taken that acid-mouthed bugger. I went straight for
the counter like a duck to water. Which, subsequently, was
to prove a mistake.

'Afternoon, Corvinus.' Zethus detached himself from a
conversation with two of the locals. 'Haven't seen you in here
for a while. How's it going?'

'Okay.' I pulled out one of the bar stools and sat on it.
'Make it a half jug of the usual, pal.'

He filled the jug and poured the first cup. It went down
without touching the sides and I gave myself a refill.

'How's the big murder investigation? I hear you've been
busy.'

'So-so.' He probably knew more about it than I did – wineshop owners usually do – but the other barflies had their ears at full stretch and after my last little run-in with Zethus's clientele I wasn't going to satisfy anyone's curiosity.

Zethus turned to put the wine jar into its rack. 'Trebbio's getting on okay, incidentally,' he said as it thudded home into its cradle. 'I sent him a couple of jugfuls and a few odds and ends from the kitchen.'

'That was good of you.' It was, and I felt vaguely guilty: they'd be holding Trebbio, of course, until the praetor's rep arrived, and although he'd be fed it wouldn't be much. Not that the old soak would be too worried about food, I'd guess, but the wine would've been more than welcome. Zethus was a nice guy. 'Uh . . . you're a local, pal. Or the next thing to it. Just out of interest and while I'm here, you happen to know of a man by the name of Philippus? Licinius Philippus?'

Pause; *long* pause. Finally, Zethus turned round. 'I've heard of him,' he said, his voice carefully neutral.

'He's Licinius Murena's freedman.'

'I know who he is.' His face was expressionless, and he was looking at something over my right shoulder. 'Turned out nice again. We may get a bit of thunder later, though.'

'Only I was wondering.' I took another swallow of wine. 'How did he get to be a freedman? Someone must know.' I glanced sideways at the other punters at the bar. 'Any ideas, anyone?'

No answer, and the punters had suddenly decided that staring at the wall in front of them was the in thing this season. Odd.

Zethus hadn't moved. He was still looking over my shoulder. 'Listen, Corvinus,' he said quietly, 'maybe you should just drink your wine and—'

He never finished. Somewhere among the tables behind me a chair shifted and a voice said, 'Maybe you should just let the man dig a fucking hole for himself and climb down into it, Zethus. If he wants to that bad.'

I turned, slowly.

Oh, shit. Oh, thank you, gods.

Yeah, well; even heavies have to have some quality time. It was just my bad luck that one of the ones I'd last seen trailing their knuckles behind me along the corridor of Philippus's gambling hall happened to have decided to spend it here.

'Ah . . . afternoon, pal,' I said. Bugger, he was big: half my size again and straining the seams of his extra-large tunic. He didn't look like he was much of a one for the social niceties, either.

The barflies on both sides of me edged away like I'd suddenly contracted a bad case of plague.

'I don't want no trouble,' Zethus said. With my back to the bar I couldn't see him, but I heard the scrape of the weighted Punter Pacifier he kept under the counter. A brave man, Zethus.

'Pity. Shut up.' Happy Horace's eyes were fixed on mine. His right hand moved towards his belt-pouch. 'Corvinus, isn't it?'

'Uh . . . yeah.' Trying not to make it too obvious, I leaned back and put my elbows on the bar top. If he rushed me – which was an odds-on-bet – I could lever myself up and kick him in the balls. Not the most stylish or gentlemanly tactic, but I reckoned getting in first and hard was the only way I was going to come out the other side of this in reasonable shape. 'Listen, I don't think your boss would approve of this.'

He grinned. I'd thought Philippus's teeth were bad, but this guy's had them beaten six ways from nothing. I'd just bet he didn't chew mint leaves, either. 'Oh, he would. The boss don't like people asking questions about him behind his back. He don't like it at all. Sooner you understand that the better. And just in case you don't—'

I'd been expecting it, sure, but the rush still caught me off-guard. I only just had time to lift myself and drive my right foot at his groin when he was on me. Only I missed because he swerved at the last moment and punched me hard in the ribs.

It hurt far worse than any normal punch should've done, like being hit with a sledgehammer. I grunted with pain, doubled up round the punch and folded at the knees.

Then there was a dull thud. I didn't know what the hell that was; I was too busy trying to get a grip on the bugger, pull him down to my level and stop him slugging me again. I'd just about managed it when I realised that he was a dead weight.

'You all right, Corvinus?' Zethus said. His voice sounded fuzzy, but that was just me.

I shoved my head out from under a sweaty armpit, tried to breathe and managed a chest expansion of about half an inch before the pain hit me and I decided any attempt at breathing with my back and ribs caught between the jaws of an invisible vice wasn't a smart move. 'Jupiter fucking god almighty!' I whispered, then coughed and *really* wished I hadn't.

Someone – one of the barflies – pulled the guy off me. He slumped to the floor and I noticed the set of iron knuckles clenched in his right fist. Yeah, that explained that one. Well, I was lucky: it could've been a knife.

'I'll take that as a no, then,' Zethus said.

I felt myself beginning to laugh – reaction, sure, it wasn't all that funny – and doubled up again clutching my side. 'Bastard's broken one of my ribs,' I mumbled.

'That so, now?' Zethus was putting the weighted stick back behind the counter like attacks on his customers by rampant gorillas were an everyday occurrence. Maybe they were. 'It's your own fault. I tried to warn you. Lucius here's got his cart outside, he'll get you away before your friend wakes up. You know any doctors?'

Did I know any doctors? Bugger. Still, it might be a good idea at that. He might be on the suspect list, but that didn't affect his medical qualifications any, and I *hurt*.

'Yeah,' I said. 'One, as it happens.' Through sheer effort of will I got a hand round my wine cup – luckily it was still pretty full, because in my present state I couldn't've hefted the jug – and swigged the lot. Not that it did much good, mind. 'Guy called Diodotus. Mean anything?'

'Fancy,' Lucius murmured, standing up and emptying his own wine cup. 'Yeah, I know where Diodotus lives, Corvinus. Come on, you brainless bastard, if you're really hurt I'll drive you over there. Not that you're going to enjoy the ride.'

'What about my mare? She's parked out front.'

'No problem. One of the guys can take her home for you. Sextus?'

A punter nodded. 'Will do. It's on my way.'

'Wait a minute.' Zethus came out from behind the counter and tied a bar towel tight round my chest. 'Not perfect, but it's better than nothing.'

'Yeah,' I said; the pain was still there, sure, but *better than nothing* was a fair assessment. Now it was only agonising. 'Yeah, thanks, Zethus. And for belting Horace here. I owe you one.'

'Don't mention it. He was warned. No one messes with my customers, even if they are idiots.'

Fair point. I grinned, and winced as whoever was

operating the vice gave the screw another turn. 'Uh-huh. Well, thanks anyway. Okay, Lucius, pal. Any time you're ready.'

Clutching my chest and gritting my teeth, I staggered to the door.

Lucius was right. I didn't enjoy the cart ride into town at all.

14

S till, even the state I was in, being jolted for a couple of miles on the front seat of a cart was better than facing Perilla. I'd have to, of course, eventually, but that was one encounter I wasn't looking forward to: Perilla gets really *intense* about me arriving home beaten up.

Diodotus's surgery, as you might've expected from his class of patient, was in the more upmarket part of the town centre, on the sea side of the square: a natty two-up two-down town house in a quiet street where the local bought help kept the cobbles clear of muck and washed so clean you could eat your dinner off them. There were even a few ornamental bushes beside the entrances and pot plants on the windowsills. Not that I was in any mood for taking in the local scenery. Lucius decanted me, knocked on the door, ascertained from the young guy who opened up – he wasn't a slave – that the doctor was in and that I'd be seen this side of the Winter Festival, then buggered off back to Zethus's to chug the rest of my wine. Sympathy for half-assed purple-stripers isn't exactly rife among the Baiae locals.

Mind you, I didn't blame him. In retrospect it'd been the equivalent of jumping into the arena and making faces at the cats.

The doorman took me through to Diodotus's treatment room where the guy himself was writing at his desk.

'Well, Corvinus,' he said, laying down the pen and

standing up. 'What brings you here? I understand from what Aristias tells me that this is a professional consultation.'

'Yeah,' I said. 'Bar-room brawl. A greaser hit me in the ribs with a knuckleduster.' That was all he was getting: Diodotus was still a suspect – very much so – and if he had any connection with Philippus then telling the straight truth was not an option.

'Hmm.' No surprise, hardly even interest. I suspected it'd take quite a bit to faze Diodotus. 'Let's have a look. Take off your tunic. Aristias, help him.'

Easier said than done. Eventually, though, Aristias – he must've been the trainee assistant – and I managed it between us.

The right side of my chest was one huge purpling bruise. Diodotus clicked his tongue.

'You have been in the wars, haven't you?' he said, putting one hand behind my back and pressing gently against the bruise with the other. 'Deep breath, please.'

I breathed in and out. Carefully: breathing was something I'd got pretty circumspect about in the last half-hour. This time I managed to up the half-inch by another quarter. 'You should see the other guy. *Ouch!*'

'Fine.' He let go of me. 'That seems satisfactory.' Jupiter on skates! Not from where I was standing. Trying to stand. 'You're not spitting blood?'

'Only metaphorically, pal.'

'Good.' Not the trace of a smile. 'Lungs intact, then. You're lucky; the rib isn't broken, but it may be cracked. I'll strap you up and give you something for the pain. Aristias, the bandages, please.'

While the two of them were busy with the bandaging and to take my mind off things I looked round the room. I don't have much truck with doctors – no one does who has any sense – and I'd never been inside an actual surgery before. It was more or less what I would've expected: couch, desk, chairs, shelves with labelled jars and bottles plus a range of mortars, a wall-cupboard fitted with little drawers for – presumably – dried herbs and so on, and a bookcase stuffed to the gunnels with tagged book-cylinders. The only bit of furniture I couldn't place – and I wasn't sure I wanted to – was a thing in the corner with as many cords, levers and pulleys as you'd expect to see on a piece of serious military hardware.

'Uh . . . what's that?' I said to Diodotus, nodding at it. 'An army-surplus catapult?'

'There are similarities in the construction.' He finished pulling the linen band tight and held it while the assistant slit along the last yard of its length with a sharp knife. 'But not in the purpose. It's a Hippocratic bench.'

'Is it, now?' The thing had straps, and parts of it were obviously designed to move apart. More torture chamber than army storeroom, then, and high-tech, at that; I reckoned whoever was behind the levers asking the questions wouldn't've had to wait too long before he got the answers. 'A Hippocratic bench, eh?'

'We use it for setting limb fractures and for traction.' While the assistant held the unslit part of the bandage in place he wound the slit ends around my chest and tied a knot.

Limb-setting and traction. I felt my balls shrink just at the thought. Shit; I was lucky that Philippus's sunny little helper hadn't broken my arm, although come to that I doubted if I'd be all that much happier on the operating side of things. Me, I could never be a doctor, no way. They say that in the army, where a good percentage of the patients tend to arrive with symptoms a bit more drastic than a dose of the collywobbles or a slight skin rash, the medics are trained to ignore the screams and just get on with the job of sawing, cutting and stitching. The really proficient ones can have a leg off, cauterise the stump and sew it up tighter than a Lucanian sausage in five minutes flat. Single-minded concentration like that takes a special kind of person, and I was damn sure it wasn't me. Diodotus, now; Diodotus was another matter altogether. Cold, clinical, efficient bastards like him are just made for the medical branch of the Eagles. I could see operating this Hippocratic bench of his wouldn't faze him one bit. He might even get a kick out of it.

That was a chilling thought.

'Where did you do your training, pal?' I said. 'Just out of interest?'

'The Cos medical school, for five years. Then Alexandria, for another ten.' He tied a final knot and then stepped back. 'There, Corvinus. That'll do you. Aristias, mix some of the Number Three. Standard strength.'

'What brought you in to it?'

'The usual. My family have been doctors on Cos for a dozen generations. One of them was a pupil of Erasistratos himself.'

'Erasistratos?' I reached for my tunic. I wasn't going to be dancing on any tables in the near future, sure, and anything but shallow breathing was not a viable option, but at least the guy with the vice had slackened off a notch.

'You haven't heard of him? One of the greatest surgeons who ever lived. He worked in Alexandria two hundred and fifty years ago. Did ground-breaking work on the brain.' He smiled. 'I have a copy of the treatise he wrote, if you'd care to see it. Fascinating stuff, especially the illustrations.'

'The *brain*? You mean he dug around inside people's f— inside people's heads?'

'Oh, yes. Although "dug around" isn't an expression I'd use myself.' He went over to a basin with a jug standing in it, poured water and washed his hands. 'And he based his operations on careful prior research, naturally.'

'What sort of research?'

'Practical research. The medical profession in those days wasn't as hidebound as it is now. Dissection was allowed, even encouraged. Vivisection, too.'

'Uh . . . vivisection? That's cutting up live bodies, right?'

'Of course.'

'Jupiter, pal!'

'Why not? What's so wrong in that? How do you expect medical knowledge – surgery especially – to advance if you forbid actual internal investigation?' He reached for the towel that Aristias was holding out and dried off. 'A corpse is well enough, and relatively easy to come by, naturally, but a dead body can't provide all the answers. Criminals, murderers – men who will die anyway under due process of law – you may as well make practical use of them if it'll help push forward the boundaries of science. It's a crying shame we're no longer permitted to do it.'

Sweet immortal gods! 'You think it's okay to cut people up? *Live* people? Just for information?'

Again the cold smile. He handed the towel back. 'Well, I'd settle happily for dead ones, myself,' he said. 'But living ones – yes, certainly, under certain circumstances. Again, I'd ask you why not, if they're to be executed in any case? Why waste the opportunity? The only way to learn properly how the body operates is while it's actually working.' My expression must've shown what I was thinking. 'Oh, I don't expect you to agree, Corvinus – you'd be in good company, even where a fair proportion of my colleagues are concerned – but the practice is at least defensible. Unfortunately, in these more unenlightened times it's an avenue no longer open to us. We have to make do with second-hand experience, and excellent though the textbooks are they're no substitute.'

Holy shit! Cold and clinical was right! Cutting up corpses was bad enough – I wasn't a religious man, but when my time came to go I wanted to be burned whole, not filleted with my bits in separate bags – but I certainly didn't approve of the idea of letting callous buggers like Diodotus slit a healthy man open just to see how his liver went about doing whatever the hell livers do. Even if the man was a condemned criminal. I struggled into my tunic.

'That should feel better now.' Diodotus went back to his chair behind the desk: consultation over, evidently. 'I'll send my bill round later. Keep the bandages on for a few days. You have a slave who can retie them? It's not a skilled job, just so long as they're firm enough to give support but not too tight to be uncomfortable.'

'Yeah,' I said. 'No problem.' Bathyllus could do that; or, at a pinch, Perilla. It'd have to be a real pinch, mind, because the lady was no gentle-handed nurse at the best of times, and on this occasion sympathy wouldn't figure too strongly. 'Uh . . . as long as I'm here, pal . . .'

He'd picked up his pen and turned his attention away from me to whatever he'd been working on when I came in. Now he looked up again, frowning.

'Yes?'

'Maybe I could just sort of check on a few things that've come up since I saw you last. That be okay?'

'What sort of things?'

'I was told you owned a half share in one of the bath-houses.'

Not an eyelid did he bat. 'That's correct.'

'Any particular reason?'

'Of course. Much of the treatment I prescribe – the treatment any doctor would prescribe – involves bathing, massage and specific exercises. Having a direct link with a bathhouse means that I can send patients somewhere I can be sure they'll be treated exactly according to their requirements.'

Yeah, and the referrals would turn a nice profit, too. Still, that side of it was fair enough. 'Your partner's Licinius Philippus.'

The frown deepened. 'Yes, he is. So?'

'His name came up the last time we spoke. You didn't think to mention the connection?'

He laid the pen down again and turned to his assistant. 'Aristias, leave us alone now, please,' he said quietly. 'I think Valerius Corvinus would like to talk private business.' He waited until the young guy had left. 'Now, Corvinus. No, I did *not* mention the connection. Nor did I volunteer the address of my banker or for that matter information on what I had for dinner the night before because none of the three was relevant. I ask you again: so?'

'Did Murena know?'

'He may have done, but I doubt it. The subject never, to my recollection, came up in conversation, but if it had it would've caused no embarrassment to either of us. Murena certainly wouldn't have minded, nor would he have had any right to say so even if he did.'

'Philippus's bag is rented rooms, girls and gambling. He steers clear of anything else, or so he told me. How come he was willing to go shares with you in a bathhouse?'

'The place was part of his wife's dowry. A family property of long standing. Two years ago I cured him of a chronic bladder infection and as a result he was very grateful. I happened to mention that I'd been thinking of investing in one of the Baian baths and he offered me a half share at a price too tempting to refuse. Does that satisfy you?'

'That your only connection with him?'

He gave me a long look, and I got the distinct impression that he was counting slowly to ten before he answered. Finally, he said, 'Yes. Yes, it is. We're not exactly kindred spirits, as you'll understand if you've met the man. Our "partnership", as you call it, doesn't go beyond two signatures on a deed. He takes no interest in the everyday running of the place, which I do where it falls within my sphere, and as long as he gets his part of the profits each month there's no reason for us to meet.'

I shrugged. 'Okay. Second question. What happened at Drepanum? With the old guy and the young wife.'

That one got through, seriously. He coloured up like a beetroot. 'Corvinus, if your intention is to goad me into—'

'I was told you left there in a hurry. That you were treating the man for the stone and he died suddenly.'

'That had nothing to do with me! Or my treatment! Holy Asclepius, how you have the nerve to come in here and—' He stopped himself, took a deep breath and let it out slowly. Then he said more calmly, 'The man went to a dinner party where – against my specific instructions – he ate and drank far more than his constitution could decently stand. As a result, and not surprisingly, he collapsed and died of an apoplexy in the litter on his way home. And I did not "leave Drepanum in a hurry". If you really want to know, I'd already bought this house in Baiae and was only waiting for a colleague to arrive and take over the practice. All of this, Corvinus, if necessary, and the gods know why it should be, I can prove, and certainly I'm ready to swear to the truth of it if you ask me to. Now, I won't ask where you got your sordid little scraps of information from, because I can hazard a good guess. Was it Chlorus who told you or Nerva?'

'Ah . . . Chlorus.'

He grunted; he was still looking pretty angry, but he'd got himself in hand: *coldly furious* would about cover it now. 'Yes,' he said. 'Yes, it would be. Not that the other wasn't as good a possibility. I should never have had anything to do with that bloody family. They're all vipers.'

'Including Gellia?'

'Gellia more than—' He stopped himself again and stood up. 'I'm sorry, Corvinus. This conversation is becoming most unprofessional. Let me just remind you of what I said the last time we talked: I am a doctor, I have sworn certain oaths and I keep to them strictly, as my family always have done. I had, despite what Titus Chlorus and his ilk may say, no relations whatsoever with Licinius Murena's wife outwith what was proper; nor, of course, was I involved in any way in his death. And, incidentally, should you require an alibi for that evening Aristias will confirm that he and I were attending a difficult childbirth in Bauli which kept us out until early the next morning. That is another fact which I didn't happen to mention at our last interview, again because I didn't deem it relevant. Artistias will provide you with details, if you wish corroboration. Now, if you're satisfied, and even if you aren't, that's all I have to say.'

'Ah . . . right. Right.' Well, if the alibi checked – and there was every reason that it should – then that was that: Diodotus was seriously off the hook. Bugger.

'Good. If there's nothing else . . .'

'One thing.' Hell; I might as well ask while I was here, even if I did get my head bitten off, and if he knew both Murena and Philippus he might have the answer. 'Philippus's background. There any information you can give me on that?'

He checked and frowned. 'In what way?'

'He's Murena's freedman, right? So why did Murena free him? And why, when he did, didn't they have the usual patron—ex-slave relationship?'

Diodotus didn't answer at first, and I thought we'd come up against the ethical stone wall again, or he was going to hand me my teeth in a bag. However, the guy was calming down, maybe even looking a little shamefaced. He even lowered himself back into the chair.

'About the freeing I know nothing whatsoever,' he said. 'The other matter – well, it's fairly common knowledge locally, and I'm surprised you haven't heard the story elsewhere before now. Philippus's father was also one of Murena's slaves. He offended his master in some way, I don't know the details; badly enough, however, for Murena to have him put to death. Rumour has it – although of course I can't confirm or deny the truth of it – that Murena subsequently had his corpse thrown into the eel tank.' He picked up the pen and dipped it in the inkwell. 'Now, Corvinus, I really do apologise, especially for my outburst which was completely uncalled for and contrary to my nature, but I have work to do. Aristias will give you your medicine on your way out.'

I left. Aristias was waiting in the hall, holding out my packet of powder like it was something the cat had dropped. Evidently, the trainee assistant had been listening in, despite Diodotus's instructions, and he wasn't looking too chuffed. They stick together, these medical types.

'Ah . . . about the evening of Licinius Murena's death, friend—' I began.

'We were in Bauli, sir,' the guy said. 'At the Servian villa. All night, from before sunset onwards. A breech delivery.' His tone would've frozen the balls off a salamander. 'Take an egg-spoonful, in water or wine, three times a day before meals, until the packet is empty.'

'Right,' I said. 'Right, thanks.' I just hoped it wasn't poison.

'You're welcome.'

The front door closed behind me.

So Murena had had Philippus's father killed and his body fed to the fishes, had he?

Gods!

I'd never felt less like walking, but at least if anything Diodotus's place was on the right side of town for home, and barring the early morning I'd got the best time for it. The streets were almost deserted, smelling of soup, frying fish and boiled greens: we were well into the late afternoon/early evening dip here, when most ordinary punters've shut up shop at least temporarily for the dinner break while the social butterflies are lounging about at the baths or being primped and painted for another hard evening's partying. The sun was only about a finger's-breadth above the horizon, so the heat was off the day, and there was a cool sea breeze. Perfect walking weather. If it hadn't been for my aching ribs I'd've been enjoying myself.

I was past the town gate and heading down the track that led off the main road for the last half mile or so to the villa when it happened. The gods alone knew what had warned me – maybe a movement in the rocks to my right that caught my eye and sent a message to my brain – but it was enough to save my life. Just. I stopped and half-turned, and something went past my left ear with the whine of an angry gnat.

Oh, shit. A sling may not look much of a weapon, but if the guy holding it knows his business he can knock your brains through the back of your skull easy as winking. I hit the ground fast, almost biting my tongue in half with the pain as my bandaged ribs met the track, and did a rapid crawl towards the safety of the bushes.

Comparative safety. A second stone whizzed through the undergrowth a scant foot above my head, ripping through the packed twigs and leaves and burying itself in the earth bank half a dozen yards in front of me. The ice settled on my spine. Bugger; we'd got a real crackshot here. If he wanted to kill me – which he clearly did – then he wasn't doing too badly.

Okay, Corvinus; panicking won't get you anywhere, boy. What we needed here, and pretty urgently, was cover. I glanced around. On a proper road there would've been a drainage ditch that I could've slid into and blown raspberries at the bastard until he got fed up and went away, or came out of hiding to try his luck at close quarters; but this track didn't have one. All I'd got on my side was bushes. They were thick enough to screen me, sure, but they wouldn't stop a sling-stone. My only chance was to stay flat, keep my head well down and hope that, now he'd lost the element of surprise, the guy over in the rocks would give it up as a bad job.

Or, of course, until he managed to put a shot through the top of my skull which, on current showing, was just as likely. More so. As if to ram home the point, a third pebble went zinging into a stone barely six inches from my ear, shattering as it hit. The fragments stung my cheek. On second thoughts, maybe playing the flatfish wasn't such a hot idea after all.

Hell; it was now or never. A good slinger – and this bastard was good – could have another shot in the pouch while the first was in the air, sure, but reloading would still take that two or three seconds. Not much, but it was all I had. And if

I stayed where I was it was only a matter of time before he drilled me. I sprang to my feet, gasping at the sharp knife-thrust in my chest, and sprinted towards where he must be hiding. At least if he did try another cast then I'd see who the bugger was before he gave me my ticket for the ferry, and if he missed I was quids in.

There was a frantic scrabbling among the rocks up ahead. Yeah, right; so chummie had decided to cut and run for it after all, had he? Fine by me; absolutely fine. I shouted and, ignoring the pain in my ribs, forced myself to make the final spurt . . .

Which was when I found out that there had been a ditch after all. Not a proper, man-made one, just a narrow channel formed by a small spring or the winter run-off on the track's further edge. It was no more than a generous hand's-breadth wide, but it was deep enough, when my foot went into it, to throw me off balance. I came down hard, right on my sore ribs, my head hit a sizeable chunk of rock flat on, and chasing phantom slingers suddenly didn't seem quite so important any more.

The combination had me out of it and gasping for a good two or three minutes. By the time the pain had faded from sheer bloody murder to agonising and I could pull myself back up and take a wider interest in things there wasn't no one left around but us chickens.

Bugger.

Yeah, well. Some you win, some you lose, and at least I wasn't lying back there with my skull smashed like an egg and what brains I had spread over half Campania. I brushed myself off and started the long limp home.

15

Bathyllus's precognitive faculties were obviously at their usual razor-sharp level, and when I hobbled up the drive he was already standing by the open door with the obligatory jug and cup, eyes fixed in horror on what was left of my mantle and tunic. No surprises there: as far as sartorial elegance went, I wouldn't've given a month-old scarecrow a decent run for its money. Not that it was altogether my fault, of course; mantles aren't exactly designed for taking violent exercise in, and when the old pukkah Romans had chosen their national dress they hadn't taken pub-fights, crawling through heavy undergrowth and generally rolling about the countryside into consideration.

I took the cup from the little guy's nerveless fingers and drained it. Beautiful!

'Dinner started?' I said.

'Yes, sir.' He poured a refill and cleared his throat. I could see that the muscle in his right cheek was beginning to twitch: a normal day's wear and tear is one thing, but having the master come back in a state that would've disgraced a third-grade Tiber scavenger offended Bathyllus to his respectable core. 'Ah . . . perhaps you'd like to change first, sir.' He sniffed. 'A wash wouldn't go amiss, either.'

I grinned: from the tone, the sniff and the look I was still getting I had the distinct impression that the finicky bugger would cheerfully have made it a hosing down at short range by the local fire brigade. Not that he was totally out of line, mind: after what I'd been through that day I'd've killed for an hour in the bathhouse. Still, with dinner already served there wouldn't be time for that, even if the furnace was lit. 'Yeah, okay,' I said. 'Fair point, pal, no arguments.' I stripped off the mantle. 'Give this a decent burial, will you?'

'Yes, sir.' He took the thing from me in a fastidious one-finger-and-thumb grip. 'A pleasure. Interesting day, sir?'

'It had its moments.'

'So I see.' Sniff.

'Sod off, Bathyllus.' I was still grinning. Disapproving major-domos or not, it was nice to be home; to be *alive* and home. That was enough for the moment. I'd think about the implications of our friendly pebble-slinger later.

I downed the refill, held the cup out for more and then went upstairs for a sluice and a change.

When I came back down the starters were already half gone.

'Uh . . . sorry I'm late,' I said, easing myself on to the couch beside Perilla as naturally as I could manage. Evidently not naturally enough, though, because Perilla was frowning at me.

'Are you all right, Marcus?' she said.

'Sure. Never better.' I reached – gingerly – for the wine. Luckily, Diodotus's bandaging was hidden by the tunic – she'd see it later, of course, but that was a confrontation I intended to put off as long as possible – and I'd managed to tidy up the worst signs of the cross with the homicidal slinger. 'Just a bit stiff from walking, that's all.'

'Hmm.' She dipped a stick of raw carrot in the fish sauce. 'So how was your day?'

'Busy.' I'd been casting covert glances at Mother and Priscus on the other two couches. Oh, hell. Evidently there had been Developments, and I didn't need to be an augur to see that the signs weren't good: the equivalent of all the sacred chickens at once keeling over and handing in their feed pails. Mother was in full-scale war rig, dressed to the nines up to and including the tiara. That she didn't do normally for family dinners, no way, and it meant that she'd used the prinking and primping as an excuse to spend the time with her maid rather than Priscus. Added to which the old guy looked even vaguer than usual, which was the standard last-ditch Priscan defensive manoeuvre. Mother was ignoring him. I cleared my throat and grasped the nettle. 'Ah . . . how about you, Mother? Anything exciting happen?'

'Don't ask, dear!' she snapped.

Jupiter! Nettle, nothing; what we had here was a combination of prickly pear, poison ivy and Medusa the Gorgon on a very bad hair day. *Seriously peeved* did not quite cover things. 'Yeah, okay, if you—'

'We went into Bauli, the three of us.'

'Hey, that was nice! It's a lovely drive to Bauli, especially—'

'Yes, it is. We were passing one of the wineshops in the square when your stepfather was hailed by Licinius Nerva and Aquillius Florus. I wasn't aware that he'd met the gentlemen, but evidently he had. How and where exactly wasn't at once apparent, although *that*' – she fixed me with her eye – 'became clear later.'

Hell. 'Is that so, now?' I said.

'Mmmaaa! . . . Vipsania, dear, I have apologised already.' Priscus blinked at me. 'I'm sure Marcus doesn't want to know—'

'Be quiet, Titus.' When she likes, Mother has tones to her voice that would make a legionary First Spear hand in his vine-staff and take up crochet. She used them now, and Priscus curled up like a salted slug. 'Marcus has his faults, many of them, the gods know, but as de facto if not precisely, thank the gods, de iure head of the family he has a duty to know what is going on under our noses. If' – she shot me another look – 'he didn't know already and was covering up for you. Which wouldn't surprise me in the least.'

Oh, bugger; so the shit had finally hit the fan. Well, I'd warned the old buffer. Twice. All that remained was to ascertain precise details re coverage and depth. 'Ah . . . maybe you'd like just to tell me what Priscus did, Mother,' I said.

'I am doing so.' Mother shelled a peahen's egg and dunked it viciously in the salt. 'The two . . . gentlemen, as I say, hailed Titus by name as a long-lost friend and insisted that he have a cup of wine with them. Naturally I didn't want to cause a scene so we arranged that Perilla and I would take a walk and pick him up on the way back in time for a spot of shopping.'

I glanced at Perilla. The lady was keeping her head down: a bad sign. 'Seems fair enough to me,' I said. 'Very reasonable arrangement.'

'So I thought.' Mother dunked the egg again, squashing it. 'When we returned Nerva and Florus had gone and Titus was sitting at the table, smelling strongly of drink.'

'It was only two cups, dear. Well watered.'

'Don't interrupt, Titus. Despite this, Marcus, since I saw no reason why the day should be irretrievably ruined, we continued to Gratianus's, which as you know is one of the better local jewellery shops. I bought, or at least I selected for purchase, a very nice little cameo brooch. Naturally, since Titus was carrying the money, I referred Gratianus to him . . .'

Uh-oh; I knew what was coming now. The daft old bugger!

'. . . only to discover that he had nothing to pay with. Of

course, I asked him why – he'd had, to my sure knowledge because I checked as I always do, at least fifteen gold pieces in his belt-pouch when we left this morning – and after a certain amount of prevarication and downright lying—'

'Mmmaaa!'

'. . . it transpired that he had lost all of it to his two wineshop friends in a dice game. Gratianus very kindly set the brooch aside for me, so that part of it is fine, but understandably I was seething. Which I still am.' She dropped the squashed, over-salted peahen's egg on to her plate and wiped her fingers. 'There. *That* is the story. Appalling, isn't it?'

'Uh . . . yeah. Yeah. Disgraceful.'

'Of course, I had everything out of him on the way home. He has been going behind my back for days, pretending to visit that Sicilian friend of his while actually frequenting gambling dens, wineshops and goodness knows where else. It is despicable and deceitful and, naturally, it stops here.' She glared at Priscus.

'Yes, Vipsania,' Priscus murmured. A six-year-old caught with his hand in the preserved fruit jar couldn't't've said it better. Well, at least that got me off the hook: with Priscus grounded, presumably for the rest of the holiday if not for life, my half-promise to take him to the gambling hall wasn't valid any longer. And because I'd already talked to Philippus I wouldn't be shedding any tears on that account.

'So there only remains, Marcus, for you to get the money back,' Mother said.

I snapped into full attention. '*What?*'

She sniffed. 'You're the head of family, dear. I understand that you know or have had dealings with these two dice-sharpers already. You may even – I don't accuse you, but I have very strong suspicions – have been instrumental in introducing them to Titus and so allowed them to take advantage of him. You therefore have a clear duty and obligation to remedy the situation by recovering the money. And don't try to weasel out of it, because you won't.'

Oh, shit. 'Mother, look, this has got nothing to do with me, right? I'm sorry, but if a guy gets involved in a dice match of his own free will he has to be prepared to—'

'The usual conventions regarding the settlement of gambling debts do not apply, Marcus. Titus was not responsible for his actions. You've known him long enough to know that he very seldom is. I'm willing to set this particular instance of his gross irresponsibility down to a temporary aberration on his part—'

'Mmmaaa!'

'. . . but as I say having talked long and seriously with him I have grave doubts about your role in the business. Someone must have led him astray and to my mind you are the obvious candidate. In fact the only possible candidate.'

'Now look here! I—'

'So I expect you – *expect* you, Marcus – to make suitable amends, at the earliest opportunity.' She reached for the stuffed olives. 'There. That's all I have to say on the subject, dear. I am disappointed in you; *gravely* disappointed. Consider the matter closed.'

I sat back. Jupiter on a fucking trolley doing handstands! How had that worked? In the course of two minutes I'd moved from uninvolved sympathetic listener to the villain of the piece, while conniving bloody Priscus came out the other end shining white as a vote-chaser's mantle. There wasn't no justice; there wasn't *no* justice! When I got my bleating, buck-passing stepfather on his own I would kill the bastard.

Typical Mother, mind. She may have a first-class brain, but in her book the direction of a logical progression is optional: you choose where you want it to go and that's where it ends up. If the destination doesn't make sense to anyone else, then tough, and there's no use arguing because that just makes things worse.

'Ah . . . right,' I said. 'Right. Okay. I'll do my best.'

'You had better. And no cheating by substituting your own money, either.'

Hell . . .

'Now.' She settled back and unshelled another peahen's egg. 'How is your case going?'

I told them, missing out the little contretemps at Zethus's and the resultant trip to Diodotus's, plus, of course, the slinger episode. It took a while – like I'd said to Perilla, the day had been busy – but at least it got my mind off the Priscus problem. By the time I'd finished Bathyllus and the minions had cleared away the starters and brought the main course. I noticed that, following a glare from Mother that would've filleted an anchovy, the wine slave skipped Priscus's cup: the old guy was obviously on strict probation. Not that I had any sympathy, mind. At that precise moment I'd gladly have recycled the duplicitous bugger for catmeat.

'They seem a *most* unpleasant family,' Mother said.

'Yeah.' I took a swig of wine. Only a small one: I'd had Bathyllus bring a dozen jars of the Special down with us, and given him strict instructions to go easy on the water – luckily, with Priscus out of things for the duration I was the only one drinking, Mother and Perilla being on some fruit-juice-honey-and-herb aberration – because Mother tended to keep count. 'That's putting it mildly.'

'So who are your prime suspects?' Perilla said.

'Almost any of them could've done it, as far as motivation goes.' I helped myself to the seafood ragout. 'The old guy wasn't exactly flavour of the month all round. Opportunity, now . . . well, that's a different matter. Gellia's still up there, for a start. Standard motive: she's a good thirty years younger than her husband, they weren't exactly compatible, and she's got an itch in her drawers that she isn't averse to scratching.'

'*Marcus!*' Mother snapped.

I ignored her. 'Also, she's got no alibi.'

'Could she have done it alone? What about the doctor?'

'Uh-uh. Diodotus is clean. He was at an all-night childbirth over in Bauli. But there's—'

'You talked to him?' Perilla said sharply. 'When?'

'Ah . . .' I slid to a mental halt. Oh, shit; there went the ball-game. 'We, uh, bumped into each other in the market square.'

The lady had put down her spoon and fixed me with her eye. 'Marcus,' she said, 'you're lying. I want to know why, please.'

'Look . . .'

'I am looking. I'm also listening. I'll find out eventually, of course, so you may as well tell me now.'

Overtones of pure natron chilled to a temperature that'd make winter in Thule feel like an Arabian July. Well, that hadn't lasted long, had it? And she was right: she'd see the bandages as soon as I took off my tunic. It was a fair cop. 'We, uh, talked while he was fixing me up,' I said. 'Round at his surgery.'

' "Fixing you up"?'

'Yeah. I sort of got involved in a bar-room brawl. A minor one. Nothing serious, no real—'

'A *brawl*?'

'Over at Zethus's. Gods, Perilla, it's only a bruised rib! Nothing to—'

'*Marcus Valerius Corvinus, I will—*'

'Perilla, dear,' Mother broke in calmly, 'no quarrelling at the table, please. You can tear his ears off in private later.' She shelled a mussel. 'Personally, I'm not surprised in the least. If I have learned anything about my son in the past thirty-six years it is that his brain doesn't function like a normal person's. If indeed, properly speaking, it functions at all.'

Jupiter on a pole! 'Now look here, Mother!'

'Quite. I totally agree, Vipsania.' Perilla sniffed. 'We'll discuss the brawl later, Marcus. In detail. Carry on.'

'Ah . . . right. Right.' I gathered my wounded dignity. Yeah, well, at least she didn't know about the sling attack. That little nugget I wasn't going to pass on, no way, nohow, never: finding out how close I'd come to having a hole drilled through my head would really put the lady off her dinner. 'Where was I?'

'The doctor.'

'Yeah.' I took a swig of the Special to help get things back on track again. 'Like I say, Diodotus is out, as the actual murderer, anyway. He'd be capable enough, sure, especially on the planning side, but even if he hadn't had an alibi I can't see him and Gellia being an item, and without that he's got no real motive. Gellia would've had to be the driving force, and Diodotus is no pushover. Florus, now, he's another matter.'

'Ah.' Mother leaned back.

'He's got the brains of a gnat, he's tied up with Gellia and I'd bet the lady could twist him round her little finger if she wanted to. He was at Philippus's gaming-house for at least part of the evening, sure, but only latterly; he could've gone there straight from Murena's place, easy. Florus is a possibility.'

'What about the rest of the family?' Perilla said.

'Chlorus is off the hook. He was at Ligurius's that evening, which alibis them both. Nerva . . . well, he tried claiming at first that he was at Philippus's until the small hours, but according to the staff he wasn't there at all. Nerva's a fair bet. Certainly he was at the villa earlier in the day, and he had a row with his father, probably over money. Also, I'd have a side bet that Nerva could've been in on it with Philippus, for business reasons.' I swallowed another mouthful of wine. 'The most interesting of the three, though, is Penelope.'

'*Who?* Oh, Marcus!'

'Hang on, lady. Middle-aged matron or not, if she believed that her father was responsible for her mother's death then she's got motive in spades.'

'But, Marcus, that's silly! The woman . . . what was her name again?'

'Fadia.'

'Very well. Fadia has been dead for thirty years. Even if your Penelope does believe she was murdered why should she suddenly decide on revenge at this stage?'

I shrugged. 'Pass. I asked myself the same question. Even so, it's a possibility, and six gets you ten there's a thread there that needs following.'

Mother had been de-shelling a prawn. She looked up, frowning. 'This all happened in Rome, didn't it?' she said. 'Not in Baiae?'

'Uh . . . yeah,' I said. 'Yeah, I assume so.'

'And there was . . . would there have been an actual trial involved?'

I felt the first tingle of excitement: now that was an angle I *hadn't* thought of. 'Maybe,' I said cautiously. 'You tell me.'

She shook her head. 'No, dear. I'm afraid I can't go quite

that far. When you first mentioned Licinius Murena's first wife the word "trial" did slip into my head, but that's all there was, and I'm afraid it's too faint a bell.'

'Never mind, Mother,' I said. 'Anything you've got.'

'I'm sorry, but there really is nothing more. After all, it's been almost thirty years. Your father and I were abroad at the time when . . . whatever it was . . . happened, and when we got back to Rome the thing was well past the gossip stage. Still, I do remember a trial of some kind being mentioned, and that Licinius Murena was not considered altogether' – she hesitated – '*welcome* any longer socially, if you know what I mean.'

'Yeah,' I said. The hairs on the back of my neck were definitely stirring now: we could be on to something here. 'Yeah, I know.'

I did; anyone from a purple-striper family would. In the circles Mother was talking about, you either fitted or you didn't, right from birth. On the other hand, even for the ones who fitted, there was a line that was as clear and precise as the sacred city boundary; cross it, and the great and good might still be polite enough to your face but socially and otherwise you were dead meat. Not that we're necessarily talking actual crime here: indulging in some crimes, such as peculation, embezzlement, vote-rigging and even treason, is just a good old-fashioned upper-class-Roman tradition, hardly even in the minor peccadillo class: getting yourself exiled or being told to slit your wrists may prove inconvenient personally, but they don't lead to loss of status, not in the opinion of the people who matter, anyway. Try cheating a partner over a business deal or welshing on a bet, though, and you're *really* in shtook. In fact, as Mother put it, you're no longer *welcome* . . .

Interesting, right? Especially so because, if my theory re

Tattius held good, Licinius Murena must've made his decision to up sticks and move to Baiae shortly afterwards.

'Marcus, you're not listening!' Mother snapped. 'Pay attention, dear!'

'Hmm?' I brought my eyes back into focus. 'Sorry. What was that?'

'I was saying that if you're really interested you could have a word with Quintus Saenius.'

'Who?'

'Quintus Saenius. If anyone remembers the details then he probably will. He has a villa on the Bauli road, just past the shrine to the Graces, if I recall. He's getting on a bit now, and almost blind, but before he retired to Baiae he had a very extensive forensic practice. If you think it's all that important, of course.'

'Uh . . . yeah. Yeah, I do.' Gods! 'Thanks, Mother.'

'Don't mention it.' Mother finished de-shelling the prawn. 'He's quite a dear. Do give him my regards when you see him.'

'Yeah,' I said. 'I'll do that.'

I settled back to my dinner, brain buzzing.

16

I slept on my back that night; rolling over wasn't an option unless I didn't mind a little excruciating agony, which I did. The lady wasn't sympathetic, either.

'Corvinus, if you *will* get yourself mixed up in bar-room brawls you'll just have to take the consequences. Now don't groan too loudly, I want to sleep.'

Oh, great.

When I crawled out of bed the next morning with gritted teeth and feeling like six kinds of vice-squeezed hell, the only consolation I had was that after the belt on the noggin Zethus had given him Happy Horace wouldn't be all that chipper either. I swigged down my dose of Diodotus's powder in a cupful of wine and water – the stuff tasted like fermented mouse-droppings, sure, but I had to admit it was effective – got Bathyllus to retie the bandages and give me a leisurely shave, grabbed a quick crust and set off for Quintus Saenius's place. Walking: the Shrine of the Graces on the Bauli road was a fair trek, but in my present state I wasn't going to risk a horse. On foot was bad enough.

I went careful, mind. Of course, it was sod's law that the day after someone had had a crack at me with a sling I should be having to give the bastard a second shot at the nuts by taking a walk across open country, but that couldn't be helped. Short of kitting myself out in full legionary armour or putting a bucket over my head, there wasn't much more

I could do than keep my eyes skinned and my fingers crossed. In any case, the risk of another attack didn't just go one way. The bugger had been lucky, last time, that I hadn't caught a glimpse of him. Now I was forewarned the chances of that happening a second time were pretty slim. If he tried and missed again then I'd have him by the short hairs.

Not that my phantom slinger was likely to be identical with the murderer, though; that was too much to hope for. Oh, sure, any kid worth his salt can throw a pebble a few yards without smacking himself round the ear with it, but if he's a townie – especially a well-born townie – then that's usually his lot, and by the time he's into his teens he has other skill priorities. To find a *real* expert you've got to look to the country, among the sheep- and goat-herders, where using a sling well is an essential part of the job. Certainly, as far as the extended Murena family were concerned, I doubted if any of them could hit a barn door at thirty yards more than three times out of five, which just wasn't good enough for chummie.

So. My bet was that whoever wanted me out of the way had done a bit of judicious hiring. Baiae might not be like Rome and have a thriving sub-population of knifemen willing to take on a commission, but there're always guys on the fringes ready to make a silver piece or two. And if he (or she) could find them, then I might be able to as well.

The villa was tucked into a fold of anonymous ground just off the main road. It was pretty typical of the houses you get inland of the bay: Baiae and Bauli themselves are rich districts, and waterfront properties tend to be flashy, OTT and only for the seriously moneyed, but the area's also popular with not-so-wealthy city types who've made their modest pile and want to retire to where the air's fresher and there's more green than grey. Saenius was obviously one of them. There were no impressive gateposts, sweeping carriage drive or ornamental fountains, but it was a tight little place with a long frontage and quite a bit of plain white marble on show.

I went up the steps. The door-slave – he looked like Tithonus's grandfather, eighty if he was a day – was sitting on a stool outside, eyes closed, dozing in the sunshine.

'Uh . . . excuse me, pal,' I said.

There was no reply.

I tried again, louder, and the guy woke with a snort. 'I'm sorry. I'm looking for Quintus Saenius. This his house?'

'Eh?' He cupped an ear.

I raised my voice another notch. 'Quintus Saenius?'

'I'm sorry, sir, you'll have to shout. I'm a bit deaf.'

Gods! '*Quintus* . . . bloody . . . *Saenius!* This where he lives?'

'You want to see the master?' The hand still hadn't moved.

We have contact! I pressed my aching ribs. 'Yeah, if . . .' I began, then nodded instead; it was quicker and less painful.

'He's in the rose garden.' The guy stood up, slowly. I swear I could hear the creak. 'What name, sir?'

Oh, hell; round two. 'Corvinus. Marc—' Shit. '*Marcus . . . Valerius . . . Corvinus.*' Nothing. '*I SAID MARCUS . . . VALERIUS . . .*'

Ouch!

'Ah.' He gave me a myopic stare. 'Perhaps you'd just like to follow me. I'll show you.'

He set off along the portico at an arthritic hobble. Yeah, well, the rose garden couldn't be all that far away, but I just hoped he didn't croak before we got there. Me, I wouldn't take any bets.

We reached it, eventually: a walled garden, opening off the

portico's far end, planted out with more roses than I'd ever seen growing in one place. The air was heavy with scent. Modest villa or not, Saenius was obviously a rose fanatic.

He was sitting on a bench set against the far wall. If I'd thought the door-slave was old, Saenius was ancient: a little, dapper man in a very formal broad-striper mantle, with about three strands of white hair carefully combed over a scalp bald and gleaming as a bronze mirror. His eyes were closed, but he can't've been sleeping because when we were still a dozen feet away they opened.

'Marcus Veranius Curtinus, master,' the slave said.

'Ah . . . that's Marcus Valerius Corvinus, sir.' I was looking at his eyes. The eyeballs were almost completely covered by cataracts. Yeah: Mother had said he was blind.

'Messalinus's son?' He was staring at a point just to the right of my ear. His voice was thin and reedy, like I'd imagine a ghost's might be. Jupiter, he must be ninety, easy!

'Yeah, that's right,' I said.

'He was a fine lawyer, your father. I heard him speak many a time.' He chuckled, with a sound like dry leaves rustling. 'Often, to my discomfiture, on the opposing side, which does not make his son any the less welcome. Sit down, Corvinus. You don't mind sharing a bench? As you may have noticed, Paulus isn't really up to fetching chairs these days.'

I sat. 'Nice garden. The roses are beautiful.'

'Oh, I've been collecting them for many years. They were always a passion of mine even before this.' He indicated his eyes. 'Now, of course, I'm very grateful to myself for my original choice of hobby. I spend most of the day out here in summer.'

The door-slave was still hovering. 'Should I bring some wine, master?' he said.

'Corvinus?' Saenius looked at me, directly this time. I

wondered if he had at least some vision left or if he'd taught himself to gauge distance and direction from the sound of a voice. 'I don't drink wine myself at all now – doctor's orders – but I have a passable Latian in the cellar if you'd care to try it.'

'No. No, that's okay,' I said. 'I'm fine.' After walking all the way from Baiae I could've murdered a cup of Latian, but I wasn't going to risk being responsible for Gerontius here keeling over into the flower-beds under the weight of a wine tray. 'Which doctor?'

'A young chap, name of Diodotus. He's very good.'

Well, it was probably chance. The guy was a high-society doctor, there weren't all that many around, and he had a large practice. He certainly got about, though. 'My mother told me to give you her regards, by the way,' I said. 'She was the one who suggested I call.'

He nodded. 'Vipsania, isn't it? She's well?'

'Very well.' Fit and punching.

'A splendid woman; beauty, brains, character and a sense of proportion. You don't get that combination very often. Your father – no offence meant, Corvinus – made a great mistake when he divorced her. One among very few. Give her my best wishes. Now.' He adjusted a fold of his mantle. 'That's quite enough of the civilities. You've come for a reason, of course.'

'Uh . . . yeah,' I said. 'Mother thought you might remember something about a trial in Rome thirty years back. To do with the death of a lady called Fadia.'

His chin came up. Old man or not, I could see he was no pushover. 'Licinius Murena's wife?' he said sharply.

I felt the first brush of excitement. 'Yeah. That's right.'

He didn't speak at once. Then he said, 'Corvinus, I am – or was – a lawyer, and I neither believe in nor trust coincidences. So before we continue let's have one thing clear. Would this interest of yours have any connection with Murena's own recent . . . death?' I noticed the pause before the last word, like he'd selected it carefully and deliberately from a range of options. Lawyer was right.

'Yeah,' I said. 'Yeah, it would. I'm, uh, sort of looking into it.'

'Officially?'

'I've got official permission, sure. And the guy who a lot of people think was responsible has asked me to represent him.'

'In court? Do you have any legal training?'

'No. I'm, ah, rather hoping it won't go that far. Which is why I'm here.'

'Hmm.' He was frowning. 'And you believe . . . Young man, I may live quite an isolated existence here, but I do keep up with the news. I'm not unwilling to help, especially if as you say you have official blessing, but I do have my own curiosity to indulge. I'm sorry, but what possible bearing can Murena's first wife's death have on his own six days ago and that ne'er-do-well Trebbio's arrest for his murder?'

Well, I ought to have known that he'd make the link: old and blind or not, Saenius was still a sharp cookie. I gave him the truth. 'I don't know, sir. Maybe no bearing at all. But I've a gut feeling that it does. I don't trust coincidences either, and there're too many connected with whatever happened thirty years back for comfort.'

The frown relaxed. 'Really?' he said. 'Are there indeed? Well, curiosity aside it's not my case and perhaps under the circumstances it would be unethical to press you.' He smiled suddenly. 'You've got a lot of your mother in you, my boy. Did you know that? Your father, too, although from what I heard of your relationship with him you may not think so, or welcome the comment. He was a digger as well, in his way. Now.' He shifted on the bench. 'It wasn't thirty years ago, it was twenty-eight, the year Silanus and Silianus were consuls. The trial, I mean. Fadia had died the year previously.'

'It was a murder trial?'

'Yes. Not before the full Senate, though, very much in camera. Murena managed things to that extent, at least. The accusation was brought by Fadia's family. Murena was the defendant. I wasn't involved personally, and I won't burden you unless you wish it with the names of the prosecutor and defender. In any event, the case for the prosecution collapsed on the first day, so the term "trial" is rather a misnomer.'

'You remember the details?'

'Of course.' He smiled again. 'I told you, I'm a lawyer. When I start forgetting things I'll go into my study and slit my wrists. Or do it out here, most probably. I'm assuming you know the circumstances of the woman's death? Do you?'

'Yeah. Or at least I know what I was told. She was sleep-walking at the time, the slave who was supposed to be watching her was asleep, and she fell downstairs and broke her neck. Murena and his daughter Penelope were witnesses.'

'Penelope? That would be young Licinia, wouldn't it?'

I nodded, then remembered and said, 'Yes.'

'Correct. Only there was another witness. *That* in the event proved to be very important.'

My guts went cold. 'Another witness?'

'Oh, indeed. We'll come to him later. Fadius – Fadia's brother – claimed that Murena had pushed her downstairs intentionally. He based the claim on two factors: one, that the marriage had been no marriage at all for a period of several years, and two – the main factor – that Murena's own daughter said she'd seen him do it.'

'Fair enough.' Pretty damning, in fact, or so it seemed to me. And, of course, it matched with what I already knew. 'So why did the case fold?'

'That was due to the third witness I mentioned. Murena's door-slave. He was downstairs at the time, in the door-slave's cubby, invisible to the other two; he came forward of his own volition, just prior to the trial. The young man confirmed that Murena had indeed stretched his arm out towards his wife when she was on the top step, but – this was important – that his clear intention had been to stop her falling.' Saenius frowned. 'Naturally, being a slave, his evidence was only admissible if confirmed by torture, and the prosecution insisted this should be administered to the full letter of the law. It made no difference: he refused categorically to change his story. That, of course, would fit the known facts equally well, and since the prosecution had no further actual evidence to offer, the judge exercised his prerogative and dismissed the case.'

'Uh . . . hang on.' Sweet gods alive! This didn't add up! 'It was still a slave's word against a citizen's. I'm sorry, sir, but things like that just don't happen. The judge would've believed the girl, even if the slave was tortured.'

'Agreed,' Saenius said quietly. 'There were, however, unusual circumstances. First of all, as I say, no one suspected at the time that he had witnessed the incident. Second, a month or so before Fadia's death Murena had had the boy's father, who was also a slave in the house, flogged to death for some misdemeanour and his corpse thrown into the tank where he kept his moray eels.' My brain went numb. 'Naturally, that put any question of the slave's lying out of loyalty to his master beyond the pale, especially since he had come forward – so he insisted, again under torture – purely in the cause of truth and justice. Any slave, the judge reasoned, who would voluntarily submit to torture to save a master who has just had his father killed, when he could easily have ensured his condemnation either by confirming his guilt or simply keeping silent altogether, could not possibly be lying.'

'So what about the girl?'

'She was just that; a girl in her mid-teens. Scarcely more than a child, and easily capable of a mistake. She saw her father stretch out his hand towards her mother – no one denies he did that – and misinterpreted the action. End of the prosecution's case and collapse of the trial. Murena was sent home without a stain on his character.'

Except where it mattered, I thought: whatever the verdict, where Rome's social movers and shakers were concerned the guy wasn't *welcome* any more. Which was why he'd had to leave Rome and move permanently to Baiae. 'The slave,' I said. 'That'd be Philippus, right?'

Saenius nodded. 'Yes. He's done very well for himself since, I hear. And I understand he still drags his left leg, even after all this time. The praetor's torturers weren't gentle, and as I say the prosecution insisted on thoroughness.'

Well, it all fitted in, sure, but even after thirty years – twenty-eight years – you could just smell the rotten fish. Me, if I'd been the judge, I would've dug a bit deeper. The guy must've been mentally impaired, which wouldn't be a first in a praetor. 'Philippus got his freedom shortly afterwards. Didn't that strike anyone as, uh, suspicious at all?'

The old guy shrugged. 'Oh, yes. Of course it did. But the trial was over, the verdict was given and the young man was Murena's to do as he liked with. And, after all, he had saved his master from exile or a very hefty fine. Besides – and I'm speaking now from hearsay, mind, not personal knowledge – Philippus bought his own freedom, he wasn't given it gratis.'

'Yeah. Yeah, he told me that himself. So he was telling the truth?'

'I have no reason to doubt it. Certainly, he has always so insisted, and Murena never denied the fact.'

'You any idea where he got the money?'

'No, none at all. Except that it was his own to spend; or, at least, so again he insists, unlikely though it may seem. In any case certainly – as you must know, if you've talked to the man – he acknowledges no debt to his former master whatsoever, and he's had very few dealings with him since, if any.'

Jupiter bloody best and greatest! The thing had as many holes as a net bag! And I could see how, as far as Roman society was concerned, it would leave Murena even less *welcome* than ever. 'Do you believe all this?' I said. 'Yourself, I mean?'

He took a long time answering. Finally he said, 'I'm an old man, Corvinus, ninety-seven years old at the Spring Festival. I've been a lawyer all my life: my first memory is of my father lifting me above the crowd to watch Cicero speak in favour of Caelius. If in all that time I have learned one thing it's that the law may sometimes be unjust and its decisions frankly wrong but it is still the law. Murena was accused, he was tried and he was acquitted; that for me, is the sum and end of it. Besides' – he smiled – 'even if he was responsible for his wife's death, then where is the real blame? I would hope, if my own mind failed to such a degree that I had no real concept of self or recognised the friends and family around me that one of them would, through kindness, do for me what I no longer had the awareness to do for myself. Does that answer your question?'

'Yeah,' I said. 'Yeah, I suppose it does.' *Through kindness.*
That's where I stuck; I couldn't imagine Murena, from what
I knew of him, doing anything through kindness. If he'd
killed his wife – and I'd bet he had – then he'd done it for his
own reasons. 'I can't agree, mind, but then I'm not a lawyer.'

'If we all agreed on what was right, then there would be no
need for lawyers.'

True; although I wasn't sure that that was any reason to
put business in the buggers' way. I stood up. 'Well, thanks
for your time, sir. And for the information. It's been very
helpful.'

'I hope so. A pleasure to meet your father's son, Corvinus.
Do give my regards to your mother.'

'I'll do that,' I said. I'd turned to go, but then a thought
struck me and I turned back. 'One more thing. Murena's
partner and son-in-law, Decimus Tattius. You know him?'

He hesitated. 'Yes, of course. Not well, but we have met
on occasion.'

'He was an old friend of Murena's. Since Rome.'

'That's right. They were colleagues together in the aedileship, but I think the friendship long predated that.'

There'd been a definite guarded note to his tone when he
answered, and it puzzled me. That wasn't all, though: the
content of the answer was odd, too. I'd known the two had
been political colleagues, sure, but not their final rank.
Tattius had told me categorically that they'd done their
junior magistracies together. Aediles are responsible for
Rome's physical side, the upkeep of the streets and buildings, public and – where they impinge on the public domain
– private. The aedileship, being the first of the senatorial
magistracies, is a Political office with a capital P: the start of
a career, not the end of one. Hardly a junior magistracy, and
if the two had been aediles together the age requirement

meant that it couldn't've been all that long before the trial. So what had happened? In Murena's case, the answer was simple: not being *welcome* any more, he'd chosen to leave Rome. Or been forced to leave, rather. But what about Tattius? He'd got his foot on the bottom rung and yet, like Murena, that was where it had stopped. Like Murena again – but without Murena's reasons – he'd thrown up a prospective career in politics and moved to Baiae. The question – and it had the back of my neck tingling – was why?

'Corvinus?' Saenius was staring past me, blank-eyed. 'Are you still there?'

'Uh . . . yeah,' I said. 'Yeah. I'm sorry, sir. I was thinking. Why did Tattius leave Rome? Do you know?'

'Not because of any . . . misdemeanour, if that's what you're implying.'

I hadn't been, or not directly, but the response was interesting. As was that pause, again, before the exact choice of word. 'Okay,' I said. 'Understood. But I really would like to know. If you can tell me, that is.'

The old man frowned, then chuckled. 'You're a digger all right, Valerius Corvinus. And stubborn. Your father would be proud of you: he was always good at spotting an unwilling witness. Very well, have it your own way; it's old history now and long forgotten in any case. I didn't give you the names of the lawyers at Murena's trial because – to be honest – I think the past is much better left buried. However, to keep it so I'm not quite prepared to go to the lengths of an out-and-out lie.'

Oh, shit; I was there before him. 'Tattius conducted Murena's defence,' I said.

'Yes.' Saenius nodded. 'Yes, he did.'

Bull's-eye! I'd got the connection!

17

I was thinking hard on the way back. If my slinger pal had been around to try it on at any point he'd've nailed me, easy.

So Tattius had defended Murena in the Fadia trial, had he? In retrospect, it made perfect sense: assuming the guy had legal training – which he must've had – that was the way things naturally went: if you're in trouble, legal trouble, the first person you approach to conduct your defence is a close friend or an ex-colleague; a social equal or a superior. And Murena and Tattius had both been aediles together, so Tattius would've been Murena's logical choice. Only in that case the rotten smell wasn't confined to Murena, far from it: whatever sharp practice had been perpetrated twenty-eight years back, Decimus Tattius had been in it up to the neck. That I'd bet on, a gold piece to a corn plaster. And the result had been that Tattius hadn't been *welcome* in Rome any longer either.

Okay. A scenario. Let's say Penelope was right: Murena took the opportunity of his wife's sleepwalking to push her downstairs and end the marriage. Why he did it – whether for Saenius's reasons or mine – wasn't all that important, but the fact was that the guy had committed deliberate murder. His problem was Penelope. I'd bet that Murena hadn't realised his daughter was there and watching until it was too late, and now instead of being commiserated with as the sorrowing but now happily released widower he'd found himself facing a murder rap and the better than likely prospect of spending the rest of his days twiddling his thumbs in Lusitania.

Enter Decimus Tattius. He reviews the case. He can argue, fair enough, that Penelope was mistaken: what she saw was Murena trying to grab his wife before she fell. That might do the job okay, sure, but Penelope, even as a kid, would've been no pushover in the witness box for a cross-examining counsel. Also, I'd bet – seeing that Fadia's brother had lodged an accusation in the first place – that Murena's attitude to his wife and her illness up to that point hadn't exactly overflowed with altruistic concern: I wondered, for a start, about the exact details of these previous 'suicide' attempts that Ligurius had mentioned. The thing would come down to the jury's choice on who to believe, Murena or his daughter, and that edge was too slim for comfort. So what Tattius needs, like the tragedians who've got their knickers in a twist plot-wise at the end of a play, is the old god-on-a-crane routine: a surprise witness, with no personal axe to grind who saw the whole thing but was invisible to the other players. And he comes up with the door-slave, Philippus.

Whether or not Philippus actually saw anything wasn't really relevant; the important thing was that it was possible, because his cubby would've been in sight of the stairs. So Tattius approaches him quietly and suggests a deal: he comes forward off his own bat and gives evidence that'll back the defence's case and Tattius guarantees he'll be set up for life. It won't be easy, mind – Philippus would know all about the slave's-evidence-only-under-torture rule – but slaves are a pretty tough breed, and freedom and the promise of serious financial backing once the cap's on is a powerful incentive. Also, although we were talking thirty years back and I'd only met the guy as a man, I'd judge that Philippus would be just the sort to jump at the chance. He'd hated Murena, sure – he still did – but even in his teens he'd've been ambitious and enough of a thinker to see the possibilities. So he agrees.

Did Murena know about the scam? Probably not, or not to begin with, at least: like Penelope, he hadn't known a third witness existed. But if the guy's evidence got him off the hook then he wasn't going to object, was he? And after the trial he'd be a fool to open his mouth at all.

Okay. So far so good. The verdict's been given, Murena's home and dry, legally at least. Then his good friend Tattius puts the bite on. He tells him about the scam; or rather (I stopped myself) he tells him about the deal with Philippus. The door-slave lied: sure, he saw what happened, but what he saw was Murena giving his wife that fatal shove. Tattius is suffering a bad attack of conscience. He did what he did out of friendship, concealing the truth in the process, but maybe he shouldn't have, and now he's sorely tempted to go to Fadia's brother and reveal all in a paroxysm of remorse.

On the other hand – he says – that wouldn't do anyone much good, would it? Fadia's dead, and that perhaps is a blessing. Murena's been punished enough by having the society door slammed in his face, and he, Tattius, is effectively in the same position. Maybe he should just leave things as they are. What does Murena think? Of course, he has suffered considerable personal damage as a result of his act of friendship, and he's sure that Murena realises this and is anxious to make it up. He's not greedy. He'll settle for marriage with Murena's daughter, a hefty dowry, a not-too-onerous partnership in Murena's lucrative family fish-farm business on advantageous financial terms, and a lump sum to defray expenses incurred by his promise to Philippus. Which he must fulfil, naturally, because who knows whether the young man might not have a crisis of conscience himself and decide to spill the beans to Fadia's brother, especially since he hates Murena's guts?

Yeah; it would work, Murena would be firmly over a barrel, not just from the blackmail side but from the *noblesse oblige* one as well: whether he liked it or not – and I'd bet he didn't – Tattius was *owed*. And it would explain everything: why the partnership, why Murena nicknamed Tattius Oistrus, how Philippus managed to buy his own freedom and get his start in business, and why he and Murena would have nothing to do with each other subsequently.

It would also explain why Penelope hated her father so much. If she guessed there'd been some skulduggery at the trial – and I'd bet she did – then knowing she was part of the price for getting him off and was married to the bastard responsible must've seriously rubbed salt into the wound. Hatred wouldn't cover it by half.

I'd have to have another talk with Penelope.

Well, I was on the right side of Baiae and Tattius's villa wasn't that far out of my way. There wasn't no time like the present.

I went through the gilded-fish gates and up the carriage-drive. A second view of the place didn't do anything to alter my first impressions: the villa definitely had a seedy look to it, as if money available for spending on repairs and upkeep wasn't too plentiful, and Tattius had had to cut serious corners, even to the extent of selling off some of the decoration he'd started out with. That, given what I knew now, was significant: if he had been milking his partner over the odds then I reckoned the milk supply had been running short recently. Which raised some interesting questions: like, had Murena finally decided to put the mockers on it himself, and if so how would Tattius have reacted? Had there, maybe, been a quarrel, with Murena claiming that he needed a slice of the cash hitherto allocated as conscience money to finance expensive business ventures such as his hotel project? And if there had been, and it had happened the night of the murder, then maybe Tattius's temper had got the better of him.

It was a theory, sure, and if it didn't provide the bastard with exactly a prior motive at least it put him well in the running.

The door-slave was sitting outside, the same one as previously. He was still, as far as I could see, wearing the same threadbare tunic.

'I'm afraid the master's not at home, sir,' he said. 'He's away on business at the moment.'

'No problem, sunshine,' I said. 'I wanted to talk to the mistress. Is the around?'

'Yes, sir. If you'd care to wait I'll see if she's receiving.'

He went inside while I kicked my heels on the portico. Business, eh? That didn't sound like Tattius. Still, like any man with a private income he wouldn't be at home all the time. And I doubted that his domestic circumstances would prove much of a tie.

The slave came back out. 'The mistress will see you, sir,' he said. 'If you'd care to follow me?'

She was sitting in a small room overlooking the overgrown back garden, with sliding window-doors that were half open to let in the fresh air. I could tell, from the decor, that it was where she spent most of her time: it had a lived-in feel to it, and there were little female touches like vases of flowers on the tables and what must've been her collection of dolls as a kid arranged round a household shrine in the corner. She stood up when I came in: neatly dressed, but still very much the dumpy matron.

'Valerius Corvinus,' she said. 'This is a surprise. I'm afraid Decimus is in Neapolis, if you wanted to talk to him. He won't be back until late this evening.'

'No, that's okay,' I said. 'It was you I wanted to see.'

'Really?' She sat down again. 'And why should that be? You look rather travel-stained. Make yourself comfortable. Stentor here will bring you some wine.'

The slave bowed and left. I pulled up another chair. 'Uh . . . I've been talking to an old guy out on the Bauli road who used to be a lawyer in Rome. About the trial that was held a year after your mother's death.'

There was a long silence while she just stared at me. Her face was expressionless. 'And?' she said finally.

This was the tricky part. 'I . . . understand you gave evidence for the prosecution.'

She sat back. 'Corvinus, let's be clear about this. I know that my father murdered my mother. I was there, I saw him do it, and I've always maintained that he did it. It's why I hated him, one of the reasons anyway. The details may be new to you, but not the result; I told you at the time of our first meeting that I was glad he was dead and I hoped he was rotting in hell. Do you expect me to retract that statement now?'

'No.' I shifted in my chair. 'But what I didn't know then was that your husband was counsel for the defence. And that . . . well, let's just say that there was something screwy about the evidence he produced.'

'You mean the slave's? Philippus's?' She was perfectly calm.

'Yeah.'

'Then of course there was. Philippus lied, and the lie led to my father's acquittal. It was as simple as that.'

'You're saying he didn't see what happened after all?'

'No. He may well have done. That wasn't what I meant. But if he did see then he lied about what he saw.'

'You didn't know he was downstairs in the hall, then?'

'No. Not at all. Not until the trial when Decimus produced him as a witness. It was possible, certainly; there were no lamps downstairs, and the atrium was in darkness. He came out of his cubby later, of course, after my mother . . . fell, but whether he was awake and watching beforehand I don't know.'

'What about the landing itself? That was lit?'

'Yes. We always kept a candelabrum outside my mother's room, plus another two either end of the gallery. In case of the sleepwalking.'

'So he could've seen, right enough, if he'd been there? Although he wouldn't't've been seen himself?'

'Oh, yes. Perfectly clearly. As could I, which is why I know he must've been lying.' She gave me a straight look. 'It wasn't a grab, Corvinus, not even a fumbled one as my father claimed. I was within three feet of him, and I couldn't have been mistaken. My father pushed my mother downstairs deliberately. I've no doubt of that, no doubt at all.'

Gods, I'd been right about the lady being no slouch as far as sticking to her story was concerned. Tattius had needed all the help he could get. 'Okay,' I said. 'Fair enough. Now what about the . . . the aftermath.' I chose the word carefully. 'After the trial. Your father engaged you to Tattius?'

Her eyes closed, briefly, and her lips tightened. 'Yes,' she said. 'Almost immediately.'

'There hadn't been any' – I hesitated – 'any prior warning? I mean, you were what, fifteen at the time?'

'Sixteen. I'd just had my sixteenth birthday.'

The right age for an engagement, maybe a bit over. 'He hadn't suggested it before?'

'No. But then of course he couldn't've, because—' She stopped. 'Never mind. It's not important.'

I frowned; why the hell couldn't he have suggested it? Oh, sure, any engagement to Tattius, old enough easy to be the girl's father himself, might not be on the cards at the time, but a lot of girls are married by sixteen, and the subject of a future husband usually comes up long before then. So why the *couldn't've*?

Unless of course . . .

'He couldn't've suggested it because you were engaged already,' I said quietly. 'So when he did engage you to Tattius, he had to break the prior engagement.'

Long silence. Finally, she glanced down at her right hand. 'Yes,' she said. 'You're very astute, Valerius Corvinus.'

'Who was he?'

'His name was Quintus. A cousin in Ostia that I'd practically grown up with and been in love with for years. It was mutual. It didn't matter in the end, because he married someone else shortly afterwards and died two years later. One of those summer fevers.'

Oh, shit; here was another reason why she should hate Murena. 'You didn't object? Refuse to marry Tattius?'

She stared at me. 'Of course I objected! What do you think? But my father was my father, my mother was dead and my elder brother Titus couldn't've cared less. And Quintus, as it happened, being from a junior branch of the family very much dependent on ours, wasn't in any position to insist that Father honoured his commitments. What choice do you think I had?'

Yeah; right. She might be a strong-minded lady, but you couldn't go against seven hundred years of social conventions. The simple answer was: No choice at all.

There was a knock at the door, and the slave came in with the wine tray – two cups, I noticed. Well, I didn't blame her. We sat in silence while the guy poured, bowed and left.

'Uh . . . just a question,' I said: it had to be asked, and now was as good – or as bad – a time as any. 'Where were you? The night your father died?'

'At home. Here.' She took a swallow of the wine. I sipped it myself: it was almost neat. 'I spend a lot of my time here, Valerius Corvinus. My husband has his own quarters.'

'Was he at home too?'

'That I can't say. You'd have to ask him, or one of the slaves.'

'Philippus. The guy I was talking to said he bought his own freedom.'

'I can't comment on that either. Possibly he did: certainly my father wasn't the most generous of men, or the most grateful. In any case, between the time of my mother's death and my marriage I had as little to do with him as possible.'

'One more question.' I didn't have to ask it, but I'd be interested in her reaction. 'Who do you think killed your father?'

She set the cup down. 'I don't know,' she said. 'But whoever did it has my blessing, and always will. He deserved to die. He deserved it twenty-nine years ago. My only regret is that whoever killed him didn't do it sooner.'

There was nothing else to say. I got up, made my thanks, and left.

*

When I got home Bathyllus was waiting with the news –
gleaned by Phormio on his daily shopping trip to the market
– that Titus Chlorus had been found early that morning in
an alleyway with his throat cut.

18

Chlorus's place wasn't far from the centre, in a cul-de-sac that opened off a small square with plane trees and a public water-fountain. I identified it straight off from the funereal cypress branches draped round the door.

'Ah . . . I'm sorry to disturb the household,' I said when the door-slave opened up to my knock, 'but I was wondering if maybe the mistress or somebody would have a word with me. Valerius Corvinus.'

The guy was no spring chicken, fifty if he was a day. The sparse condition of his forelock showed that he hadn't stinted the dead his due, and he looked genuinely upset; which having met Chlorus and knowing at least by hearsay how he treated his slaves surprised me. 'The mistress is in, sir,' he said. 'I don't know whether her grief will allow her to talk to you, but I'll ask. If you don't mind waiting.'

'Sure,' I said. 'No problem.' He disappeared inside.

Interesting: had there been the barest smidgeon of sarcasm? It was pretty well-hidden by the deadpan delivery, but I could've sworn it was there, all the same. I remembered Mother saying that Titus Chlorus and his wife – what was her name? Catia, right – didn't exactly hit it off together. If the friction between them had gone to the lengths of being commented on to a stranger, albeit indirectly, by the family's door-slave then it must've been pretty considerable.

There wasn't any doubt where the door-slave's sympathies lay, either. Considering Chlorus's reputation, that was interesting, too.

The guy came back. 'The mistress will see you, sir, but only for a few moments. Come in, please.'

She was lying on a couch in the atrium, dressed in a mourning mantle that satisfied the conventions as far as colour was concerned but was so sheer and tight-fitting that at its most strategic points of coverage what showed was Catia. Grief-stricken the lady might be, but she hadn't let it spoil her appearance. Or her make-up. Even in deepest mourning, Titus Chlorus's widow was a stunner, and she knew it. The look she gave me was frankly assessing.

'Valerius Corvinus,' she said. 'Gellia told me all about you. I've been expecting to meet you for several days. A shame it has to be under such tragic circumstances.'

'Yeah.' Well, *tragic circumstances* notwithstanding I'd seen more genuine grief on a face for the death of a pet sparrow. There was a stool opposite the couch, next to a very nice bronze of Actaeon, half man half stag, being ripped apart by his hounds. I sat on it. 'My condolences, Catia.'

'Thank you. It was quite a shock.' She said the words like you might say, *It was a very disagreeable party*. 'Hebe and I are quite devastated.'

' "Hebe"?'

'My daughter. Licinilla, really, but that's such a mouthful that we don't use it. She's marrying young Manlius Torquatus, you know. Terrible tragedy for the poor girl.'

'Why? No chin and a nose like a trireme's, eh? Yeah, you get that in these old families.' I couldn't help it; it slipped out and the woman was beginning to grate on me already.

She glared at me and tugged at the mantle, obscuring a couple of the more pertinent curves. 'I *meant*,' she said, 'Titus's death. Murder.' The last word was breathed with relish. 'He was murdered, you know. But then I expect that's why you're here. To question me.'

'Uh . . . right.' Well, she might not be the typical grief-stricken widow, but that was all to the good. I couldn't help drawing parallels with her pal Gellia. The loving family motif evidently extended sideways. 'Maybe you could tell me what happened.'

'Certainly.' She tugged at the mantle again; I noticed that she wore her fingernails long, and the fingers themselves were covered with rings. 'Titus went out last night just after dinner saying he had to meet someone. That was the last I saw of him until the local Watchman called round this morning with the news that he'd been found in an alleyway about two hundred yards off, with his throat cut.'

I waited. There was nothing else. 'Uh . . . is that all you know?' I said.

'Yes. That's all. I was totally distraught, of course.'

'He – I mean Titus – didn't say where he was going? Who he was meeting and why?'

'Oh, I wouldn't have expected it. He never does. Titus is very secretive.' She caught herself. 'Was. I suppose I'll have to start using the past tense when I speak of him now. It's very annoying.'

'Yeah. Yeah, right. Ah . . . the alleyway. Which direction was it in?'

'Towards the centre, I think. I'm really not sure. I always use a litter when I go out.'

'He know anyone in particular that way, do you know?'

'Not that I'm aware of. Although of course it would take him to the main road, and from there he could go anywhere.'

'How about Ligurius? He lives near here, doesn't he?'

'Ligurius?' She frowned. 'Why Ligurius, especially?'

'Your husband told me he often went round to his place

on business in the evening to save going all the way out to the fish-farm. It'd be an obvious possibility.'

'Yes, I suppose it would. And yes, he did. But I think Ligurius lives in the other direction. In fact, I'm sure he does. Over a fuller's establishment, on the outskirts. Not a very salubrious address.'

'And he didn't give any indication at all?' Catia was still frowning; not Baiae's greatest brain, obviously. 'I mean, that the appointment was unusual. Or that it was business, rather than social.'

'No. I said. He didn't say anything about it. He never does, just that he's going out and not to wait up.' She sniffed. 'Not that I would. Mind you, it wouldn't've been social. Titus isn't – *wasn't* – a very social person. We didn't go out together half enough, or have people round to dinner. I had to manage that side of things practically single-handed.' She gave me a slightly bitter look. 'He could have been visiting a mistress, I suppose, but I very much doubt it. Titus wouldn't have either the interest or the energy for an affair. And no woman with any scope for choice would've bothered starting one.'

'He didn't have any particular enemies? Anyone who'd want him dead?'

'Who'd want Titus dead? I've just told you, Corvinus: he was the blandest, most boring man imaginable. His work was his life. It was all he was interested in, and all he ever talked about. Oh, I've no doubt he had enemies, the usual business sort, but no one who'd actually go the length of killing him.'

'Someone did.'

She blinked; maybe she'd suddenly realised that she wasn't behaving quite how a dutiful wife whose husband has just had his throat slit down an alley was expected to, and it was getting a little too obvious. 'Yes,' she said slowly. 'Yes, I suppose that's true. How awful; poor Titus. But really I haven't the faintest idea who, or why.' She gave the fold of the mantle another tug: a fiddler, Catia, I decided; her fingers hadn't been still since I came in. Unless it was nerves. 'Now I'm afraid that's all the time I can give you. I have to arrange the funeral, of course, and all that unpleasantness, and I really must write a long letter to Manlius's father telling him what's happened. The wedding may have to be postponed, which is absolutely dreadful but it can't be helped: there are conventions about these things, and Torquatus senior is a *very* conventional man. So nice to have met you, Valerius Corvinus.'

So that was that. *A few moments* was right. Gods! You'd think even a bubblehead like Catia would've shown a bit more respect for her dead husband than she had done. Or even interest in how the poor sod died. And the interview hadn't left me much wiser than when I started, except for the fact that I'd got a bit more of an insight into Chlorus's family life, or lack of it, than I'd bargained for. I almost felt sorry for him. Still, like I say, it was par for the course as far as the family were concerned. Maybe Catia and Hebe were all he deserved.

The door-slave let me out and I started back for home. I'd gone about a hundred yards when I heard hurrying footsteps behind me.

'Sir! Valerius Corvinus!'

I turned. It was the door-slave. 'Yeah?' I said.

'Wait a moment, sir, please. Until I get my breath back.' He was beetroot red and panting: whatever the guy's name was it wasn't Pheidippides. 'I couldn't let you go, sir. Not without telling you.'

'Telling me what?'

'The master was always good to me, sir. He had his faults, but he was good to me. It isn't fair.'

'What isn't fair?' The guy was practically weeping.

'The mistress didn't tell you, did she? About the note? She knew about it; I swear she knew!'

My guts went cold. 'What note was this?'

'A man brought it round last night, sir, for the master. Just after dinner. The seal was broken; the man said he'd done it accidental when it caught against his belt. I'm afraid I read it – I can read, sir, and I like to get what practice I can – and—'

Jupiter in a basket! 'Look, sunshine, forget the excuses. Just tell me what this note said, okay?'

'Yes, sir.' He took a deep breath and glanced behind him again. 'It said, "Come round straight away. We have something to discuss," sir. Just that.'

'Was it signed?'

'Yes, sir. That's the point. It was signed "Aulus". The master's brother.'

Oh, shit! 'You're sure it was from him?'

'No, sir. It had his name on it. That's all I know.'

'The man who brought it round. Did you recognise him?'

'No, sir. He wasn't one of the Nerva household's usual messengers, but that don't mean nothing. The master and his brother aren't really on social terms, as it were, so the households don't mix as a rule. Most of his slaves I've never seen.'

'Where does Nerva live?'

'Near the harbour, sir. He's got a house near the harbour.'

The other side of the town centre, in other words: the direction Chlorus had been going when he was murdered. Sweet gods! I gave the guy a couple of silver pieces from my pouch and he darted off back to the Chlorus property. The front door closed behind him.

I needed half a jug of wine, and a place to think. Fast.

*

I found it just round the corner: a small wineshop in another
tree-shaded square, with tables outside and a board that
didn't promise the earth, just two or three good local wines;
luckily, we were a bit too far from the fashionable part of
Baiae for the golden set to venture. I ordered up a half
of Gauranum and a plate of cheese and olives – it was getting
late now, and what with Bathyllus's news I'd skipped lunch
– and settled down with my back to the wineshop wall.

Aulus Nerva. Oh, sure, he'd been on the cards from the
start – the quarrel that evening with his father, the business
over the grain barge (I'd still have to go into that one) – but
he was still running light as far as hard proof was concerned. Okay; I wasn't completely gullible, there was always
the obvious possibility that someone had used Nerva's
name as a blind just in case things went pear-shaped. All the
same, the original note had been sealed against casual eyes,
and it had his signature, which presumably had been
genuine enough not to cause Chlorus any suspicions, at the
bottom. And if he did plan to slit his brother's throat Nerva
wasn't stupid enough to send the thing round via one of his
own slaves: there were plenty of guys, slave and free,
knocking around the streets who'd deliver a message for the
price of a cup of wine, no questions asked. I'd be equally a
fool to assume it *wasn't* from Nerva. So. Let's start with that
angle.

First, the most generous scenario: the whole thing was
completely innocent. The two men may not have got on all
that well, but they were business partners, after all, and there
wasn't anything particularly remarkable about one of
them asking for a meeting. Only in this case there was. What
could be so urgent, business-wise, for Nerva to write a note
to his brother for delivery after dinner telling him to drop

everything and come round straight away? Especially since in the event Chlorus had ended up dead in an alley five minutes out. And Baiae, unlike Rome, doesn't have a problem with casual knifemen and muggers.

So scratch the most generous scenario.

Second: what Nerva wanted to discuss had something to do with his father's death. *That* scenario was pretty interesting, to say the least. The problem was, I'd no idea what the hell the 'something' could have been. From my experience of Nerva and Chlorus, what they were *really* into was planting knives in each other's backs. Pulling on the one oar in fraternal harmony was something the two bastards just didn't do. Except . . .

I stopped and took a thoughtful swig of the Gauranum.

Except on the subject of Gellia. They both hated her, even to the degree of forgetting their differences. It was all, as far as I could see, that they *did* agree on.

That was another avenue that I hadn't finished exploring. Oh, sure, Diodotus was off the hook as an accomplice, but where Gellia was concerned he wasn't the only fish in the sea. There was Aquillius Florus with his lack of alibi, for a start, and I hadn't forgotten that when I talked to Diodotus he'd implied that, although the whole family were vipers, Gellia was the worst of the lot. The fact remained that as far as motive went the lady had as good a one as any for putting her husband into an urn, and unlike others the opportunity as well, both personally and through lover-boy Florus. So. Let's say Nerva had found out something definite to link his stepmother with the killing. He'd want to consult with Chlorus first before going public with it, because although Chlorus might not be exactly sympatico or overflowing with brotherly fellow-feeling he was the family lawyer, he was the thinking type, which I'd bet

Aulus wasn't, particularly, and he'd know about these things. Yeah; new info on Gellia as a reason for the projected meeting was a definite possibility . . .

Only, like the first scenario, that one didn't explain why it was Chlorus who'd ended up dead in an alley. Or who had killed him.

Right. Scenario three, the most obvious – and likely – of the lot. Nerva didn't want to discuss anything with his brother. What Nerva wanted was to get the guy out of the house and somewhere he could murder him in safety and comfort.

Only, again, we were left with the why? What had Chlorus done to deserve it? Or – which was maybe more likely – what did he have it in his power to do? What had Chlorus *known*?

I hadn't the slightest idea. Worse, I didn't even know if we were talking here about Nerva at all. It could be someone completely different, and probably was. Bugger. I sank another quarter-pint of the wine.

On the other hand . . .

Mother had said – hadn't she? – when I first asked her about Murena's family that, according to local gossip, Aulus Nerva had the hots for his brother's wife, and it went both ways. Now I'd seen Catia for myself, I could believe it: she was definitely Nerva's type, the bubblehead *par excellence*, radiating sex even through a mourning mantle. And she didn't seem even partly cut up about her husband's death. Okay. Scenario four, last of the bunch. Let's say Chlorus's death had nothing to do with Murena's murder at all; that Chlorus had finally tumbled to it that his brother had his feet under the table at the very least with Catia, and had taken it seriously amiss; that the 'something' Nerva had to discuss with him was the future of his marriage, only in sending the note discussion wasn't exactly what he had in mind . . .

Shit, no, that was rubbish. Lovers didn't kill husbands to get them out of the way any more, certainly not in cosmopolitan Baiae where some married couples don't wake up in the same bed two nights running, let alone sharing. If Nerva and Catia wanted to screw they could do it no problem, without having to go to the lengths of killing Chlorus. And even if they wanted something more permanent, divorce was simple. It might still be sniffed at as infra dig in a few real, old-fashioned, high-pukkah Roman families, but for ninety-nine hundredths of the civilised world . . .

I stopped.

Old-fashioned, high-pukkah families.

'*Torquatus senior is a very conventional man.*'

I almost groaned. Oh, hell. Oh, no; it couldn't be that straightforward. That was putting things *way* out of proportion, even if Catia was a complete snob.

Still, where ultra-pukkah was concerned, you didn't get better than the Manlii Torquati. They might be broke nowadays, but they still had a pedigree that went back as far as you liked to go. And if push came to shove I could make a case which if it wasn't sensible was at least rational.

Say Nerva's interest in his sister-in-law *had* got beyond the starting line. Chlorus finds out. Being Chlorus and a real poker-up-the-rectum type, he confronts Catia and threatens divorce. Me, having seen both of them now, I'd bet Catia was the real social climber of the pair. Papa Torquatus, she knows, is not exactly going to be turning cartwheels when he hears his boy is marrying into a family where his future mother-in-law is in the process of getting the heave for adultery, and there's a better-than-average chance that the old guy will decide to blow the whistle on the whole thing and look elsewhere. Having failed to dissuade Chlorus Catia goes to Nerva: can he, um, persuade his brother to see sense and leave things as they are? Maybe Nerva tries it; maybe he doesn't bother because the two brothers hate each other like poison anyway. And – there was another point in the theory's favour – if he *had* killed his father for money and control of the business, knocking off his brother wouldn't be all that much of a step, and it'd net him – through his brother's widow, if the grief-stricken lady should choose to remarry – twice his present share of the actual cash and no problems over future business policy . . .

Yeah; it worked, at least as a theory. We'd definitely have to think a lot more carefully about Aulus Nerva.

I'd be going in the direction of the harbour anyway, on the way home. I might as well pay Chlorus's brother a visit.

19

Nerva was closeted, so his major-domo told me, in the study with a business friend when I arrived, so I kicked my heels in the atrium until he was free. Nice decor, but flashy, like the guy himself: plenty of busty, long-legged nymphs in that transparent-drapery style you get among the statuary, and some of the wall paintings were straight out of that part of the pattern-book that the artists don't show when they're going through the options for staid matrons and the more poker-rectumed pillars of the community. I noticed, too, on a side table beside one of the couches a pricey Twelve Lines board, of cedarwood inlaid with ivory, set out for a game. Instead of the usual bone counters this one had gold and silver pieces. The guy evidently brought his love of gambling home with him. There was a small statuette next to it, of the Greek goddess Luck.

The door to the study opened, and Aquillius Florus came out, followed by Nerva. Nerva was wearing a mourning mantle, but like Catia he didn't seem exactly upset. He didn't seem all that pleased to see me, either.

'Corvinus. What the hell are you doing here?'

'Just dropped in on the way home,' I said. 'Hi, Florus.'

That got me a nervous nod. Florus slipped past me like I was suffering from something infectious and headed for the front door at speed.

'We'll talk again later, Sextus,' Nerva called after him.

Then he turned to me. 'I'm sorry, Corvinus. I'm not myself today.' He indicated the mourning mantle. 'Had a bit of bad news this morning.'

'Yeah,' I said. 'I know. My condolences.'

'Thank you. It came as a—'

'Great shock. To all the family.' I couldn't resist that, even if – as I'd known it would – it did put the bastard's back up. 'Right. I've just been talking to Catia, as a matter of fact, and she said the same. She's as upset as you are.'

Was it my imagination, or had his eyes flickered when I mentioned Catia?

'Of course she is,' he said irritably. 'It's a terrible business. Terrible.' He went over to a side table with a jug and wine cups on it. 'Some wine?'

'Yeah. That'd be great.' I stood while he poured. 'How did it happen? You know?'

'No idea. All I know is that Titus went out, yesterday evening, after dinner. His body was found in an alleyway near the Shrine of Mercury.' He handed me a cup. 'Catia sent a slave round with the news early this morning.'

I sipped. The wine was second-grade Falernian. 'You any thoughts on where he might've been going at the time?'

'None. He didn't say anything to Catia, but then he never does.' He drank. 'Sit down, Corvinus. Make yourself comfortable.'

I stretched out on one of the couches. Well, when in doubt go for the throat. 'Word is, you sent him a note asking to meet,' I said.

Nerva went very still. He put his cup down on the table with the gaming board and stared at me, his face expressionless.

'Who told you that?' he snapped.

'Did you?'

'Of course I fucking didn't! Who told you?'

'The note had your name on it.'

'I never sent Titus any note. And if he got one supposed to be from me then it was a forgery. Or whoever gave you the information was lying.'

I chanced my arm. 'Even if it was Catia?'

That stopped him. 'Catia? Catia wouldn't—' His mouth shut with an almost audible snap and he turned away. 'That's impossible. There wasn't any note. Or if there was like I say it was a fake.'

'Good enough to fool your brother?'

'Maybe. But then why should he think it wasn't the real thing in the first place?'

Fair point. The handwriting'd have to be at least similar to Nerva's, mind. Which, if I were inclined to give him the benefit of the doubt – which I wasn't, particularly, at that juncture – was a point that needed following up. 'So who do you think could've sent it?' I said.

'How the hell should I know?' He sat down on the other couch, reached for his cup and swigged half the wine straight off. 'Obviously someone who wanted to shift the blame for Titus's murder on to me. My guess – for what it's worth and if the fucking thing existed in the first place, which I doubt – would be Gellia.'

I leaned back. 'Yeah? Why her in particular?'

'Come on, Corvinus! She hates my guts. She hated Titus's guts. She killed my father because she hated *his* guts and wanted her freedom and her widow's cut. She's a cunning, conniving little bitch. Something like this would be just her style.' He swallowed the rest of the wine at a gulp. 'That do you?'

'Okay. Only why should she want your brother dead, particularly?'

'I don't know. Maybe he found out something.' He waved the empty cup. 'Maybe he was blackmailing her. Titus wouldn't be above a little blackmail on his own account, the hypocritical bastard. She couldn't arrange a meeting under her own name – Titus wasn't stupid – so she forges mine and uses that indeed.'

'And kills your brother herself?'

'She's got that fancy doctor friend of hers. They've already committed murder. She could've got him to do it.'

'Diodotus isn't Gellia's lover.'

Nerva laughed. 'He tell you that? Don't believe him, Corvinus. She made a dead set at him from the very first, and unless he's a boy-lover or a eunuch – and I wouldn't bet on either – he'll've caved in pretty quickly.' He got up, walked over to the wine tray and lifted the jug. 'Greeks are all liars. They're proverbial for it.'

'He couldn't've murdered your father,' I said. 'He was over in Bauli at an all-night childbirth.' No answer. 'Okay. If we're talking in terms of a murdering lover what about your pal Florus? Story is, he's got a vested interest there as well.'

The hand holding the jug paused for an instant. 'Sextus wouldn't harm a fly,' Nerva said. 'Besides, he hasn't got the brains to commit a murder.'

'He wouldn't need brains, just to be in the right place at the right time with a knife. He'd've had all the thinking part done for him. If' – I took another sip of my wine – 'we're talking about Gellia as the motive force, naturally.'

Nerva was frowning. 'You leave Sextus alone. He may not be clever, but he's a good friend of mine. And he knows where he is with women, at least, even if I don't admire his taste. As far as that side of things goes, Gellia'd be wasting her time.'

'You sure?' I said. 'You like to bet on that, maybe?' He

didn't answer, but the frown deepened. I shrugged. 'Yeah, well, Gellia was your suggestion anyway. Leave her. You have any other ideas?'

'No. Fuck off, Corvinus.'

I set my wine cup on the table and stood up. He was rattled; seriously rattled. I could see that. 'Fine,' I said. 'If you want to play it that way then it's fine with me. Thanks for the drink. I'll see you around, pal.'

I left.

So. That had been interesting. Nerva could've been telling the truth about the note, but I wouldn't bet on it: the guy, like I say, had been seriously rattled, especially when I mentioned Catia as a possible source, and his swipe at Gellia had been pure knee-jerk reaction. The theory held good.

What *really* interested me, though, was Aquillius Florus. I'd've given a lot to know just what the two of them had been discussing when I turned up, and the look the guy had given me when he left – plus the scared-rabbit run – had me thinking. The lad had beans to spill, that was sure; the question was, what sort of beans? And why had Nerva warned me off him? Knee-jerk reaction or not, Nerva's theory about Gellia being responsible for Chlorus's – and Murena's – deaths wasn't all that far off the wall: she'd be capable of murder, sure, although in Chlorus's case she'd definitely have needed an accomplice. Failing Diodotus – and I was pretty certain Nerva's accusations in that quarter were prompted by pure malice – Florus was a prime candidate. Nerva, if he was innocent, must see that too: my shot about the guy not needing brains just to wield a knife had gone home. So where did Florus fit? Which side of the fence was he on, Nerva's or Gellia's? Because he sure as hell was on one of the two. I'd have to lean a little on Florus in the very near future and see which way he jumped. Plus find out more about his and Nerva's business dealings.

Nerva's suggestion of blackmail on his brother's part was a distinct possibility too, and it meshed with my third scenario. Not that it didn't raise problems of its own. Whether Chlorus's victim was Gellia, as Nerva suggested, or Nerva himself, like I'd thought, was a moot point; what I was missing, and what was central, was the reason for his death. We were back to the vital question of what Chlorus had *known*. Or what he had it in his power to do. Maybe we'd better think about that.

So let's lay it out and see what we'd got, maybe take a back bearing. Before he'd been chopped, where *had* Chlorus fitted into the case? As one of the Murena family, sure, with all the petty jealousies, dislikes and not-so-petty mutual slaggings-off that went with the badge. But then we were looking for an actual hard motive here, and bad-mouthing a stepson or brother's a long way from slitting his throat. The same went for murder by his wife's lover; the cause just wasn't strong enough for the effect. Or not as things stood, anyway.

Okay, scrub murder for family reasons pure and simple. Next there was the business side. Chlorus had been the company's lawyer and accountant. That angle was the most promising, especially since if I didn't miss my guess things were taking a distinctly financial turn. Chlorus could easily have been killed for something he knew about there, an irregularity or some kind of secret deal; in which case the finger naturally pointed at either Nerva or Florus or both. That, personally, would be my bet.

So what was left as a motive for stiffing Chlorus? *Anyone* stiffing Chlorus? Nothing much, barring the outside chance that he'd witnessed something to do with Murena's murder

itself, either hadn't realised its importance or kept shtum for
his own reasons, and finally made the mistake of tackling the
murderer about it in private. Only that wasn't likely, because
Chlorus hadn't been anywhere near the villa that night. He'd
been the other side of town, discussing defaulting customers
with—

I stopped. Oh, shit.

Ligurius.

Now *there* was a guy who, given certain circumstances,
had a prime motive for shutting Chlorus up. Alibis went two
ways: if Ligurius had alibied Chlorus then it'd been the other
way about as well. If Chlorus, for some purpose of his own,
had originally fixed up a phoney alibi with the farm manager,
not suspecting that Ligurius was the actual killer, and subsequently begun to smell a rat . . .

Gods. Sweet immortal gods. I hadn't considered Ligurius
at all, not since the start. Like Chlorus himself the guy had
been off the hook for Murena's murder simply because he
couldn't've been there at the time. Only maybe, now, he
could've been. All I'd really got, when push came to shove,
was his and Chlorus's otherwise unsupported statements
that they'd been together, at Ligurius's house. And if
Chlorus, for reasons best known to himself, was telling
porkies and had got Ligurius to back him, not realising that
he was the killer, then . . .

It was a possibility, sure it was. Certainly one that needed
to be checked, because if the visit had never happened then
it gave Ligurius at least the opportunity to kill Murena. Sure,
the question of motive was something else again, and it was
one I couldn't answer. Ligurius hadn't liked his boss, that
was obvious, and he made no bones about it; but neither,
from what I could see, had half of Baiae. There was the
added fact of the nickname, of course; that may've rankled,

but again it didn't exactly provide him with a strong enough reason to stiff the bastard. On the other hand, how about a threat to his job? Ligurius had been Murena's manager for years, and his father and grandfather before him. The job was part of his life. Say Murena, for some reason, had decided to fire him; maybe he'd caught him fiddling the accounts, or with this new hotel scheme he was planning changes to the existing fish-farm arrangements that meant Ligurius was getting the heave. That might've done the trick, all right, especially with an unambitious stay-at-home type like Ligurius; and with Murena dead the chances were that his hotel plan would die with him. So Ligurius could've gone round after sunset when he knew his boss would be alone by the tanks, feeding the fish and . . .

Oh, hell. Yeah, sure, it was all possible, but I was building sandcastles here. Given the opportunity Ligurius could've killed Murena, no question, and as far as Titus Chlorus was concerned he had as good a reason for wanting rid of him as any, if not a better one than most. He'd certainly have been able to forge Nerva's signature, arrange delivery of the note and lie in wait. All of that, no argument.

Still, whether or not he was the actual villain was another matter. That in their infinite wisdom the gods alone knew, and the bastards weren't dropping any hints.

Even so, this possible lack of alibi was another angle, and one I'd have to follow up. Catia had said Ligurius lived further up her way, near the edge of town, over a fuller's shop. Not the best of directions, but it'd have to do. Tomorrow I'd take a walk over, see what I could find out on the ground and take it from there.

Tomorrow. Meanwhile, I was dead-beat and hungry. The sun was almost down: enough sleuthing for one day.

I went home.

★

I just made it in time – again – for dinner. Or almost in time. Mother, Priscus and Perilla were already couched round the table. I put down Bathyllus's welcome-home drink beside my place, kissed Perilla and settled in beside her.

'You're late, Marcus,' Mother snapped.

'Uh . . . yeah.' I reached for the bread: the cheese and olives at the wineshop near Chlorus's house hadn't gone far, and I was starving. 'I'm sorry. I called in at Aulus Nerva's on the way back.'

'Phormio told us,' Perilla said. 'That Titus Chlorus had been murdered, I mean. It's absolutely dreadful. Do you think—'

'Perilla, *not* at the table.' Mother helped herself to some of Phormio's seafood mousse. 'Don't indulge him.'

'Mmmaaa! These little crayfish are superb.' Priscus was sucking the last of the meat from a shell. 'Try one, Marcus.'

So the prodigal was allowed to join in the cut and thrust of dinner-time conversation again, was he? Still, Mother didn't hold a grudge. Once she'd ripped your chitterlings out and fed you them in slices that was it. As long as Priscus didn't reassume his evil dissolute ways he'd be as safe from first-degree sarcasm burns as the rest of us.

'I trust, dear' – Mother had turned back towards me – 'that when you interviewed Aulus Nerva you introduced the subject of your stepfather's fifteen gold pieces.'

Oh, shit. 'No, actually I—'

'They're a simply appalling family. I'm not surprised that another of them has had the bad taste to have himself murdered. Why not?'

'Why not what?'

'Why didn't you ask for the return of the money? I would

have thought even under the circumstances it was the ideal opportunity. You could've raised the matter tactfully in some way, I'm sure.'

Jupiter on skates! 'Mother, I told you; Priscus lost the cash in a dice game. It was a legitimate gambling debt. I can't just—'

'And *I* told *you*, Marcus, that Titus, being Titus, was not responsible for his actions. Furthermore I suggested that you, to a great extent, were.' She put the crust down. 'Now. I suspect you may be indulging in a little shilly-shallying over your promise to me, and I feel justified in exerting some pressure on you to fulfil it.'

'Look, it was a fu—' I stopped myself in time. 'It was a dice game, all right? I can't ask Nerva and Florus to hand back money they won fair and square.' Especially under the present circumstances: Nerva for one didn't owe me any favours. 'You just don't do things like that.'

'It wasn't fair and square. That is the point. They took advantage of Titus's innocence, and they cheated.'

This was a new one on me. 'How do you mean, "cheated", Mother? *Actually* cheated, with rigged dice? Can you prove that?'

She looked a bit discomfited for a moment, which for Mother isn't saying much, mind. 'No. Not as such. But from Titus's description of how the game went I would not be at all surprised, and that is *quite* good enough for me. Actual proof would be a confirming factor, certainly, but it's not strictly necessary. They frequent that place you mentioned, don't they? The gambling den?'

She'd fazed me for a moment, because I was still mentally gasping over that 'actual proof' bit. 'Uh . . . Nerva and Florus? Philippus's? Yeah, as a matter of fact they do, but—'

'Then if you don't want to ask them outright to return the money – and why you don't, Marcus, escapes me entirely – then you'll simply have to win it back from them, won't you?'

I stared at her.

Priscus was dismembering another crayfish. He beamed. 'Mmmaaa! Good idea, Vipsania! Nerva and Florus told me they were in Philippus's most evenings. I'll take Marcus along with me and—'

She gave him a look that shut his mouth with a snap that probably had serious implications for his remaining teeth. 'Titus you are *not* going anywhere! You've done quite enough already. Marcus can go on his own.'

'Uh . . .' I began.

'Of course' – she pulled the salver of crayfish away from Priscus's questing hand – 'it's hardly likely that Nerva will be there – mourning is mourning, after all, even if he is a poisonous little squirt and didn't get on with his brother – but there's always the chance of the other fellow.'

It was time to knock this one on the head right now, before she *really* got the bit between her teeth. 'Listen, Mother,' I said carefully. 'This is important. We're talking about dice, right?'

'Correct.'

'Now, the odds in a dice game are pretty even, unless the bones are shaved or loaded, and me, I'm not going to play anyone using doctored bones of my own, not for you or anyone else. Especially somewhere the boss takes the house's reputation really, really seriously and who's already not exactly a bosom buddy of mine. Understand?'

'Yes, of course, Marcus! I never suggested that you should—'

'Fine. This means that if I play Florus or Nerva at dice it's just as likely that I'll lose as win. And frankly I don't feel like risking one copper piece of my income just on the off-chance of getting back what that dozy old bugger over there shouldn't've bet in the first place.'

'*Marcus!*'

'Mmmaaa!'

'So you can just—'

'How about Twelve Lines?' Perilla said brightly.

I spun to face her. '*What?*'

'Twelve Lines. People gamble playing that, too, don't they?'

'Whose side are you on, lady?'

'I mean' – she shelled a clam – 'it would be much better than dice, wouldn't it? It involves more skill than luck. Or at least as much, anyway.'

Holy immortal gods! Was I the only sane one here? 'Perilla, watch my lips. I haven't the slightest intention of playing either of these bastards at Twelve Lines, okay? No more than I have of playing them at—'

'I would hope not, dear. Certainly not if they're any good. They'd walk all over you.' She laid down her knife. 'I *was* going to suggest that I play them – or one of them – myself.'

I goggled; Mother, to give her her due, goggled, and that's a thing you don't see often. Priscus almost swallowed his last crayfish whole and went off into a protracted bleat.

'You, lady,' I said, 'have got to be joking.'

'Why? I can beat you nine times out of ten, and only because the tenth time you cheat and I don't let on I've spotted you.'

Jupiter in a bloody sack! 'Perilla, it's got nothing to do with skill! Philippus's is a gambling hall!'

'So?'

'Women don't go into fu— . . . into gambling halls! At least, uh, not your kind of women.'

'You mean they've got three arms and two heads?'

'Gods, lady, you know what I mean! Mother, you tell her!'

Mother sniffed. 'I'll do nothing of the kind, dear. I never interfere between man and wife as you well know' – *hah!* – 'and I'm not going to begin now. I can't say I altogether approve – you're perfectly correct there, Marcus, and I wish you'd show similar delicacy in other circumstances – but that is up to Perilla. Besides, I've played Twelve Lines with her myself in the past and she beats me hollow every time.'

'Oh, come on, Marcus!' The lady was grinning at me. 'Don't be a spoilsport! I'm good, you know I'm good, it'd be fun, and there's no actual law against it, is there?'

'Uh . . . now you come to mention it—'

'Nonsense. We can go after dinner in the carriage. If neither Nerva nor Florus is there Lysias can bring us straight home.'

Bugger; I knew that tone, and I'd got about as much chance of changing the lady's mind as walking across the Bay of Baiae juggling three elephants. I was nailed, and I knew it. Well, at least it would get Mother off my back.

She was right about the cheating, too.

20

We scared up Lysias, the carriage and four torchmen and headed off for Philippus's. On the way, I conquered my sulk and told Perilla about recent developments.

'You think Nerva could have killed him?' she said when I'd finished. 'His own brother?'

'It's possible. After all, he's a fair bet for pushing his father into the fish tank. From parricide to fratricide ain't a big step. And like Mother said they're an appalling family.'

'But why? Why should he kill Chlorus?'

'That I'm not sure of. My guess – and it's only a guess – is that if he did then his reasons boil down to money and control of the family business. Me, I'd really like to know the details of this grain barge scheme.' I looked out of the window. Philippus's wasn't far – I could've walked it, easy, in under half an hour if I hadn't had Perilla – and we were almost there. 'There again, he may be the front runner, but he's not the only one in the family. There's Penelope, for a start. If the Fadia trial's relevant to all this – and I'll bet that it is – then it gives her motive in spades for the Murena side of things, certainly, even after all this time. She might not look much, but that lady *hates*, and she's got good reason to. I didn't know just how much.'

'Penelope may have killed her father, but why Chlorus? I get the impression she despised him rather than hated him. Contempt doesn't lead to murder, Marcus.'

'Could be from the motive Nerva gave me for Gellia: that he found out something and was blackmailing her. Certainly she'd know her brother's handwriting, well enough to forge the note, but then so would anyone else connected with the case. Then there's Gellia herself. If Nerva didn't kill Chlorus she's a reasonable bet, because she had both the motive and the opportunity to kill her husband. That's if the two deaths are connected, of course.'

'They must be, surely.'

'Yeah. I agree. I just haven't got the link yet, that's all, or at least if I have then I don't know it. On the other hand, I've got a better possibility than Gellia lined up, for Chlorus's murder at least.'

'Oh? And who's that?'

'Ligurius.'

She spun to face me. '*Ligurius?* Marcus, why on *earth* would Ligurius want to murder Chlorus?'

'To hide the fact that he hasn't got an alibi for the time of Murena's murder.'

'But . . .' she began. Then she paused and frowned. 'Oh. Oh, I see. You mean that if Chlorus was lying about spending the evening with him—'

'It'd be in his interests to shut the guy's mouth, permanently. Right.'

She was still frowning. 'But he'd only do that if he'd killed Murena. And why should Ligurius want to kill Murena?'

'Gods, Perilla, I don't know! I've got a few theories, but that's all they are. All the same, he's on the list again with a vengeance, at least for the time being. The alibi question's something else to check, and settling it one way or the other's not outwith the bounds of possibility.' I glanced out of the window again. We were just turning into the street with the gambling hall. 'Forget the case for now. Here we are, lady; up and at 'em. Blow on your dice-hand for luck.'

'Superstition doesn't come into it, dear,' she said primly. 'Winning at Twelve Lines is a science.'

'Just do it, Aristotle.'

The big fat German bouncer was standing outside. He opened the carriage door for us and pulled down the steps. Then he saw Perilla, and his eyebrows rose the inch that separated them from his hairline.

'No women,' he growled. 'Is not allowed.'

I'd been ready for this. 'That's okay, pal,' I said easily in my best purple-striper drawl while I helped Perilla out. 'It's all arranged. The boss knows we're coming.'

Perilla gave the guy one of her best smiles – I could almost see his moustaches crinkle – and slipped past him before he could answer. I followed, a hand on her arm. So far so good.

The place was a lot busier than last time, and lit up like an oil-shipper's wedding: yeah, well, in a gambling hall that'd be important, because if you can't see the spots on the dice everyone's in shtook. Upmarket clientele, too, but I'd been expecting that as well: most of the mantles in evidence had purple stripes to them, and the conversations round about us were thick with patrician vowel-sounds. A few straight-bridged noses turned in our direction and there was an almost audible clunk as the corresponding weak chins hit the tables. The noise in the immediate vicinity shifted down an appreciable notch. Maybe this was going to be fun after all.

One of the girls – not the African, this time, but she was pretty well-endowed all the same – was heading towards us at speed, bowsprit well to the fore.

'Just smile, lady,' I whispered to Perilla out of the corner of my mouth, 'and keep it buttoned, right? I'll do the talking.'

'Good evening, sir,' the girl said. 'I'm afraid—'

'Are either Licinius Nerva or Aquillius Florus here tonight?' I said.

'No, sir. I'm sorry, but—'

'They be in later, do you know? Either of them?'

'It's possible, but—'

'That's okay. We're in no hurry, we can wait a bit.' I went to move past her, but she didn't shift.

'I'm afraid ladies aren't allowed in here, sir,' she said firmly. 'I'm sorry, but it's the house rules.'

'Oh, come on, sister! Surely . . . ?'

'I'm sorry, sir.'

Impasse. Bugger. This was going to be even more difficult than I'd thought. Well, I'd tried. Maybe there'd be another opportunity to—

'Corvinus! I want to talk to you, boy!'

I turned round. Philippus was making his way between the tables, and he didn't look too happy, either. Double bugger.

'Ah . . . right. Right,' I said.

We were practically nose to chest now, and he was glaring up at me. He'd changed his tunic, sure, but it hadn't improved his general appearance any: he still looked like he'd been dragged over a hurdle backwards. He jerked his chin to one side without taking his eyes off mine. 'It's okay, Calliope,' he said. 'I'll handle this.' The girl disappeared like magic. 'Now. What the hell are you doing here?'

Ditto for the bad breath. I stepped back a pace. 'Uh . . . I sort of thought from what you said last time I had an open invitation, pal,' I said easily. 'I just thought I'd take you up on it.'

'You want to *play*?'

'Not me. My wife. She's . . . ah . . . pretty good.'

'A pleasure to meet you, Licinius Philippus.' Perilla gave

the guy another of her best smiles. 'Marcus has told me such a lot about you.'

He was still frowning and his eyebrows had shot up like the German's outside. 'How'd you get past Siegfried?'

'We lied,' Perilla said.

He stared at her for a good ten seconds. Then, suddenly, his face split into a grin, and he laughed. 'Well, you've got nerve, boy, I'll say that. And in the lady's case that goes double. The pleasure's mine. How're the ribs?'

'Still tender.'

'Good. I'm glad.' He sucked on a tooth and leaned back, considering. 'Well, now, Valerius Corvinus. Calliope told you: we don't let women in here. House rules. But maybe under the circumstances we'll make an exception. Like I said, I wanted to talk to you, and throwing you out won't help either of us.'

'Suits me, pal.' I'd things to say to Philippus myself, and now was as good a time as any.

'Right. Upstairs, same as before.' He looked at Perilla. 'Your wife'll be okay. I'll have one of the girls look after her while we have our chat. Give her a game, too, if that's what she wants.'

'Actually, uh, we were hoping to run across Aquillius Florus or Aulus Nerva.'

That got me a long, considering stare. 'Is that so, now?' he murmured. 'Makes two of us. Well, I doubt if Nerva'll be in tonight. He's had some family trouble. No doubt you've heard.'

I didn't say anything.

'It's early still for Florus, but he may be along later. Hey, Calliope!' He raised his voice. The girl with the bowsprit came back over. 'See to the Lady . . . what was her name, Corvinus?'

'Perilla,' Perilla said.

'See to the Lady Perilla. Anything she wants, anything at all. She's my honoured guest. Right, Corvinus. You come along with me, boy.'

We set off between the hushed tables and goggling punters towards the staircase, Philippus moving at his fast limp. Yeah, that'd be the legacy from the city judge's strong-arm department twenty-eight years back that Saenius had mentioned, all right. Jupiter, the guy must be tough! Me, I doubt if I could've stuck to a lie with those bastards working on me for five minutes. Philippus had done it right through to the end, no sweat, and whatever his reasons that'd taken real guts. Bastard or not, I admired him.

The mezzanine was heaving, but this time no one so much as looked up. Philippus took the key from his belt and unlocked the office.

'In you go,' he grunted.

I sat down in the chair I'd had the last time. Philippus closed the door and limped to the one behind the desk. 'Right,' he said. 'You're a proper nosey bugger and no mistake, aren't you? Persistent too.'

I grinned. 'Yeah. You could say that.'

'I'm persistent myself. Not enough of us around. So tell me what you've found out and we'll take it from there.'

'You were Murena's door-slave, thirty years back. You saw – or at least you claimed you saw – his first wife Fadia fall downstairs. You gave evidence for Murena at the trial, under torture.'

' "Claimed"?'

'My bet is you did a deal with Murena's lawyer Tattius. You help him get his client off the hook and he'd see you got your freedom and enough cash to start you up in business.'

Silence. *Long* silence. There wasn't any friendliness in the guy's face now. Finally, he said softly, 'You're a clever, clever bugger, Corvinus. But Murena didn't free me. I bought myself out. I told you that last time we spoke.'

'Yeah, sure. But that was a technicality, wasn't it? Tattius screwed the purchase price out of Murena after the trial and got him to agree to the sale. Murena may not have given you your freedom but he paid the money for it to himself.'

Philippus scowled. 'It was no technicality. I earned that money fair and square. Wherever it came from, it was mine at the time, and I paid it over in hard coin. You remember that, boy!'

Jupiter! Back off, Corvinus! 'Yeah. Yeah, okay.'

'The bastard murdered my father. Had him flogged to death for dropping a fucking vase. You knew that as well?'

'Not the details, no, but—'

'Then he had the corpse fed to the fish. What I got through Tattius was blood money, owed twice over. Murena wasn't doing me no favours, and I wasn't doing him any, either. It was pure quid pro quo. I'm a businessman, Corvinus, and I've always played fair. I do it now and I did it then.'

'Tell me something,' I said. 'Did Murena push his wife or not?'

That got me a long, considering look. Finally Philippus said, 'Sure he did. I was there all right, down below in my cubby. I saw it all. He pushed her, no question.'

'If you hated him bad enough you could've told the jury that.'

Philippus laughed, then spat to one side. 'I could've done. I thought of it at the time. Holy Mercury, I thought of it! So what would happen then? I'd have to give my evidence under torture, and at the end of it I'd still be a slave. If I lived. Worse, I'd still be Murena's slave because the bastard was a purple-striper and all he'd get was exile for a few years. Even if the dead woman's brother had pushed for the death penalty and got it, I'd be his son's slave, and Titus Chlorus was as bad as his father. How long do you think I'd live then, Corvinus? And if I did, where would it leave me?'

Yeah; right. Still, it showed a train of logic you didn't expect from your average skivvy. Certainly not from one the age Philippus was at the time. He'd been special, even then. 'So when Tattius approached you you agreed to the deal,' I said.

Philippus laughed again. 'Fuck that, boy! Decimus Tattius couldn't find his way out of a sack open at both ends. I went to him. I told him that I'd seen, what I'd seen, and if he wanted to save his pal I could do it for him. At a price. No haggling, take it or leave it. And if he didn't agree, or welshed on me later, I'd take the real story to the mistress's brother, whether it killed me or not. I meant every word, too, and he knew it. I owed my father that, at least.'

Well, that made sense – more sense, I had to admit, knowing both Philippus and Tattius, than the other way round – and it came to the same thing in the end in any case. 'You knew Tattius had been blackmailing Murena ever since? Or at least bleeding him for all he could get?'

Philippus grinned. 'Sure I did. Good luck to him. It was no skin off my nose, and the more the bastard bled the better I liked it. I hated Murena, Corvinus, and don't you forget it. I was finished with him – I wouldn't've touched that piece of shit with gloves on – but if he was still paying then that was fine by me. The two deserved each other. And the day I heard he was dead, and how, I sacrificed to my father's ghost. You can't tell me the eels were coincidence, and you needn't try. You don't buck the gods, boy.'

'So who killed him? Do you know?'

'No. Not me. I wouldn't dirty my hands, and like I say he was still paying. I don't know who killed his son, either, and I care less, because apart from the girl they're all filth in that family, the new wife included.' He scowled. 'That's the only thing I regret, Corvinus. The girl had spunk; she'd seen what happened, too, and she spoke up against her father. For what good it did her. I'm sorry about young Licinia, I always have been.' He stood up. 'Well, you've got the whole thing, whether I like it or not, and I can't say I do. It's water under the bridge. What happens now?'

He was watching me carefully, and I knew despite the easy manner that the answer I gave him would be important. Maybe terminally so. I shrugged. 'Nothing. Not as far as the Fadia case is concerned, anyway. If the guy did murder her then he's dead and burned himself. That's the end of it.'

'So long as you don't spread the story around.'

'Why would I want to do that?'

'You wouldn't, boy. Believe me. You really wouldn't.' Our eyes locked. Right.

'Message understood,' I said.

'Fine.' He held out his hand. 'Deal?'

'Deal,' I said, and shook.

Philippus grunted. 'I've got business up here for a while,' he said. 'Go back downstairs, see if that young bastard Florus is in yet. I'm not asking the whys and wherefores, but if your wife can take him for everything that's in his purse you've got my blessing. That lady has spunk, too. I saw it straight off.'

'Yeah,' I said. 'Yeah, she has.'

'And when you're finished with him you hand him over to me. Me and Florus – and that shyster Nerva, when he's got over crying for his brother – we've got a little chat coming to do with that scheme of theirs you mentioned involving the converted grain barge.'

'Apropos of that,' I said, 'I thought maybe you and Aulus Nerva might have a deal going already.'

I was watching him carefully. He didn't even blink.

'Did you, indeed?' he said. 'Such as?'

'A three-way arrangement, with Florus. Co-financing.'

He laughed. 'I don't need to co-finance with nobody, boy! I told you: I've got all the money I need already for any investment I want to make. And even if I hadn't I wouldn't deal with Aulus Nerva. He's his father's son and that's enough for me. I said I wouldn't touch any of that family with gloves on, not for any reason. They're all shit, and I wouldn't trust any of them the length of my arm. No, believe me, this is one conversation Florus is not going to enjoy, but if he's got any sense he'll listen. Him and Nerva both.'

I grinned. Well, maybe that particular theory had been misplaced after all. Still, I didn't feel all that cut up. I was beginning to like Philippus, and if you can spread a little sunshine then life ain't too bad. 'One last thing,' I said. 'If I wanted to hire a slinger in Baiae how would I go about it?'

The dagger-point eyes fixed me. 'A slinger? What kind of slinger?'

'Just the usual. Good, not top-notch military standard, but one who knows the pouch from the strings. And who doesn't have any qualms about his target wearing a mantle.'

'Hold on, now, Corvinus!' He was frowning. 'You buying or complaining here?'

'Complaining. One of the buggers nearly took my head off on the way home yesterday.'

His eyes widened. 'Is that so, now? Not doing too well, are you?' I didn't answer. 'Okay. Leave it with me. You may not believe me, boy, but I'm straight. I'll put the word around, sure, but at present I haven't got any more idea than you have. Now push off; I'm busy.'

I went downstairs.

21

Perilla was waiting for me when I came back down, in a corner with Calliope. She smiled brightly.

'Finished, Marcus?'

'Yeah. All done.'

'Philippus is a charming man. Not at all as you described him.'

Gods! There was no answer to that. 'You been enjoying yourself?'

'Very much so. This is all fascinating. Quite a different world. And Calliope and I have been having a very interesting chat.'

'Yeah. I'll bet.' I glanced at the girl. She was looking pretty red about the ears and carefully avoiding my eye.

'Did you know that the men here sometimes play for sex?'

'Jupiter, lady!'

'In place of their winnings, I mean. The girls pocket those, or at least a part of them. Philippus doesn't mind, so long as both parties play fair, and—'

'Perilla, just shut up, okay? No sign of Florus, presumably?'

'No, not yet. But Calliope says he—'

'There he is now, madam,' Calliope said. 'Excuse me, sir. I've got work to do. If you need anything, just call.'

She escaped.

I'd turned round. Florus was chatting to one of the punters near the entrance. He hadn't seen us.

'Come on, Aristotle.' I pulled Perilla to her feet. 'Now's the time to put our money where your considerable mouth is.'

He looked up when we were about three tables away: too late to run, which from his horrified expression he'd've liked to do.

'Hey, Florus,' I said. 'How's it going?'

His eyes moved. *Definitely* shifty. I wondered again what the guy had to hide. Still, he recovered well. 'Corvinus. And . . . your wife Perilla, isn't it?' He smiled, showing a lot of teeth. 'We met in Bauli. With Helvius Priscus and your mother-in-law.'

'Yes.' Perilla gave him another of the bright smiles back. 'That's why I'm here, in fact. I'm deputising. Priscus said you and Licinius Nerva suggested a rematch, but he can't play any more, so you have me instead.'

The expanse of teeth vanished. Florus looked fazed. Yeah, well, Perilla's go-straight-for-the-jugular approach can have that effect, and the guy wasn't exactly the sharpest cookie in the box. 'Uh . . . Corvinus?' he said weakly.

'Nothing to do with me, pal.' I grinned. 'It's the lady's show. I'm just here to watch.'

He turned back to Perilla like he'd been hit a whanger with a sockful of damp sand. 'You . . . ah . . . want to play me? At dice?'

'Twelve Lines. If you don't mind, that is. Yes, I do.'

He blinked, twice. 'But the house rules don't allow—'

'Oh, that's all arranged. Calliope!' The girl with the bowsprits came over with a Twelve Lines board and a box of counters. 'Where would you like to sit?'

Times like these, you just stand back and marvel. I'd seen Perilla take on a pack of tourist sharks on the quayside in Antioch and reduce them to forelock-tugging submission in ten seconds flat. A weak-chinned bugger like Aquillius Florus didn't stand a chance. There was an empty table just beside us. He collapsed on to one of the chairs like he'd been hamstrung. Perilla and I sat opposite. Calliope laid the board between us, opened the box and began to set out the jet and ivory pieces in the usual three rows of five either side.

'Now,' Perilla said. 'The rules, before we start. No reneging, agreed? A piece once played is played.'

'Uh . . . agreed,' Florus mumbled. 'Are you sure—'

'We use the full dice throw whenever possible. If it isn't possible, for whatever reason, then as many pieces move as can, highest numbers the priority. Fifteen gold pieces on the game. Or call it twenty: the house takes a tenth of the winnings, that's right, isn't it, Calliope?'

'Yes, madam.'

'Fine. Twenty it is, then. You agree, Aquillius Florus?'

'Ah . . .'

'The wager. Twenty gold pieces. Does that suit you?'

He swallowed. 'Uh . . . yeah. Yes, twenty's—'

'That's excellent. Then let's begin, shall we?'

'Ah . . . some wine? Please?'

'Certainly.' She gave him another dazzling smile. 'Marcus?'

'Sure. The Rhodian was good last time. Okay with you, Florus?'

He nodded, dazed. I suspect that I'd've got the same nod if I'd suggested fermented goat's milk.

'And a fruit juice of some kind for me, Calliope,' Perilla said. 'Thank you.' The girl went off. 'Now. White starts. Shall we throw for white? Highest wins.' She picked up one of the three dice and rolled it. 'Four. *Not* very good, but never mind. Your turn, Florus. Oh, dear, a three. Black for you, then. Ready?'

Here we went. I noticed that play around us was stopping, like a ripple spreading across a pool. Perilla threw the dice.

A six, a one and a four.

Not a bad total, but that didn't matter: there was a long way to go. The basic aim of Twelve Lines – if you don't know the game – is to get all your fifteen counters round the board and take them off the other end while your opponent's doing the same in the opposite direction. Singletons can be hit and sent back to the start, so it's a good idea, especially when you get within hitting distance, to secure lines with two or more men. Unless, of course, you get to the point where you know you're going to lose in a straight race and decide to play a back game. Back games are chancy things, and I've never mastered them myself. Which is, like the lady said, why Twelve Lines isn't my bag and she always thrashes me.

The six and the four made Perilla's seventh line, and she moved a single piece on to line four.

Florus threw: six, double three. The rule's one die per piece – and you can't double up in Twelve Lines – so I'd expected him to move a singleton to the seventh and use the two threes to make one of the lines immediately beyond his starting position, but he played from the second and third to the fifth and sixth, which with his seventh singleton gave him three on consecutive lines. Interesting: safe enough at the moment, sure, with Perilla still well over to her side of the board out of hitting range, but it suggested the guy intended to play an aggressive game. Which might be good or bad, depending on the run of the dice. We'd have to wait and see.

This time Perilla threw five, four, one. She covered the singleton on line four with the one, used the five to add another man from the second rank to her seventh line and put a single counter from the back on to line five. The lady, obviously, had decided on the slow, cautious approach, waiting for Florus to make the first mistake.

Calliope brought the wine. Florus gulped his first cupful down, held it out for a refill and gulped that one, too. Yeah, well, I knew the feeling: after being Perilla'd the bugger needed it.

I sat back for the long hard slog.

'Slog' was the word. I'd been wrong about Florus. Weak-chinned and intellectually challenged in other respects though the guy might be, when it came to Twelve Lines he was no pushover, and with half a pint of the Rhodian under his belt he settled in and played a very nice game indeed. Too nice by half for my liking: I was glad it was Perilla who'd taken him on, because I could see even at this early stage that he'd've creamed me without breaking sweat. The lady had noticed it as well, and she wasn't happy: fifteen minutes in she'd lost a lot of her bounce and was twisting a stray curl at her left temple, something she only does when she's tired or thinking hard. That worried me. Shit; we might have bitten off more than we could chew this time. Twenty gold pieces wasn't a fortune, sure, but it wasn't peanuts either. And if Florus won the game, unless Mother accepted that we'd given it our best shot – which, knowing Mother, was about as likely as an oyster winning the hundred-yard sprint – I'd have to make good my promise in another way.

This could get expensive. If I ever got Priscus alone some-where dark and quiet I would murder the bugger myself.

We were at that point in the game where things begin to

get complicated. Perilla had all her counters on the top six lines her side, with no singletons but the tenth and eleven lines clear. Par for the course: when you're covering lines in the top half of the board you need to leave some space for your opponent to move to, or because of the one-die-one-piece rule the game's deadlocked. Also, because you have to use all the numbers on the dice where possible, there's a good chance of getting an opponent's singleton where you can hit it and send it back to start. Florus was almost in the same position, but with only one line free – the tenth – and a singleton killer back on his fourth line. This is when the luck of the dice really matters: if you can move a piece to your opponent's side of the board and cover it without leaving a singleton on your own side vulnerable, then great. If you can't, then that's when the game starts to hot up, because the chances are one of you will be hit on the next go. Which may, of course, leave the hitter himself vulnerable.

I took a swig from my wine cup and crossed my fingers. Florus's throw: five, three, one. Good and bad: it left him a singleton on Perilla's eleventh and opened up his own eighth line, but it meant that to make a safe hit Perilla would need a four, a three or a two plus another of the same numbers in the roll to cover.

Six, three, one. The three gave her the hit, sure, but it was a forced move that left two of her men vulnerable on her own eleventh and Florus's tenth. Florus threw three, two, two. Good and bad, though mostly good for him because it meant he had the option of hitting – and covering – both of his target lines. Perilla's eleventh would give him an island on her half of the board, but his own singleton on the fourth was still vulnerable and he was allowing her a good chance of getting the first man of the game off the end. On the other hand, if he chose to hit that one instead he'd close his own tenth line, leaving only the eighth open. Tricky.

Florus chose the first option, leaving his singleton still exposed and using the spare two to move a man from his ninth to his eleventh line.

Okay: so we were into the rough stuff now.

Perilla threw again: six, five, four. Decision time again. The six was good: it meant she could either hit Florus's singleton or cover her own on his tenth. She covered, brought her man on with the four and moved a piece from her seventh to her twelfth. Florus's next throw was four, two, one. Easy-peasy: the four covered the singleton and he shifted a man from his seventh to his ninth line and another from eleven to twelve.

Level pegging, more or less: both of them had islands on the other one's side, plus an empty line, and killing pieces within striking distance of it at the back.

I looked up. The play around us had stopped altogether, and a few of the punters had drifted over to watch. Yeah, well: a woman playing at Philippus's was a first, and it was shaping up for a good match. I didn't blame them.

'Marcus, do you *have* to sit there breathing into my ear like that?' Perilla snapped.

'What?'

'You're putting me off. Go away, I need to concentrate.'

'What about all these other guys?' There were six or seven of them now, standing around the table.

'Them I don't mind. You I do. You're making me nervous. Now just go away and let me get on with it.'

Gods! Yeah, well, if she didn't want the moral support she didn't, and it was the lady's prerogative. And the game still had a long way to run. I stood up, picked up my wine cup and went walkabout.

Outside our little circle of interest there were plenty of

other games going on: dice, mostly, but a few of the more cerebral punters were playing Twelve Lines or Robbers. Like I say, Twelve Lines isn't my bag, and I didn't bother at all with the Robbers guys – it's a slow game, with lots of thinking between moves, and the real aficionados get pretty sarky with onlookers, especially when they offer unsolicited advice – but a few of the dice games were real needle matches. Played for high stakes, too. I hung around one or two, but when curiosity got the better of me I drifted back over to Perilla's table and did a bit of rubbernecking from where she couldn't see me. It didn't look all that good, not from a cursory glance, anyway, and Florus was looking a lot happier. Shit. I moved away again.

'Hey, Corvinus.'

I turned. Philippus was beckoning from an empty table in the corner by the stairs. I went over.

'How's it going?'

I shrugged. 'Could be better. I don't know for sure; the lady doesn't want me to watch.'

'That so, now?' He grinned. 'Well, don't let it worry you too much, boy. I'd be the same myself. So would you. And if not having you there sharpens her game it's all to the good. Right?'

'Yeah. Yeah, I suppose so.'

'I thought I was finished with you, but I've been thinking again and maybe I haven't after all. This won't take long, so we needn't go back to the office. Here's fine. Okay with you?'

'Sure.'

He pulled up a chair and sat down. 'Now. I said I didn't want to know, but I've a reason for asking, so maybe you'll tell me. This game your wife's playing with Florus. It has something to do with your stepfather?'

I sat down opposite him. 'Uh . . . yeah. You could say that.'

'Rooked him, did they? Florus and Nerva?'

'Yeah, maybe. That's what Mother thinks. I don't know for sure myself, but—'

'They rooked him. Oh, I know these two buggers. Not here, though, they know better than that because they'd be out on their backsides if they tried it. Somewhere else.'

'Bauli. A wineshop.'

Philippus nodded. 'Fine. Then like I said to you upstairs I hope your wife takes that bastard Florus for everything he's got. Good luck to her. Thanks, Corvinus. That's all I wanted to hear.'

I stood up. 'Okay. In that case—'

'Sit down.' Philippus hadn't moved. 'I haven't started yet.' I sat. 'I don't like customers of mine cheating each other, wherever it happens, my place or someplace else. And I *really* don't like customers who I know are bastards doing it to someone I've brought here myself in good faith. I don't like that at all. So I reckon, boy, that I owe you. A big one, because it covers your grain barge tip as well.' He sucked on a tooth. 'Here's the payoff. You get yourself over to Puteoli tomorrow. Street just off the market square, I can't remember offhand what it's called but you'll find it. The man you want to talk to is Gaius Frontinus.' He stood, suddenly. 'That's it. Like I say, I hope your wife wins.'

'Hang on. Who's this Frontinus?'

'That's all I'm telling you. We've a deal. You stick to your part of the bargain and I'll stick to mine. The account's clear now. You just talk to Frontinus, hear? And don't forget, I want to see Florus when you're done. Calliope'll come and get me.'

Before I could answer he'd limped off.

I stood up and moved back over to the game. Florus was sitting back in his chair grinning, and one look at the board showed me why.

It was bad; very bad. In fact, it could hardly be worse.

Hell.

22

The game was almost over: there were only three counters still on the board, black ones, two on Perilla's fourth line and one on the third, ready to be moved off. Plus – and this was the point – one white, waiting to come on.

Florus leaned forward and picked up the dice. So it was Florus's throw, on top of everything else. Oh, shit, there went the whole boiling. Still, we'd tried our best; even Mother would have to admit that.

I would *kill* Priscus!

I pushed my way through the crowd of punters – it was a crowd now – and sat down next to Perilla.

'Hey, Corvinus.' Florus gave me a big grin. 'How's the boy? Back in time for the finish, right?'

'Yeah,' I said.

'Hello, Marcus,' Perilla said listlessly; the lady looked done in. 'I'm sorry, but we seem to have lost.'

'Someone's got to. Luck of the game.' Florus was still grinning and jiggling the dice, prolonging the agony. My fist knotted. 'It's just my night, that's all.'

'Just shut up and throw, pal,' I said. Twenty gold pieces and it all to do again. I could've wept.

He shrugged and threw. The three dice clattered across the board.

Two sixes. And a two.

Behind me, I could hear the breath go out of the punters,

but I was watching Florus. His grin had slipped. Two sixes got his back two men off. The two . . .

The two left him one to go: a vulnerable singleton on the last line. And now it was Perilla's turn.

Suddenly, I felt angry. Anything else and she'd lost, sure, but if she threw a one we were back in the game. The hell with science now; let's go with the luck. As Perilla reached for the dice, I put my hand over hers, stopping her.

'Hold on, lady,' I said. I was still looking straight at Florus.

He frowned. 'Come on, Corvinus, this is your wife's game! No interfering. Let her make the throw.'

'In a minute. You want to raise the bet?'

'Do I *what*?'

'Marcus!' Perilla whispered.

I didn't look at her. 'You stay out of this,' I said. There had been a murmur from the punters behind me, but I ignored that too. My eyes were still on Florus. 'Okay. Here's the deal, friend. We double the wager—'

'*Marcus, have you totally lost your senses?*'

' . . . only if Perilla hits your man and goes on to win after all we take half in information.'

Long silence; you could've heard an ant cough.

Florus's eyes shifted. A lot of the bounce had suddenly gone out of him. He licked his lips nervously.

'What kind of information?' he said.

'The answers to any questions I care to ask you, ten minutes' worth. Straight, full and delivered under oath.' I waited, but nothing came. His face had gone grey. 'Come on, pal! A ten-minute chat saves you twenty gold pieces. And that's only if we win. If we lose, you get forty. Now are you a gambler or aren't you?'

It was a close thing. For a minute I didn't think he'd bite. On the other hand, he'd been called upfront, and no gambler worth his salt likes to knuckle down under these circumstances. Plus the fact that half of Philippus's was there watching to see him do it. And the odds were fair: Perilla would still be using all three dice. Three chances at a one.

I'd got the bastard by the short hairs, and both of us knew it.

'Treble,' Florus said. I doubt if you could've prised his teeth apart with a crowbar.

'Fine with me,' I said. 'Treble it is. Same deal: twenty in cash, the rest the other way.'

'*Marcus, have you gone completely mad?*' I could feel Perilla staring at me. '*That's sixty gold pieces!*'

Yeah, well, maybe she had a point at that. But it was too late to go back now. 'Just throw, lady,' I said.

She shook the dice. I crossed my fingers, held my breath and prayed to whatever god protected half-assed, brain-dead purple-stripers who didn't know when to cut their losses and go home gracefully.

A five, a three and a one.

Perilla squealed, two of the punters behind me cheered, and one plummy-voiced senator type murmured, 'Oh, good show, madam!' Florus just looked sick.

I breathed out and grinned. Jupiter! That had been close! We weren't out of the woods yet, sure, not by any means, but at least we were back in there and punching. Now it was a straight race; except, of course, if one of them hit the other's piece on the way round . . .

Perilla's five and three took her to the ninth line. Florus's turn, coming on from scratch. He reached automatically for the dice and threw: a six, a two and a four, putting him straight up to his twelfth, halfway round the board. Shit; he had the edge, three lines ahead. And if Perilla didn't get the four that would send him back again then it was all in the dice. The chances of three ones I just didn't like to think of.

She got them all the same.

Behind me, there was a hiss of indrawn breath and one of the punters swore fluently. I knew how he felt. Me, I just gritted my teeth and said nothing.

Florus was grinning again. A one would give him a hit and put us back to the start, and I doubted if we'd be lucky a second time. There again, anything over twelve and he'd won the game anyway. Bugger. He jiggled the dice and threw.

A five, a four and a two. Well, at least we were off the hook for the moment: he'd missed her singleton and fallen short of the straight win. Still, it only left him two lines shy of home, and with three dice that was it.

So it was all on this throw. And, like Florus had been, Perilla was only on her twelfth line.

'Come on, lady,' I said. 'Thirteen or better. Can you do that for me?'

She smiled faintly. 'I'll try, dear. But no promises.'

She picked up the dice and rolled them.

Two sixes and a five. She whooped, and hugged me.

Yeah, well, when the lady does something she does it with style. The punters erupted.

'Okay, pal,' I said to Florus through the hubbub. 'You and me are going to have a little talk.'

The three of us ('I'm not being left out now, Marcus. Not after I've done all the work') went over to the table I'd been sitting at with Philippus. Florus was looking sick as a dog. I'd brought the wine jug over with me and I filled both our cups. No point in being cruel, and the bastard looked like he needed it just as badly as I did. He sank his in a oner.

'Right,' I said. 'Give. Let's start with that grain barge deal. And you're on oath, remember. Gambling debts are sacred.'

'There's nothing to tell! It's all above board!'

'Fine.' That didn't explain why he'd practically filled his pants when we'd bumped into each other at Nerva's a few hours ago, mind. Or why he'd looked like running when he'd caught sight of me that evening. Or why he was sweating now like a pig in a steam bath. However, we'd take things as they came. 'So we'll just begin with the straight facts, okay?'

'Aulus and I are partners. We're going to buy the barge – it's one of these big ones that go from Egypt to Puteoli – do it up and moor it offshore as a floating gambling hall and brothel.' He glanced sideways at Perilla. 'I'm sorry, but he did ask.'

'That's all right.' Perilla gave him a bright smile. The lady was looking chirpy as hell. Jupiter, it'd be months before I took the bounce out of her for this! 'I'm not offended, Aquillius Florus. A brothel is a very good investment, and it keeps girls off the streets.'

I ignored her. 'Equal partners?' I said.

'Yes. Yes, of course!'

'It sounds pricey to me. Where's the money coming from?'

Florus coloured up. 'That's none of your damn—' he began.

'Oh, yes it is, pal. As of five minutes ago. Gambling debt, remember? Just answer the question, okay?'

He subsided. 'I already had my share. A legacy from an uncle.'

'Congratulations. What about Nerva?'

This was the sticking point, and both of us knew it. Florus's eyes shifted. 'He . . . was hoping to get it from his father,' he muttered.

'Yeah. Only his father wouldn't oblige. Wouldn't and couldn't both, because he'd got plans of his own. Expensive plans, connected with the new hotel he wanted to build. Right?'

Florus didn't answer.

'Which was why they had the slanging match the day Murena died.'

'He didn't tell me about that!'

'Maybe not. But believe me, it happened. Fine. So if Nerva wasn't getting the money from his father, and if your barge scheme was still a viable option, which it was and is because you're talking about it in the present tense, then where did he propose getting the cash?'

He hesitated.

'Come on, Florus! Give!'

'From a money-lender in Puteoli. Gaius Frontinus.'

I kept my face expressionless. 'Is that so, now?'

His eyes widened. 'You know him?'

'I've heard of him.' Shit. 'On what security?'

The shifty look was back. 'Aulus has a house of his own. A good one.'

'No one puts his own house up as security for a dodgy business venture, pal. Not unless he's desperate, or an idiot. And you haven't answered the question.'

'All right!' Florus glared at me. 'Then I don't know! Whatever the security was, Frontinus accepted it. The why isn't my business. How he came up with his half of the capital was Aulus's concern, not mine.'

'Yeah. Only in the event he doesn't need a loan now, does he? Not with his father and his brother both dead.'

'Titus's share of the estate goes to his widow. They've got a daughter. That's the law. If the marriage has produced children then—'

'Yeah, I know all that,' I said. 'But with his brother dead Aulus Nerva controls the family company's finances. Together with his father's partner, sure, technically, at least, but Decimus Tattius isn't going to make any waves. The widow Catia neither, for different reasons. Oh, and we might add Gellia, too, while we're on the subject. I understand you've got a bit of influence there.'

If Florus had looked green before he went three shades greener. 'You leave Gellia out of this,' he muttered. 'She's got nothing to do with it.'

I'd touched a nerve somewhere. Maybe it was time to probe a little deeper. 'She'd have a prime motive for killing her husband, wouldn't she? Mind you, she'd need help.'

Florus stood up; or tried to, at least, because I grabbed his arm and forced him down again.

'I'd nothing to do with Licinius Murena's death, Corvinus!' he said. 'Nor Chlorus's. I swear that. If Gellia had, then I know nothing about it. If you think—'

'Yeah. Right. Still, it's a thought, isn't it?'

'Put it out of your head. We're . . . friends, certainly, I admit that, but I wouldn't . . . I couldn't . . .' He swallowed. 'Gods! You've got to believe me! It's the pure and honest truth!'

Shit, he was probably right; this long streak of cowardly lard wouldn't have the guts to murder anyone. Which left one interesting alternative.

'But Aulus Nerva would, right?' I said softly.

All the colour drained out of his face. He didn't say anything.

'Okay,' I said. 'Stop faffing around. Just tell me what you know.'

'I don't *know* anything! That's the trouble!'

'Fine. Tell me what you guess.'

He was quiet for a long time. Then he said, 'Aulus wasn't here the night of the murder. He tried to tell you he was, but he wasn't.'

'Yeah, I know that. I checked. And?'

'He wasn't here last night, either. When Chlorus died. He should've been: we had an arrangement. When I talked to him this afternoon he said he'd had a head cold and decided to stay in.'

'Did he? Have a head cold, I mean?'

'He gets them sometimes. But you talked to him yourself, after I left. What's your answer?'

Yeah; I saw the guy's point. Not a sniffle. Still, it might've cleared up. All the same, it meant that Aulus Nerva didn't have an alibi for either the evening of his father's death or his brother's. And he'd lied, or tried to lie, about both. Interesting. 'Is that all?'

He hesitated.

'Come on, Florus! Gambling debt, forty big ones, remember, and I'm not getting value for money here! Cough it up, pal!'

'He . . . said he wished his father would drop dead. Or that someone would kill him,' Florus muttered. 'The day we agreed on a price for the barge. He said it would . . . simplify things. He was serious, Corvinus. Really serious.'

The guy was still white as a sheet, and shaking. Yeah, right: I reckoned we'd got to the heart of that one, finally: Aquillius Florus was scared out of his skin. 'So,' I said, 'you think Nerva murdered his father. And his brother. To get the money for your grain barge scam.'

'Corvinus, I swear to you I don't know anything more about it! Whatever he did, it's got nothing to do with me, I'm not involved, okay? If Aulus is a killer then—'

'Right. Right.' Jupiter, I felt sick myself.

'All I ask is you don't tell him I've told you any of this. If he finds out he'll kill me too.'

'Fine.' The only thing I wanted now was to go. 'Okay, pal. Interrogation over. You still owe us twenty gold pieces in cash. Pay the lady.'

He took out his purse with a shaking hand and counted out twenty big ones. Then he stood up. 'Corvinus, I swear—' he said.

He stopped. His eyes were fixed on something behind me. I turned.

Oh, yeah, I'd forgotten: Philippus.

He was waiting by the stairs, with his two heavies in attendance. I noticed that one of them was the guy who'd punched me in the ribs, and he was wearing a fetching little bandage round his head. I grinned at him and got a glare back.

'Looks like you're popular tonight, friend.' I smiled at Florus. 'We'll just leave you to it, shall we?'

He was still staring. Philippus limped forward, flanked by the heavies. He didn't look too chuffed, either.

Me, I know when I'm not wanted. I stood up.

'Okay, Perilla,' I said. 'Fun's over, lady. You had enough excitement for one evening, or should we go somewhere else?'

She got up and kissed me. 'Yes, thank you, Marcus. It's been fascinating. Home, I think. Goodnight, Aquillius Florus, and thank you for the game. I enjoyed it immensely.'

Florus gave a strangled grunt. His eyes hadn't moved.

'Finished, Corvinus?' Philippus said.

'Yeah, you could say that.'

'Good.' He turned to Florus and jerked his thumb. 'You. Upstairs.'

*

We dropped off the house cut with Calliope and went outside. Lysias had turned and was parked just up the street, waiting.

We drove home. It'd been a long, long day, and I was knackered.

Still, I reckoned we'd got our killer. It was only a question now of wrapping things up.

23

The next morning I took the mare into Puteoli.

With Ostia silting up fast, and despite the distances involved, Puteoli's Rome's main port, especially for the grain ships that ply across the Med from Alexandria, so it's a far bigger place than Baiae, practically a city in its own right like Neapolis. Even so, Philippus's directions were clear enough for my purposes. I found the market square, mentioned Frontinus's name to a friendly vegetable-seller and was directed to a two-up, two-down house in a street just off the centre.

'Gaius Frontinus's?' I asked the door-slave.

'Yes, sir. The master's out at the moment, though. On business.'

Hell. 'You know when he'll be back?'

'Can't say, sir. Was it urgent?'

'Yeah. You could say that.'

'Then you'll probably find him at Cleisthenes's emporium. In Five Cedars Street.'

'Where's that, sunshine?'

He gave me directions. Luckily it wasn't far: one of the streets the other side of the square. I slipped him a few coppers – door-slaves can always do with a contribution to the liberation fund – and set off back the way I'd come.

I couldn't've missed Cleisthenes's. It was one of those big emporia that sell everything for the house, from snail dishes to man-size storage jars, and it filled practically the whole of the block. I parked the mare at a convenient horse-trough and went in. One of the sales skivvies directed me to a back room on the far side of the central hall.

I knocked on the door.

'Come in.'

It was a small office. There were two men there, going through a stack of tablets: a tall lanky one with 'Greek' written all over him and a small dumpy one with an Aventine face and rheumy eyes. Despite the Aventine face, what was written all over him, from his pricey Cordoban leather sandals to the pearl earring in his left ear, was money. Yeah, right: that had to be Frontinus.

'I'm sorry to disturb you, gentlemen,' I said. 'Valerius Corvinus. I was told I'd find Gaius Frontinus here.'

'That's Gaius *Calpurnius* Frontinus,' the little guy said. Obviously, he was proud of the name, but if he was one of *the* Calpurnii then I'd eat my mantle. 'How can I help you? I'm afraid I'm rather busy at present, as you can see, but if you make it brief . . .'

'Ah . . . I was given your name by Licinius Philippus in Baiae,' I said.

The effect was magic. The guy literally flowed over. 'How is Philippus?' he said. 'Well, I trust? Cleisthenes, you'll forgive us for a moment.'

The lanky guy didn't have much choice – I reckoned from the way he was acting he owed Frontinus serious money, and that the account had just become due – but he put a brave face on it. 'Certainly. I'll just . . . that is, I'll . . .' He gave me a nod and slipped out, closing the door behind him.

Yeah, well; I couldn't fault the value of Philippus's introduction, anyway. Frontinus beamed at me. 'Now, Corvinus,' he said. 'How can I help you? I assume it's a loan.

Let me say now that I'm sure there will be no difficulty where anyone recommended to me by Licinius Philippus is concerned.'

'No, I'm fine at present, thanks.'

He looked blank. 'Really? Then I don't quite see why—'

'Philippus said I should talk to you about a guy called Aulus Licinius Nerva.'

'Did he, indeed?' The tone was guarded. 'In what connection?'

'Was he one of Philippus's recommendations too?'

'No, he wasn't. I get very few recommendations from Philippus. He's a very discriminating man, *very* discriminating, and most careful who he lets use his name.' He frowned and looked at me like he was reconsidering that particular judgment. 'In actual fact the recommendation came from one of my other customers who is, I understand, a cousin of Licinius Nerva's business partner.' He blinked at me. 'Now, Valerius Corvinus. Could I possibly ask you what your interest is?'

'I understand Nerva was arranging to borrow some money.'

'That is certainly the case.' The guy was wary now, no question, and I reckoned that he was within a hair's-breadth of telling me to get lost, but obviously Philippus's recommendation was still working its magic. The guy had paid off his debt right enough. 'Of course. Quite a considerable sum, in fact.'

'To finance buying a decommissioned grain barge. Yeah, I know that. What I don't know is what security he offered.'

Silence; *long* silence. 'I do not believe,' Frontinus said at last, carefully, 'that that's any business but his and mine. Not even if you are a friend of Philippus's. I'm sorry, Corvinus, but if you've come all the way from Baiae just to ask me that then—'

'Nerva's father was murdered seven days ago. His brother was murdered the day before yesterday. Maybe that's relevant.'

'Murdered?' I'd rocked him; I could see that. The rheumy eyes – they had traces of ointment in the corners – opened wide.

'Yeah. The old guy was found in a fish tank. The brother had his throat cut in an alley. I'm looking into both deaths.'

'Oh, my goodness.' There was a chair beside the desk. Frontinus collapsed into it. 'Oh, my! That does put a . . . rather different complexion on things. A completely different complexion, in fact. You're sure? That the deaths weren't . . . accidental?'

I nodded.

'But that's terrible! Simply dreadful!'

'Yeah,' I said, and waited.

'You see, Nerva wanted to raise the money on his future prospects.'

The hairs on the back of my neck stirred. 'Is that so, now?' I said carefully. 'And how would that work, exactly?'

'Oh, it's a common enough arrangement.' Frontinus was looking sick. He took a handkerchief from his mantle-fold and dabbed at his lips. 'The principal is guaranteed by a promissory note payable in full when the borrower comes into his inheritance. Subject to verification that the amount involved will be sufficient to cover it, of course. Interest is paid by the calendar month, naturally; that's quite separate. The rate depends on the age and . . . durability of the testator.'

'What happens if the borrower dies before he inherits? Or if something goes wrong?'

'He signs a paper allowing me to sell up his own assets to the value of the amount borrowed, before the estate passes to his own heirs. And, of course, I'm very careful to ensure that these assets are sufficient in themselves to cover the debt, which Licinius Nerva's were, if only just.' The ointment-smeared eyes blinked at me anxiously. 'Murdered? You're *sure* they were murdered?'

'Yeah,' I said. 'No doubt of it. Believe me.'

'Oh, my!'

'So did Nerva actually borrow the money from you?'

'Oh, yes. The contract was signed and I handed over the draft on the spot. Mind you, when he gave me his receipt he did say' – Frontinus faltered – 'he *said* – oh, my goodness! – that he hoped to repay the principal in full very shortly. That he had . . . prospects in view.' Another anxious blink. 'Both of them? The father *and* the brother, both murdered?'

'Uh-huh.' Sweet holy gods! I'd got him! 'When was this, by the way? When he signed the contract?'

The guy swallowed. 'Ah . . . seven days ago,' he said.

The day of the murder.

Bull's-eye!

I left Frontinus having a fit of the horrors in Cleisthenes's chair and went back outside. It fitted; Jupiter, did it fit! With Frontinus's draft in his mantle-fold Nerva legally had the cash he needed to fund his half of the barge scheme, sure, but there were strings attached. Pretty considerable strings. Money-lenders like Frontinus weren't in the business for their health, and interest rates were crippling, especially if the loan was a big one, and it had been: Frontinus's mention of the fact that Nerva's own total assets were just enough to cover it proved that. The interest rate couldn't be less than ten or eleven per cent, which meant that the monthly repayments wouldn't be peanuts, and I knew that Nerva had a serious ongoing cash-flow problem already. So if the length of the loan was tied in with his inheritance the cost of waiting until his father dropped off the tree naturally, or until the grain barge started turning enough of a profit to pay back both interest and principal, if it ever did, would've made a serious hole in his bank balance. Possibly even a fatal one. And he'd be involved in a hell of a lot more ongoing expense before that happened.

On the other hand, with both his father and brother out of the way he could use company money to pay off the balance immediately. No need even to wait until his actual inheritance came through. And he would've saved what would amount over time – if he could put off bankruptcy, that is – to a small fortune in the process. For a guy like Nerva I'd say that the combination of factors was a pretty fair incentive to murder. Good enough for me, anyway.

I picked up the mare from where I'd left her fraternising with a couple of carters' mules at the horse-trough, mounted up and set off for the four-mile ride back towards Baiae.

Short as the interview with Frontinus had been, it'd been a good morning's work. We'd nailed the bastard, no question: borrowing money on his future prospects was the clincher. And the fact that he'd signed the contract the day of the murder and told Frontinus that he hoped to pay off the principal almost before the ink was dry put the lid on things.

Okay; so how had it worked on the ground? What was the order of events here?

First of all, Nerva approaches Frontinus. He isn't thinking yet of murdering his father – at least, *pace* Florus, not seriously – but he needs a lot of money that he doesn't have, quickly. On Florus's cousin's recommendation he goes to

Frontinus. Frontinus suggests the inheritance option, and Nerva jumps at it because it gets him off the hook. Only in the short term, though: once he has the cash in his pocket he knows he's home and dry as far as the barge deal is concerned, sure, but he still has the interest to worry about, and in his current financial position finding that on a regular basis is going to be no joke. So he decides – this was where Frontinus's info re the early repayment prospects came in – to sound out his father again and put the scheme to him as a proper business proposition meriting company funding; maybe, this time, dangling the bait of a preferential deal. Only in the event it's no go: Murena – this is the afternoon of the murder – tells him to forget it; he's up to his neck in expense already with the Juventius estate, planning on more, and he can't afford to fund his son's pie-in-the-sky projects. There's a quarrel, and Nerva stalks out, stymied.

Right. So far, so good. On his way home, he does a bit of thinking. He's got no love for his father – neither of Murena's sons do – so that's no barrier. Murena isn't going to budge now, that's certain, and without him Nerva is screwed, or as near to it as makes no difference. On the other hand, if his father were out of the picture he'd have control of the company purse-strings. Except for his brother Titus, of course, but maybe he can get round Titus. Or something. Okay; so say Papa Murena meets with an unfortunate accident. He's subject to fainting fits, and it's his habit to visit the fish tanks of an evening after dinner. Say he has one of his turns, falls into a tank and drowns . . .

Nerva goes back to the farm, waits for his father and kills him, tipping his corpse into the eel tank. Job done, inheritance and so loan secured.

Then, five days later, when things have died down a little and suspicions are elsewhere – he's still pressed for time,

remember – he sends his brother a message: he's got something to say to him; would Chlorus come round at once?
He's decided that he won't bother trying to persuade him; or
maybe – which seemed more likely, from what the guy had
said when I talked to him myself in the wineshop – he's tried
already and Chlorus won't play ball. Worse, he knows the
approach has been made, and he may have guessed why,
plus gleaned the implications. So Chlorus has to go too, and
quickly. Message sent, Nerva lures his brother down an
alleyway and slits his throat.

Yeah; it would work. Sure it would. The theory fitted like
a glove – motive, means, opportunity, the lot. According to
Florus, who was too frightened and too stupid to lie, Nerva
had no alibi for either of the two evenings in question, he'd
motive in spades, and in either case means weren't a
problem. Aulus Nerva was the man, and thanks to Philippus
I'd got him.

All I had to do now was prove it. That was the tricky part.

When I got back to the villa, Mother and Priscus were just
getting into the carriage. She stopped when she saw me.

'Hello, Marcus. Did you have a nice ride into Puteoli?'

'Yeah. Yeah, it was okay.' Mother has never really got to
grips with the idea that horses and me don't go naturally
together, and riding isn't something I do because I enjoy it.
I dismounted and handed the mare over to one of the stable
skivvies. 'Where are you off to?'

'Neapolis, dear. *Not* my favourite town, but Titus has a
friend there with a unique collection of Samnite arms and
armour. There's a cuirass he wants to look at. At least' – she
fixed Priscus with a beady stare – 'that's what he *says* he
wants to do, and it had better be.'

'Mmmaaa!'

'I shall be keeping a very close eye on Titus. When I've dropped him off at his friend's I intend to do a little shopping. The shops in Neapolis are excellent, and I have the fifteen gold pieces which you and Perilla so kindly recovered to spend.' She sniffed. 'Perilla told me all about that at breakfast, by the way. Well done, dear. Perhaps you have your good points after all, although they are rather unconventional.'

'Ah . . . right. Thanks, Mother.'

'They really are a dreadful pair, that Florus and Nerva. Quite beyond the pale. Perilla says that you think Nerva murdered his father and brother for control of the business.'

'Yeah. At least, that's how it's beginning to look.'

'I'm not in the least surprised. I've never trusted those flashy types, and Licinius Nerva is altogether too louche to be anything but a bad hat. What do you intend doing about him?'

I'd been wondering that myself. Theories were one thing, but hard proof was another. 'I don't know,' I said. 'Go round and face him with it, I suppose. The main thing is the guy's alibi, or lack of one. If I can push him on that then maybe we'll get somewhere.'

'That's it, dear. Exert a little pressure. He's bound to crack. That sort always do.'

Well, I wasn't absolutely sure about that. Still, it was worth a try, especially now with what I'd got from Frontinus. Murena dying the same day Nerva signed the loan contract was just too pat, and the fact of the quarrel put the lid on it. 'Where's Perilla?' I said.

'Inside. But she's coming with us. She was just leaving a message for you with Bathyllus in case you got back after we'd gone.'

I went up the villa steps and met Perilla coming through into the lobby from the atrium.

'Oh, hello, Marcus,' she said. 'You've just caught us leaving. Or would you like to come to Neapolis too?'

I kissed her. 'No thanks, lady. I've been halfway there and back already this morning, and another couple of hours in a carriage would finish me. Besides, if the options on offer are Samnite armour and Mother's shop-till-you-drop then I'll pass.'

'Hmm,' Perilla said. 'So what *are* you doing?'

'I thought I'd take a walk down to the harbour, drop in at Aulus Nerva's and do a bit of cage-rattling.'

She frowned. 'Marcus, I wish you'd be less flippant. And more careful. You think Nerva is the killer, don't you?'

'Yeah. I'd put a fairly hefty bet on that.'

'Then he's a very dangerous man. He's murdered twice, in cold blood, and I doubt if he'd have any compunctions about murdering again. I do *not* want to come back from a shopping trip in Neapolis to find you laid out in the atrium with a pair of coins over your eyes.'

I laughed. 'Don't worry, lady. I'm not booked for the urn yet. Nerva wouldn't dare touch me.'

'I wish I was as sure of that as you are, dear. But be careful, anyway. Now I really must be going. We're late enough starting as it is.'

I waved them off and set out for Nerva's.

24

Actually, I didn't go straight there. I'd got one loose end to tie up first, and checking Ligurius's alibi wouldn't take me all that far out of my way. The guy himself wouldn't be at home, sure, but that was all to the good: if he was the killer (and it was still possible; I was keeping an open mind on that one, even with Nerva firmly in my sights) and he had been fibbing then he sure as hell wasn't going to change his story for the asking now, not when he was home and dry with Chlorus safely in his urn. I'd just have to hope he had nosey neighbours.

The first problem was finding the place. 'Not a salubrious area', Catia had said, and even allowing for the lady's snobbishness she wasn't far wrong. That part of Baiae was a maze of tiny streets and seriously run-down property, as bad as the Subura in Rome, easy. Also, because trades like the fuller's tend to bunch for obvious reasons – if you've ever smelled a fuller's vat you'll know what at least one of these is – even when I'd got the right bit I was spoiled for choice.

Mind you, Baiae's not Rome, and we were working on a much smaller scale here. I had to ask at only three possible addresses before I struck lucky with the fourth. It was a one-man business, and the guy stripped to his loincloth and treading a small vatful of half-submerged mantles was evidently the owner, proprietor and staff.

'Uh . . . excuse me, pal,' I said.

The guy stopped treading. 'Yeah?'

'Someone called Ligurius live here?'

He grinned. 'Ligurius? Sure. Flat above. He won't be around at the moment, though. Not until after sunset. Works over at that fancy fish-farm on the Bauli road.'

I was trying hard not to breathe: fullers like their piss well-matured, and I reckoned this guy was *really* choosy where the selection of his raw materials was concerned. 'Yeah, I know that,' I said. 'I didn't want to see him personally. I just wanted some information.'

The grin vanished. 'What kind of information?'

I took out my purse and extracted a couple of silver pieces. His eyes went to them, but he was still frowning.

'You friendly with him at all?' I said.

'We split a jug of wine together in the evenings, some-times. He's on his own, like me, and he's a good neighbour.'

'You actually live here? On site, as it were?'

'Where else would I live?' He jerked his chin towards the shop. 'There's a back room. Big enough for me, I'm not married either.' Yeah, well; I could see – or rather smell – why that might be. Still, there were worse trades, and fullers' wives tended to be ladies with pre-cauterised sinuses. 'Most of the time, though, I'm out here in the fresh air.'

Great. Perfect, in fact. Maybe this was going to work after all. 'Uh . . . he have many visitors?'

That got me a glare. The guy was looking *really* suspicious now. 'Look,' he said. 'What's this about? If you're some sort of town officer you can keep your money and clear off. Quintus Ligurius never done nothing illegal in his life. He's not the type.'

'No hassle, friend,' I said. 'Absolutely no hassle. And this isn't official, I'm just checking up on something he told me. I was just wondering if you remembered a particular visitor, in the evening, seven days back.' I described Chlorus.

The frown vanished and his face split into a gap-toothed grin. 'Scowler? The boss's son, Chlorus? Sure. He comes round a lot on fish-farm business. I do his mantles, sometimes. Yes, he was here, no problem.'

'You're certain?'

'Sure I am. Something about a chancer in Pompeii ordering fish and not paying for them. Ligurius told me later, after he'd gone and we got the wine out.' He spat neatly to one side. 'These Pompeian buggers, I wouldn't trust them that far.'

Well, there went that theory. Still, it'd been an outside chance, at best. And at least it finally cleared Ligurius from the list. Which left Nerva.

I thanked the guy, left the two silver pieces on a convenient stone, and pushed off back towards the centre of town.

Nerva was out.

'He's in Bauli, sir,' the door-slave said. 'He left early this morning and he won't be back until late this afternoon.'

Bugger. I should've gone to Neapolis after all. I'd've had no intention of sitting in while Priscus and his friend discussed the finer points of Samnite cuirass fastenings, mind, let alone tagging along with Mother and Perilla on their shopping spree (I'd done that once before, and it still gave me nightmares. Forget being strapped to an ever-revolving wheel or suffering torments of hunger and thirst: hell is making up a third to two women shopping); but Neapolis had some pretty good wineshops in the tree-lined streets that led off the main square, and I could quite happily have parked myself in one of them while the ladies bought up half Campania. Or didn't, rather. That's what *really* gets me about women shopping. Me, if I want something I go to a shop and buy it, finish. Women can quite happily spend hours drifting from shop to shop and end up buying something in maybe one out of every fifteen. Crazy.

'Fine,' I said to the slave. 'It doesn't matter. Thanks, pal.' I turned to leave.

'Valerius Corvinus, sir!

'Yeah?' I turned back.

'Perhaps you don't know. Decimus Tattius was found dead this morning.'

My guts went cold. '*What?*'

'Yes, sir. Stabbed through the heart. At least, that's what the slave who brought the message said. The Lady Penelope Licinia only sent to say he was dead.'

Sweet gods alive! 'Whereabouts was he killed?'

'At home, sir. Or outside in the grounds, rather. I don't know for certain.'

'Ah . . . right,' I said. My brain was whirling. 'Right. Thanks for telling me, friend. Oh, incidentally. Just a small question. Was your master at home two nights ago?'

I'd left it casual intentionally, and the door-slave answered without thinking. 'No, sir. He was out all evening.'

'You know where?'

You could almost see the brain kick into gear: two nights ago was when Chlorus had been killed, and peaching on the master is not a good career move in bought-help circles. The guy's expression went suddenly blank. 'No, sir,' he said.

I took a silver piece out of my purse. 'You sure?'

He was staring straight ahead. 'Yes, sir. I'm afraid I can't help you.'

Yeah, well, it'd been worth a try. And at least I knew now for certain that Nerva had lied to Florus about staying in with a head cold the night of Chlorus's murder. That made twice, by my counting, and twice was two too many. I flipped the silver piece at the slave and he caught it neatly. 'Never mind, sunshine,' I said. 'Thanks again anyway.'

So; what now? Well, that was obvious. Forget Nerva for the time being. I'd have to go over to Tattius's place, pdq.

Bugger! What a mess!

'One of the slaves found him by the little grotto of Pan at the far edge of the grounds,' Penelope said.

We were in the room we'd been in last time, the lady's sitting-room. Penelope was wearing mourning; triple mourning, I supposed it would be now, for a father, a brother and a husband. Knowing what she'd thought of Tattius – and why – I hadn't expected her to be too cut up about his death, but her face was flushed and she'd obviously been crying. Yeah, well, I supposed it must have been a surprise.

Or had it?

'The door-slave at your brother's said Tattius'd been stabbed.'

'Yes. That's right.' She stood up suddenly. 'Would you like to see him?'

That fazed me for a moment. 'You mean the – he's still here?'

'In his room, yes. I had the slaves carry him there until the men from the undertakers arrive.'

'Ah . . . yeah. Yeah, if it isn't too much—'

'Follow me, then.'

It was a big house. We went upstairs to one of the bedrooms. Tattius was lying on the single bed covered to the chin with a sheet, the coins on his eyes. He looked smaller than he had in life, but then laid-out corpses often do, and what little I could see of him was older. I looked around for the usual pair of scissors and bowl to collect tufts of hair from the mourners, but they weren't in evidence.

Penelope must've noticed, and guessed. 'That won't be necessary, Corvinus,' she said briefly. She took hold of the top edge of the sheet and pulled it down.

Straight through the heart, like Nerva's door-slave had said. He hadn't bled much, or if he had a lot of the blood had been soaked up by his tunic and under-folds of the mantle before it could spread to the surface.

'When did it happen?' I said.

'This morning, just after breakfast. He had it late, because he hadn't got back from Neapolis until after midnight.' Yeah; I remembered when I'd been here yesterday – Jupiter! Was it only yesterday? – she'd said he was away on business in Neapolis. 'He usually takes a constitutional walk in the garden first thing. Does the rounds of the property. He had an appointment at noon in town and Stentor – you remember Stentor? He brought you your wine yesterday – went to find him, to remind him.' Her lips twisted. 'Which he did. As far as the finding was concerned, anyway.'

'Who was the appointment with?' I asked. 'Do you know?'

'Yes. My brother Aulus.'

'But Nerva was—' I stopped. Yeah, well, he could've forgotten, I supposed. There again, pigs might fly.

'He was what?'

'Nothing. It's not important.'

'You've seen enough?'

'Yeah. Yeah, thanks.'

'Then we'll go downstairs again.' She pulled back the sheet. For a moment, her hand paused. Then she whispered, under her breath, so low I could hardly hear, 'The silly, silly man!'

She'd said it gently, almost lovingly.

We went back down. While we'd been away, someone –

Stentor, presumably – had put a tray with a jug and two cups down on the side table. Penelope went across to it, poured and handed me a cup.

'To Decimus's memory,' she said.

I drank. It was the same stuff as last time, with just as little water.

'Sit down, Corvinus. Make yourself comfortable.' She settled in her chair and adjusted the folds of her mantle. 'Decimus wasn't a real husband – I won't pretend that – but he was the only one I'll ever have. Rest his bones, I've no quarrel with him now.'

'Who do you think killed him?' I said. 'Do you know?'

She watched me carefully. Then she said simply, 'No.'

'Or why?'

'Not that either.'

'What was the appointment with your brother about?'

She smiled. 'I'm sorry, I'm not being very helpful, am I? I really can't say. The only reason I knew of it at all was because Stentor told me, after he'd found Decimus's body. My husband, as you'll realise, Corvinus, didn't take me into his confidence very often. But I assume it was something to do with the business.'

'Did that happen often? I mean, from what I've gathered your husband didn't take much part in that side of things.'

'No, he didn't. But with Father's death, and Titus's, he was the only other surviving partner. I'd imagine they'd have some things to discuss at least.'

'Why did you call him silly?'

She looked blank. 'What?'

'Upstairs. Before we left. You called your husband a silly man.'

'Did I?' She frowned. 'If you say so. Yes, well, he was silly, wasn't he? Completely ineffectual. But I must have been talking to myself. I do that, sometimes, Corvinus, but I don't always listen to what I'm saying.'

'Is there anything you can tell me, lady?' I said gently. 'Anything at all?'

'About Decimus's death? I don't think so, beyond what I've told you already. As I say, I wasn't in his confidence.'

'The business in Neapolis yesterday. What was that?'

'Oh, nothing. Nothing relevant, I don't think. Decimus goes there every so often to see his banker.'

'Regularly? Or only now and again?'

'About once every two months.'

'And yesterday was about the right time?'

'Yes. The last time was late May. Just after his birthday.'

'He didn't seem worried about anything at all? Preoccupied?'

'Not that I noticed. But then I didn't have the opportunity to notice.'

There was a knock on the door and the slave came in. Stentor.

'I'm sorry to disturb you, madam,' he said quietly, 'but the undertakers' men are here.'

'Oh. Yes. Very well, Stentor.' Penelope stood up. 'I'm sorry, Corvinus, I'll have to go and talk funeral matters. Was there anything else you'd like to ask before you go?'

'No, I think that about covers it,' I said. 'Unless . . .'

'Unless what?'

'I was wondering if I could get Stentor here to show me where it happened.'

'If you like. There's nothing to see, though. Stentor?'

'Yes, madam. Of course.'

Like the rest of the place, the grounds – you couldn't really use the word 'garden' – had obviously been left to fend for themselves, and outwith the bit immediately by the house that meant they'd run wild. I didn't believe a gardener could've been here for months, and in places it was difficult just walking along the path.

The grotto to Pan was the wildest part, which I suppose was fair enough given the god's preferences: a small cave, partly natural, partly artificial, with the god's statue more than half hidden by greenery and the water that seemed to seep through the walls collecting in a shallow basin at the front, then led off through a stone channel into the undergrowth.

'This is where I found him, sir,' Stentor said. 'Lying on the path with his face to the shrine.'

I looked around. No problem with cover here, that was for sure: you could've hidden a dozen men among the bushes and high weeds beside the grotto, and the amount of free-flowing water around made for thick foliage. We were a long way from the house, too; two hundred yards, easy, and most of that was trees, bushes and assorted green stuff. He could've yelled, and someone might've heard him, but I doubted if his killer had given him the chance. And if he'd known the person he wouldn't think of yelling until it was too late.

'Any other way in here, pal?' I said. 'Barring the way we came?'

Stentor smiled. 'Oh, yes, sir. Lots. The wall on this side of the grounds has been crumbling away for a long time, and we've woods behind us, as you see.'

'Who knew your master took these morning walks?'

'Everyone in the household, sir. Other people – well, it was no secret, and he's had the habit for many years.'

'And no one saw or heard anything? None of the other slaves?'

'No, sir. That time of day we all have our jobs inside. And there isn't really a gardening staff as such. The master isn't – wasn't – much concerned with the garden, except for keeping the part most visitors would see tidy. It wouldn't've been likely that there would be anyone on this side of the house at all.'

Fair enough, and it answered most of my questions. I hadn't just got Stentor out here, though, to show me the scene of the crime. 'This appointment your master had with Aulus Nerva. You know anything about that?'

'Only what the master told me, sir. That the gentleman was expecting him at noon at his house in town.'

'Who made the appointment? Your master or Nerva?'

'That I can't tell you, sir. I only know it existed.'

'Was he looking forward to it, do you think?'

Stentor shook his head. 'I'm sorry, sir. I really know nothing about it more than I've said. The master asked me to remind him if he forgot, that was all.'

Only it wasn't Tattius who had forgotten, was it? It was Nerva. According to his door-slave he'd gone off to Bauli. The question was, why?

'Who do you think killed your master, Stentor?'

He opened his mouth to say something, but then he seemed to change his mind and he shook his head again instead. 'I've no opinion, sir. And I'm my mistress's slave, not my master's. A wedding present.'

'She . . . doesn't go out walking herself in the morning, does she?' I said. 'Your mistress, I mean?'

He might be a slave, but he wasn't thick. He delayed the answer long enough to show me just what he thought of the question and then said, 'No, sir. The mistress isn't a walker. And to my certain knowledge this morning she went straight to her room after breakfast, as she always does, and remained there until I brought her the news of the master's death an hour or so later.'

'They had breakfast together?'

'Yes. They always do, sir. And dinner, when the master's at home. He's always insisted on that. Whatever the other . . . separate arrangements.'

'Fine, fine.' Well, that just about covered it. I'd got all I was going to get, for what it was worth, and that wasn't much. I reached into my purse, took out a couple of silver pieces and handed them over. 'Thanks a lot, pal. You've been really helpful.'

'You're welcome, sir.'

What next? A place to think, and a half jug of wine to help me do it; apart from the quick swallow I'd managed in Penelope's room I hadn't had time for a drop all day.

Zethus's.

One thing did occur to me, though. Stentor had said his mistress had gone straight to her room after breakfast, before Tattius had been killed, and she'd still been there an hour later, after he'd found the body. Which was fair enough, and it should've been conclusive, because I'd bet Stentor hadn't told a lie from beginning to end.

The only flaw in the chain of logic, though, was that Penelope's room was downstairs, facing the garden. The back garden, where – eventually – the grotto was, and where, according to Stentor none of the household slaves would be at that time of day, if ever.

And Penelope's room had door-sized sliding shutter-windows.

25

I hadn't been to Zethus's for a couple of days, not since the punch-up with Philippus's heavy. This time of day – late afternoon, by now – there was a fair smattering of regulars drinking round the bar, including the loud-mouthed Alcis and my pal Lucius who'd driven me to the doctor's.

'Hey, look what the cat's dragged in,' Alcis said. Original as ever.

'How's the rib, Corvinus?' Lucius raised his wine cup at me.

'Not bad.' I went over to the bar, opened my purse and put the money on the counter. 'Still there, last time I looked. Half a jug out of that, Zethus.'

'Sure.' Zethus hefted the wine jar out of its rack and filled the jug. 'How's the case going?'

'All right.' I poured, sank the first one down and poured again. 'We're getting there.'

'Only Trebbio was asking.'

Shit. I kept forgetting Trebbio, and he was the reason for this after all. Still, he couldn't blame me on the effort score. 'He okay?'

'Happy as a kid in a sandpit. He's made pals with the jailers and decided he's better off where he is than he would be at home. Sobered up, too, although that isn't all his doing. We see he gets his wine regular, but not too much.'

Yeah, well, if he was doing well and becoming a model

citizen then that was fine. At least he couldn't've done the other two murders, but until the local authorities had someone definite to pin the Murena rap on they wouldn't be too keen to let him loose.

'Hear there's another of these bastards gone,' Alcis said. 'The son. Chlorus. Unlucky family, that.'

'Make that three,' I said. 'Decimus Tattius was killed this morning.'

There was a hushed silence. Then one of the other barflies – I didn't know his name – whistled softly between his teeth and spat on the sawdust.

'What happened?' Zethus said.

'Someone knifed him in his own garden.'

'Really, *really* unlucky.' Alcis shook his head. 'There'll be none of them left soon. Pity.'

'Who do you think did it, Corvinus?' That was Zethus again. 'You got any theories?'

'Uh-uh. Nothing definite, anyway.' Nothing I wanted to share at present with the loose-mouthed clientele in this hotbed of gossip, certainly. I picked up the jug and wine cup. 'Now if you'll excuse me, gentlemen, I want to sit and think.'

'Cerebrate,' said Alcis.

'Right. Whatever.'

I took the wine to the table in the corner and sat down.

Okay; so what had we got? Where Tattius's murder in isolation was concerned, once you discounted Stentor's evidence about the lady being in her room all morning Penelope was the odds-on favourite by a mile. She knew Tattius's habits, she knew up there by the grotto the chances of an accidental witness to the stabbing were pretty slim, and she had easy – and private – access to the back garden through her own windows. So opportunity – and motive – both in spades. On the other hand, if she had murdered her husband – and she'd hated him bad enough – we were back to the old objection: why do it now? Also, I wouldn't put her down as the murdering type. Her father, sure, I'd stretch a point on him if I was pressed, but not Tattius, and certainly not Chlorus, not unless she'd had a really strong reason for getting rid of him that I didn't know about. There was that . . . softness as well, when I'd talked to her earlier. I could be wrong, sure, and certainly it went against all my expectations of how things ought to have been, but I'd say that Penelope genuinely regretted her husband's death.

Not Penelope, then. The obvious candidate for Tattius – by extension, anyway – was Nerva. After all, I'd practically made him for the first two killings, and the third fitted the pattern.

So first the how. That was simple: I only had his door-slave's word for it (or rather he only had Nerva's) that the guy had gone to Bauli at all. He could easily have sloped up to Tattius's villa, waited for him to take his usual consti-tutional in the grounds – there was no reason to assume he *couldn't* have known about that – stepped out of cover and stabbed him. Then ridden on to Bauli – it wasn't far, only two or three miles, and he was on the right side of town – to establish some sort of alibi.

The why was more tricky.

Me, I'd like to have known who suggested that appoint-ment. The situation wasn't like it'd been with Chlorus: a note sent to get the guy out of the house, going in a particular direction at a particular time when he could be waylaid and murdered. Tattius's appointment had been for noon, and he'd been killed at home long before he was due to set out.

So my guess was that it wasn't Nerva who'd suggested the meeting but Tattius.

That would make sense. With Murena dead, Tattius has

lost the goose that lays the golden eggs. Sure, as a partner he'd still get his fair cut of the profits, but Nerva wasn't his father. Whether Tattius was actually blackmailing Murena or, more likely, that the old guy just felt he owed in the good Roman tradition wasn't relevant: the upshot – until latterly, anyway – was that Tattius was raking money in over the odds; certainly more than he was putting back. He wouldn't get away with that with Nerva. To begin with, he didn't have anything on the guy . . .

I stopped, my scalp prickling.

Or there again maybe he did. Which was what killed him. Or helped to kill him.

Put that one on hold for a moment, stick with the main theory. I took a long swallow of wine to lubricate the brain cells.

Okay. Tattius didn't have anything on Nerva that he could use as a lever. Worse, Nerva wasn't the generous type, and he couldn't afford to be, not with his up-and-coming expenses re the grain barge, so what money there was lying around was carefully earmarked. The last thing Nerva's going to do under the circumstances is hand out cash he badly needs himself as capital investment to a neverwozzer who hasn't done a hand's turn for the company since he became a partner. If Tattius tries to put the bite on this time he's going to get the dull thud. Consequently, he's further up shit creek than ever, there ain't a paddle in sight, and he knows it.

Yeah. So maybe he *does* have something on Nerva. Or thinks he can con him into thinking he does, which would be shyster Tattius all over. The meeting with his banker in Neapolis, I'd bet, wasn't coincidence. Or not pure coincidence, anyway: he'd've wanted to make sure just exactly what his current financial position was before he talked to Nerva, but he'd arrange the appointment for as soon after that as possible. So he drops some heavy hints before he goes that Nerva had better see him, for his own good, as soon as he gets back, and be prepared to fork out a realistic amount of the readies when he's asked for them. Or else. Which in the event was a very silly thing to do with a guy like Nerva, because—

I stopped again, this time like I'd run into a brick wall. Gods!

She'd known! Penelope had known!

That comment she'd made, under her breath, when she'd pulled the sheet up on her husband's corpse. She'd called Tattius a silly, silly man. Sure he had been: he'd tried to blackmail Nerva, and it'd got him an urn.

Only, if Penelope knew that much, then what else did she know that she wasn't telling? And why wasn't she telling it? There was no love lost between her and her brother, not her and any of the family, including her husband. Why should she protect Nerva? Fear? Yeah, well, that'd be reasonable, even sensible, especially if she knew more than she was saying; but from my assessment of the lady she wasn't afraid of very much. She'd publicly accused her father of murder when she was hardly any more than a kid, after all. And I'd bet even then she was aware of the possible consequences.

I took another swallow of wine, emptying the cup, and poured myself a refill.

No, not fear. Not Penelope. Maybe just a simple sense of decency.

That, when you got right down to it, was the central thing about Penelope: the lady was *decent*, in the best sense of the word: a real straight-down-the-line, old-fashioned, stiff-backed Roman matron. Even though she hated her husband

and knew why she'd been married to him she'd kept to the conventions – publicly, at least – for almost thirty years. Even at the end she could say, almost in the same breath, 'I hated him' and 'Rest his bones'. So what could a lady like that have told me? That her husband was a blackmailer and her brother a murderer? Uh-uh; she wouldn't do it, not for their sakes but for her own. If I wanted to find those things out, I could find them out for myself.

That didn't excuse Aulus Nerva, though. No way. It was time me and Nerva had a serious chat. 'Late afternoon', his door-slave had told me. Well, it was late afternoon now, and if he wasn't back from Bauli yet I'd camp on the bastard's doorstep until he was.

There was another cupful in the jug. I finished that, took the jug and cup back to Zethus at the bar, said goodbye and left.

He'd arrived, just, and – so the major-domo said – was changing into a lounging-tunic upstairs. If I'd like to wait in the atrium he'd be right down. He brought me a cup of the second-grade Falernian and I passed the time looking at the wall paintings.

Like I said, they were heavy on the nymphs-and-seductive-gods theme, with lots of boobs and bare thighs on view: Daphne and Apollo, Leda and Zeus, one biggie with a general free-for-all between nymphs and satyrs. Strong stuff for a public atrium, although maybe less so in Baiae. The quality of the painting, though, was like his choice of wine: flashy and second-rate.

He came down about twenty minutes later.

'Ah, Corvinus,' he said. 'Admiring the artwork? I had it done last year. Quite a promising young painter, I thought.'

'Yeah.' I turned away. The major-domo followed him in

with the wine jug, poured and handed him a cup, topped mine up and exited.

'I hear you – or rather your wife – took a packet off Sextus Florus yesterday evening at Philippus's. Congratulations.'

'Thanks. You've . . . uh . . . talked to him? Florus, I mean?'

'No. I ran into a mutual friend in Bauli who saw the game.' So he wouldn't know yet that Philippus was after him with a rusty hatchet. A pleasure yet to come. Well, maybe that was the least of the bastard's troubles, and I wasn't surprised that Florus wasn't exactly busting a gut to make contact, either. Knowing you've peached on a multiple killer is a pretty compelling reason for keeping your head down.

'Yeah,' I said. 'It was a good match. I'm sorry you missed it.' I was; seeing Florus getting his comeuppance had been good, but Nerva would've been better.

He was watching me, frowning. 'I understand you made a rather curious side bet. Towards the end.'

'That's right.' I took my wine over to one of the couches – red plush upholstery and too much gilding – and lay down. 'That's why I'm here. Plus the fact, of course, that Decimus Tattius was knifed early this morning.'

'So my major-domo told me. Dreadful business.' He settled down on the couch opposite. 'I was away too early to get Penelope's message, naturally. The news came as quite a shock.'

Again. Yeah; they'd had quite a few *quite a shocks* in the last few days, that family, and I didn't believe in the shock element for any of them. 'You don't seem too upset about it. If you don't mind me saying so.'

He shrugged. 'Tattius was my father's friend, not mine. I never did care for him much, and he's certainly no loss business-wise. The fact of his murder, though, that's another thing entirely.'

'You, ah, had a meeting arranged with him, I understand. For noon today.'

That got me a long considering stare. Finally, he said, 'Yes. Tattius proposed it before he left for Neapolis.'

'But you went to Bauli instead?'

'The meeting was Tattius's idea, not mine. I'd already made my arrangements. And frankly there wasn't any point changing them to suit him.'

'What did he want to talk about?'

'Money. What else did Decimus Tattius ever want to discuss?'

'Specifically?'

Another long stare. 'I'm sorry, Corvinus,' he said, 'but that's really none of your concern. It was private, between him and me. Now he's dead it doesn't matter anyway.'

'He wanted a bigger slice of the company profits?'

He hesitated, like he was weighing up whether to answer or not. Then he said, 'Yes, as a matter of fact. Tattius always wanted more than his fair share. Under my father's regime he got it, but times and circumstances have changed. If he'd done a corresponding share of the work I might've been more amenable. As things are, I wasn't inclined to be, or even to discuss the matter. That's the end of it. Now if you've got any other reason for this visit I'd be glad if you'd state it. If not—'

'I was through in Puteoli this morning. Having a talk with a man called Gaius Frontinus.'

He put down the wine cup. '*How dare you!*'

'Seemingly you took out a loan secured against your future prospects. Payable on your father's death and your inheritance.'

He was coldly furious now. 'Corvinus, this is—'

'You signed the agreement the same day as Murena's

murder. Oh, sure, you'd be responsible for the first month's interest, but you're in a position now to pay off the principal straight away. That's pretty lucky, isn't it? The way things have worked out.'

He was on his feet. I thought he was going to come across and go for me, and I stiffened. However, if he was he thought better of it, because he sat down again.

'Did Sextus tell you this?' he said.

'You mean, did he point me towards Frontinus? No.' He had, sure, but he hadn't been the first. And much though I despised Florus I didn't want to put the finger on him where I didn't have to. 'But the information's right, isn't it?'

'If you're accusing me of murdering my father just so I could—'

'It gives you a prime motive, pal.' Masks off; we were glaring at each other now. 'You were stuck for cash to finance your grain barge scheme. Paying the interest on a loan that size, long-term, would've crippled you. You tried your father the afternoon of his death, but he turned you down in spades. You've got no alibi for that murder, or your brother Chlorus's, and I bet, *friend*, that if I was to do a bit of checking in Bauli you wouldn't have an alibi for this morning, either. Now tell me I'm wrong.'

He was quiet for a long time, and if looks could kill I'd've been cold pork. Finally, he said, 'All right, Corvinus. I will. What makes you think I don't have an alibi? For all of these times?'

'Oh, come on, pal! It's a bit late now, isn't it? You could've—'

'Actually, I do. A perfectly good one. Three, in fact, although they all involve the same person.'

Gods! Well, I had to give him full marks for nerve, anyway. 'Look, pal,' I said. 'Let's just tick them off, shall we?

Two days ago, when I met you and Florus in Philippus's gambling hall, you tried to claim that that was where you'd been the night your father was killed. I checked with the staff, and you didn't set foot in the place all evening. Now do you want to move on to the second on the song-sheet, or can we just cut the crap?'

I thought maybe that might've fazed him, but it didn't. Not at all. 'Oh, yes,' he said. 'That's right. Yes, I did try to lie on that occasion, although not for the reason you may think.'

'Is that so, now?'

He picked up the wine cup and took a swallow. 'The lady's name is Pollia Rufina,' he said. 'She's Sextus Florus's cousin's wife. The man we're negotiating to buy the barge through.'

My brain went numb. 'What?'

'We – ah – met in the early stages of the deal. The husband works at the fleet headquarters in Misenum, but they live in Bauli, so he's away from home quite a lot. Rufina gets lonely. I go over there when it's convenient to cheer her up.' He drank some more of his wine. 'That's where I was this morning, if you're interested. Where I was, in fact, on both previous occasions. Rufina won't exactly be thrilled about providing confirmation, but I'm sure she will, if you ask nicely.'

Oh, shit. He sounded convincing as hell. 'So why the secrecy?'

'I'd've thought that was obvious. The lady's husband doesn't know and would be livid if he did, probably to the degree of divorce. Nor does Sextus, and I can't trust either that idiot's sense of family loyalty or his flapping mouth far enough to tell him.'

'I thought you were involved with Catia.'

'Oh, I am.' He smiled. 'I have been for some time. But Catia does get rather . . . tiresome with prolonged exposure. You'll appreciate that, you've met her. She also has an extremely jealous and possessive nature. On the other hand, she does have her good points, and the fact that she's – she was – Titus's wife added a little spice to the affair. So as you'll understand I didn't and don't want her to find out, either.' The smile broadened to a grin. 'Don't look so surprised, Corvinus. These things are commonplace in Baiae. Even Brother Titus had a mistress.'

'He *what*?'

'Oh, yes. He didn't know I knew. He didn't think anyone knew, which I doubt if anyone did, including Catia. Or would care, for that matter. It wasn't exactly a grand passion in any case. She's in her late forties, very plain, married to a haberdasher near the Puteoli gate, and she's got a most unwomanly interest in finance. I suspect they spent their evenings when hubby was out discussing bookkeeping, because I doubt if either she or Titus would be interested in anything more strenuous. Or up to it, either.' He put the wine cup down. 'As I said, you can check on me with Rufina if you like. I'll tell you where she lives and give you a note for her which you can read before I seal it. Or dictate the wording yourself, if you prefer and don't trust me. Under the circumstances, I don't think I have any option. Only do be *very* discreet, please. As I told you, the husband doesn't know, and it would be very embarrassing for me personally and business-wise if he found out. Now, if that's all you wanted I won't keep you any longer.'

He stood up, still smiling.

Me, I was feeling like the bottom had dropped out of the world.

Bugger; there went the case.

26

It was getting late now, but Perilla and company wouldn't be back for dinner anyhow. I walked back home, had a quick snack while the stable lads got the mare ready and rode out to Bauli with Nerva's note to Rufina in my belt-pouch.

I felt like crying, but this was something that couldn't wait, and putting it off would just make matters worse. If the bastard's alibi checked – and I had a horrible suspicion that it was going to – then we were well and truly screwed.

I found the place no bother: a small, newly built, squeaky-clean villa on the Misenum road the far side of Bauli itself, on the very edge of the fashionable stretch; the sort a middle-ranking government clerk would buy to show that he knew exactly which rung he was on on the Establishment ladder and how the residence of a conscientious, sober-minded middle-ranking government clerk should look. Which I reckoned would sum up Rufina's husband in a nutshell.

Even the flower-beds were colour-co-ordinated.

'Uh . . . is the mistress at home?' I said to the slave who opened the door.

'She's at dinner, sir.' The guy gave me an unwelcoming look. Fair enough: dinner-time wasn't exactly within the usual visiting hours. 'With the master.'

Hell. 'This'll only take five minutes,' I said. 'The name's Valerius Corvinus. She doesn't know me but I wondered if I could have a word with her in private.'

'What about?'

'A mutual friend asked me to call round in passing. Name of Catia. Seemingly there's been some mix-up over the dates for a women's honey-wine klatsch.' Thin, sure, but it was the best I could think of on the way over. And the mention of Catia should get me a hearing if nothing else. Assuming the lady knew about her.

It seemed she did. Not that that made me persona any more grata, mind. When Rufina stormed into the little sitting-room where the slave had taken me to wait she was purpled up to the eyeballs and fit to be tied.

A stunner, though. I had to admit that. Mid-twenties, five foot two, curves like a Praxiteles Venus and a bust that wouldn't't've disgraced the Leda on Nerva's wall. Currently, it was heaving. Rufina was not pleased.

She closed the door carefully behind her. 'Valerius Corvinus,' she hissed, 'I don't know why you're here, but—'

'I'm sorry,' I said, handing over the note. 'Maybe you'd better read this first.'

She snatched it out of my hand, tore it open and read it. I'd dictated it myself, and stood over Nerva while he wrote it, so I knew the contents were pretty bald: just who I was, a request for Rufina to answer my questions truthfully, and Nerva's signature. No mention of an alibi.

'Well?' she snapped. Her colouring had gone up another notch. 'What's this all about?'

'Aulus Nerva says he was here on the night of the twentieth, seven days ago, again two nights back and all of this morning. Was he?'

'*Valerius Corvinus!*'

The hell with that. I wasn't in any mood for going round the houses. 'Just answer the question, lady,' I said. 'Please. It's important.'

'I don't see why I should!'

'Was he here or not?'

She fizzed for a bit, biting her lip and glancing nervously towards the door. Finally, she nodded. 'Yes. Yes, he was, as it happens.'

'All night? The first two, I mean?'

'He . . . arrived just before dinner on the first occasion and stayed until the morning. On the second, he was slightly later, but not by much. Today . . . yes. Publius was at home last night, but Aulus . . . called round after he'd left for the day to Misenum.' She'd coloured up like a beetroot and she thrust the note back at me like it was red-hot. 'Now. I want to know what right you have to walk in here and—'

'That's all, lady.' I shoved the note back in my belt-pouch. 'Thanks a lot. No hassle.' Shit!

'If my husband finds out there'll be trouble! You can tell Aulus from me that—'

I backed away, one hand reaching for the door handle. 'No hassle. Honestly. Thanks for your help.'

'*How* I'm going to explain this to Publius I just do not know! He *knows* I'm not friendly with anyone called Catia, and that fool Eupolis said right out when he came into the dining-room that you'd—'

I escaped while she was in mid-flow, past the door-slave and out the front door. Jupiter in bloody rompers! Well, I'd done my best, and I'd got what I came for, but I suspected that the next time Aulus Nerva came calling – if he ever did – he'd be lucky to get clear with his eyes unscratched-out. Not that I'd much sympathy.

Fuck; where did that leave us now?

The sun'd gone down in earnest when I reached the villa. Gods, I was knackered! Two hard days in a row, and the case in shreds. I stabled the mare, noticing while I did it that the carriage was back. Bathyllus was waiting by the door with the usual jug of wine.

'Satisfactory trip, sir?' he said.

There was no answer to that, not one that wouldn't've made the little bald guy's hair curl, so I didn't make one. It wasn't his fault everything had just gone down the tubes.

Perilla was sitting reading under a candelabrum in the atrium.

'Oh, hello, Marcus,' she said brightly. 'Enjoy your day?'

I grunted, kissed her, took the wine cup and jug over to the couch opposite, and lay down.

'Ah.' She let the book roll up and put it aside. 'I'll take that as a "no", then.'

'We're stymied, lady. One hundred per cent, gold-plated, spit-on-your-granny screwed. The whole case has gone pear-shaped.'

Her eyes widened. 'Oh, dear. It can't be as bad as that, surely.'

I took a gulp of the Special. 'Nerva's out of the game. He was comforting a lonely office widow in Bauli. Which she's just confirmed. Oh, sure, he might by some stretch of the imagination have killed Chlorus, but he couldn't've done the other two murders.' I punched the couch-back. 'Hell's bloody bells and fucking upper canines!'

'I see. Then who's left?'

'Search me. Tattius and Chlorus are dead, Ligurius is alibied, so's the doctor. Aquillius Florus wouldn't have the guts to kill a chicken. That leaves Gellia and Penelope. Both of them have motive enough, sure, but I'd bet a sack of gold pieces to a plugged copper that Penelope's no murderess.'

'So it's Gellia, then.'

'Yeah.' I took another morose swallow and refilled the cup. 'Only can you see that lady in her fancy mantle and three-hour hairdo stalking Chlorus through the streets of Baiae and slitting his throat in an alley? Or hanging about in the shrubbery for Tattius to come along then stabbing him through the heart? Because I fucking can't.'

'Don't swear, dear. It's not necessary,' Perilla said. 'Anyway, I've never met the woman. I can't judge.'

'Take my word for it. If she didn't have help from Florus or the doctor, then Gellia's a non-runner.'

'You're sure about Diodotus?' Perilla was twisting her curl. 'After all, he only has an alibi for the first murder. And Gellia could have done that one herself.'

'Diodotus is clean. He's got more sense than to get himself mixed up with a bubblehead like that. And I don't think he likes the woman much, let alone fancies her.'

'Florus, then. Despite appearances.'

'Florus has as much backbone as a slug. You've seen him for yourself, Perilla. You think he could commit a cold-blooded murder without pissing himself and dropping the knife out of sheer funk before he used it? Let alone three of them?'

'Very well. Then it must be Penelope.'

'Or someone outside the circle altogether. In which case we're right back to where we started.'

I took a third gulp of the Special.

'Hmm.' Perilla was looking thoughtful. 'I did wonder, Marcus. Apropos of that. Why Penelope?'

'Why Penelope what?'

'No. Her name. I've always found that curious, and we've never really asked ourselves where she got it from.'

'It's just a pet name, lady. Every family uses them. Actually, she's a Licinia.' Something tugged at my subconscious, but when I reached for it it was gone. 'What does that matter?'

'It's just . . .' She hesitated. 'Probably not at all. But what does "Penelope" mean to you? The name, on its own?'

'Ulysses's wife, of course. Gods, Perilla, what the hell does—'

'Yes. Who waited for twenty years for her husband to come home, spurning the suitors. The faithful wife. Patient Penelope.'

Patient Penelope. Twenty years. The tug had become an itch, and everything had gone very still.

I sat up.

'Go on, lady,' I said quietly.

'I don't think I can. There isn't anything more, really, just that. But it has been puzzling me, and it is curious, isn't it? I mean, when you consider that so much of this business has come back to names. Murena, dead in a tank of moray eels. Ligurius, the manager, with the nickname Anchovy. Tattius, Oistrus. And didn't you say that the old man had given the rest of his family nicknames too?'

The itch was there in spades, and I was getting that slow, cold feeling spreading through me that was my subconscious's way of telling me something was important, somewhere. Oh, shit! So he had! Gellia was the Butterfly, Nerva the Scoundrel and Chlorus the Scowler. So why not Penelope? Just because it was a harmless, everyday girl's pet name didn't mean—

Hang on, Corvinus! Think! Saenius, when he'd talked about her, had called her Licinia. So had Philippus, who'd known her when he was Murena's door-slave. Both Philippus and Saenius were talking about the girl as a teenager, before or immediately after her mother's death and the trial. Why hadn't they called her Penelope? Girls got their pet names when they were kids, not on the verge of adulthood. Look at Catia's Hebe. She was really Licinilla – which she'd have to be, being Chlorus's daughter, that or Licinia again – but Catia had said that that had been too much of a mouthful, so they hadn't used it right from the start.

Giving pet names didn't always happen. That was just the point. It hadn't, as far as I could see, happened where our Licinia was concerned until she was well into her teens . . .

So why had teenage Licinia, settled with her name, suddenly become Penelope?

The hook caught me right in the gut, along with the answer.

'Because it wasn't a pet name at all,' I said. 'It was a nickname, like all the rest of them. A fucking nickname!'

'*Marcus!*'

I ignored her. It made sense; Jupiter best and greatest, did it make sense! 'Murena gave it to her,' I said. 'After she was betrothed to Tattius. And he used it – the rest of the family used it – ever after. They still do.'

Perilla was looking puzzled. 'But Penelope uses it herself, dear,' she said. 'If it was a nickname and she hated her father, then surely if he gave her it then—'

'Penelope used it because it fitted, and she didn't mind. Quite the reverse, she was proud of it. In fact, she preferred it to Licinia, because Licinia connected her with her father.'

'But why did Murena give her it in the first place? Surely calling a girl Penelope is a compliment, if anything.'

I shook my head. 'Not the way he meant it, lady. It couldn't've been, ipso facto, because none of the bastard's other nicknames were complimentary. There was always something nasty about them, and my guess is that Murena was about as fond of his daughter as she was of him. He nicknamed her Penelope as a sneer because she was faithful and patient. Twenty-nine years patient, as it turned out. And she didn't give in to the suitors, not really, not in herself. She still hasn't.' Gods! I'd been an idiot! A total, purblind fucking moron! She'd *told* me! She'd told me herself, the very first time I'd interviewed her, right down to using the guy's actual name, even if she had lied about the rest of it . . .

The silly, silly man. Right. I'd go with her on that one all down the line. That made two of us.

'Marcus?' Perilla was staring at me anxiously. 'Marcus, what is it?'

'I know who committed the murders,' I said. 'All three. And why.'

She asked me the obvious question. So I told her.

27

I didn't go round to the Tattius villa next morning until well after breakfast. There was no point in hurrying now. Besides, to yank the lady out of bed for what amounted to an official confrontation would've been unnecessary and cruel, and I felt bad enough already about how this business was ending to risk that. Why the hell couldn't the killer have been Nerva? Him I could've handed over to the praetor's rep without a qualm, and society could've done without the bugger, easy.

Instead I got this.

The door-slave passed me on to Stentor, who took me through to Penelope's sitting-room. She was there already, in her mourning mantle, and she looked up as I came in. There must've been something about my face that told her why I'd come, because when our eyes met I saw her flinch and then sort of settle into herself, like a boxer who's taken a hard punch shakes his head to clear it and squares up again for the rest of the match.

'Stentor,' she said quietly. 'That message I asked you to deliver. Do it now, please.'

'Yes, madam.' He bowed and went out.

I watched him go. Yeah, he'd told me he was the mistress's slave, not the master's. And I knew now who the friend had been who'd given him to her as a wedding present. I considered my options. I could stop him, sure, but it wouldn't matter in the end, however it panned out, and I hadn't cared much for any of them. Either from personal acquaintance or, in the first one's case, by repute. Leave it.

I turned back. Penelope hadn't moved. She was sitting still as marble. I nodded, slightly, and it seemed that some of the stiffness went out of her.

'Valerius Corvinus,' she said. 'What brings you here?'

'Ligurius,' I said.

She'd been well prepared for it. This time, she didn't even blink. 'Come in. Have a seat.'

I sat down on the chair facing. The window-doors were open again and there was the hint of a breeze blowing in from the garden.

'He was the Quintus you mentioned,' I said. 'The one who you were promised to originally. Only he wasn't a cousin, and he didn't die of fever.'

'Yes,' she said quietly. She looked down at her hand, at the plain brass ring on her engagement finger, the only one she wore. 'How did you find out?'

'Your name. Penelope. Ulysses's wife.'

She nodded. 'Ah. So simple.'

'Your father gave it to you, didn't he? As a nickname, when you were betrothed to your husband?'

'Yes.' She was quite composed. 'I told him I'd do what he wanted, marry Decimus, but that I'd always regard myself as engaged to Quintus.'

'What did he say?'

'He laughed. Said I could please myself who I thought I was engaged to, as long as the marriage went ahead. Then he said he was minded to call me Penelope in future. The faithful Penelope. I told him I didn't care, that I'd welcome it, in fact. He didn't like that.'

'The original engagement. It was official?'

'Yes. Of long standing, although not a well-publicised one. Quintus and I had been brought up together as children. Quintus's father was the manager of the farm before him, and his grandfather before that. Not slaves, never slaves, and by that time they were almost family. We'd loved each other for years. It wouldn't've mattered to Father if we'd married: he had two sons already, and an engagement to someone of Quintus's class would save him an expensive dowry. That was the way he thought.'

'And Quintus – Ligurius – accepted the situation?'

She smiled. 'He had no choice. I told you, when we talked before. He was an employee, I was the master's daughter. Running away together would've been pointless, and at least we'd still see each other.'

'You didn't . . . continue the relationship?'

'No,' she said simply. 'Not in the way you mean it. That wouldn't have been right. But Quintus never married. We saw each other, secretly, from time to time – we still do, of course – though never in compromising circumstances. And Quintus gave me Stentor, so we could keep in touch that way as well. He cost him nearly a year's wages.'

Jupiter, this was weird! 'So Ligurius carried on as your father's manager while you married his partner? And you never started a proper affair?'

'Never. I suspect Father knew all along that we still kept up, but if he did he didn't care. He despised Quintus. He called him Anchovy, little fish. Something not worth bothering about.'

'Yeah,' I said. 'Yeah, I know. How did Ligurius feel about that?'

'He shrugged it off. Quintus despised my father at least as much as he despised him. He expressed his contempt by doing his job to his own satisfaction and simply ignoring my father otherwise. And my husband.'

'Murena never thought of sacking him?'

Penelope's eyes flashed, but she answered in the same level voice. 'No. Or at least, not to my knowledge. If he had, or if he'd even tried to, he knew I'd make the whole affair public at once, whatever the cost. It might not have caused him any legal problems after all that time, but it would've finished him socially in Baiae.'

'So you knew about Philippus's deal with Tattius?'

'Yes, I knew. Too late to do anything about it, but I knew. And I didn't – don't – blame Philippus. He was a slave, he took the only chance of betterment that offered. And the result was that my father was being punished after all, in a way. Besides, Quintus is an excellent manager. The farm would have gone into liquidation long since if it weren't for him. My father knew that too.'

'Okay.' I shifted in my chair. 'What about the actual killing? Your father's, I mean. Tell me about that.'

'It was an accident. Or partly so.' For the first time, she lowered her eyes. 'There had been an . . . estrangement for several months between Decimus and my father. Father had bought the Juventius estate and he was planning to build a hotel. It would've cost money, of course, a lot of money, and although Father was reasonably well off he couldn't afford to do it without making economies elsewhere. He told Decimus that he intended to plough the profits from the business for a year or so – all the profits, barring the minimum living expenses – back into funds, to finance the project. My husband was a very greedy man, Corvinus, and also a very stupid one. He accepted the situation at first, or said he did, although with a very bad grace. Finally – we're talking a few days before the . . . death, you understand – he had a terrible argument with my father, in Quintus's presence, over what he called his "allowance". My father was not a man to be bullied. He told Decimus that he was fed up supporting him and that if he didn't like it he knew what he could do. He also said – and I believe he was joking, but that's the way Father was when he was angry – that he was surprised that his daughter stayed married to him, and that if she was thinking of a divorce then she had his blessing. Quintus, as I say, heard all of this. He thought things over later and without telling me decided – rather foolishly – that perhaps the time had come to approach my father and suggest we get married after all.'

'So he went to see him. Privately, and when he knew there'd be no slaves around to overhear. When Murena went down in the evening after dinner to feed the fish.'

'Yes. He had his own key to the fish-farm gate, of course, so he didn't have to go through the villa entrance.'

'What happened then?'

'They talked, and Father laughed at him. Like he always did. Said he hadn't been serious, and he'd never consider a little fish like Quintus marrying his daughter, under any circumstances. Quintus lost his temper and hit him.'

'And Murena fell into the tank.'

She was quiet for a long time. Then she said, 'Yes.'

'He could still have pulled him out.'

'He tried to. He got one of those poles with the nets on the end; you know, the ones the slaves use to take out the fish.' I nodded. 'Anyway, he was clumsy, and Father was struggling too hard because he couldn't swim. Besides, the eels got in the way. The end of the pole caught him on the head and knocked him out. Quintus panicked. He tried to use the net end to snare him in, but the net was too small and Father was too heavy. He only succeeded in pushing the body deeper and further away. By the time he did manage to get him close enough to the edge to grab his mantle it was too late, and Father had drowned.'

'So he decided to leave him where he was, for the eels.'

Her eyes came up, and there were tears in them. Not for her father, though; I knew she wouldn't cry for him. 'There was nothing more he could do, Corvinus! Father was dead, Quintus had killed him and as I say he panicked. He went back to the gate and let himself out.'

Yeah, well; it all made sense. Mind you, I had my doubts about the details. I was getting this second hand, from a woman who was in love with him. Me, I wouldn't've put it past Ligurius to have at least helped nature take its course. Although, to be fair, I wouldn't've blamed him much, either. 'Fine,' I said. 'What about Chlorus?'

A definite hesitation. 'Titus's death was . . . unfortunate,' she said finally. 'But there was nothing Quintus could do there either. He had to kill him.'

Right. Anyway, I reckoned that now I could answer that question myself. 'Chlorus needed to give himself an alibi,' I said. 'He had one already, sure, but it wasn't one he wanted to use. He was out that evening at his mistress's, and that was something he didn't want to become public knowledge. So he went to Ligurius, explained the situation in confidence, and asked him to do him a small favour: say that they'd been together that evening discussing a defaulting customer. Which they genuinely had done, only not that night, the one before. Am I right?'

She nodded, but didn't speak.

'Okay. Backing Chlorus's story would get Ligurius off the hook where I was concerned, no problem. He wasn't married, he lived alone, so there'd be no other way I could check up. Except via the neighbour, of course. There was that possibility, sure, but it was a risk he had to take, and unless for some reason I chose to disbelieve both him *and* Chlorus – and why should I do that? – he reckoned he was safe enough, even if I did get round to asking his laundry pal. One evening's very like another, especially after a few days've passed, unless there's anything to mark it out, like a murder, say. And when I talked to him the guy didn't mention the murder at all. I should've noticed that, and wondered why not; after all, finding your boss half eaten in an eel tank is news your average punter would be itching to pass on. Only I didn't do either.' Yeah, right; *moron* wasn't the half of it!

She smiled. 'No. Quintus didn't mention Father's death at the time, for obvious reasons. Then, for the reason you've given, he was very careful not to be the first to introduce the subject. His neighbour hardly ever goes out, and there was a good chance he wouldn't hear of it at all. Which, from what you say, he evidently still hasn't. Being asked to back my brother's story was a godsend for Quintus.'

'Except that when he had time to think things over Chlorus began to smell a rat. Ligurius didn't owe him anything, they weren't pals and they didn't even like each other; so why should he agree to lie on his behalf so easily? Especially where a murder was concerned. Chlorus knew damn well that Ligurius hadn't been with him that evening like he'd told me, so as things developed he started wondering what he *had* been doing. And the answer, naturally, was killing Murena.'

'Yes.' Penelope's face was expressionless. 'Titus . . . broached the subject with him in private two days after my father's death. Delicately: Titus had no liking for Father anyway, remember, and he couldn't care less who had murdered him. Also, I suspect, he rather hoped the crime would be fixed on Gellia or Aulus, and that would have been to his advantage. Having Quintus accused and condemned wouldn't have benefited him at all, quite the reverse.' She half smiled. 'My brother, Corvinus, was not a nice man. Quintus killed him, yes, but it was in pure self-defence, and he was no loss. Believe me, I'd known him all my life.'

'Yeah.' Well, I let that one go. They don't describe Cupid as blind for nothing. And, again, she had a point. Philippus had been right: that whole family was rotten. Even Penelope had a callous streak a mile wide, and she was the best of them. 'Now tell me about your husband. Tattius.'

For the first time, she seemed genuinely reticent. If the word wasn't inappropriate, I'd've said she was embarrassed.

'Decimus was a mistake.'

Yeah, well, I'd guessed as much myself, but the lady was telling this, not me, and I owed her the chance to do it in her own way. I waited.

'Quintus thought that with my father and brother dead he'd have' – she hesitated – 'he would have a chance of our finally marrying. He'd killed twice already. My father's death, as I told you, was an accident. Titus's was a necessity. The third . . . well, the third would be for the good of both of us.' The tears came again. She made no attempt to hide them, and her face didn't change. It was still hard as marble. 'He shouldn't have done it, Corvinus. It ruined everything. He was a silly, silly man.'

Right. Maybe Ligurius had got a bit too blasé about killing, too, but I didn't say that. The lady had enough problems without me adding to them. 'Would you have told me?' I said. 'If I hadn't come round today?'

She shook her head. 'No. I don't think I could have gone that far. Not even to save this Trebbio. All the same, I'd never have married Quintus, not now, whether you'd found out or not. He wouldn't be the same person. He is – he *was*, before all this started – a very gentle man. But then, he knows

I wouldn't marry him, not after Decimus. It's over, for both of us.'

'You've talked to him? Since your husband's death?'

'No. Not directly.' She glanced towards the door; yeah, right: Stentor. 'I'm glad you came, though. To a certain degree, it takes things out of my hands.'

I stood up. 'What do you want me to do?' I said.

She smiled. 'You mean I have a choice?'

'I think,' I said gently, 'you've already made it.'

This time, she didn't answer. She was staring straight ahead at nothing, lips set tight in a firm line, like a statue, but for the tears on her cheeks.

Patient Penelope. Only what happens when the husband who comes back isn't the same one that set out?

I paused, hand on the doorknob. Maybe this wasn't exactly the time, but there was still a loose end to tie up and if I didn't ask I knew that I'd regret it later.

'Ah . . . just one more question,' I said.

'Yes?' The head didn't turn.

'The evening Chlorus was killed someone tried to knock me down with a slingstone. It could've been Ligurius himself, sure, but he'd've been pushed to get back to the town centre for his rendezvous with your brother. Compared to everything else it's not really important, but I was wondering—'

She half-smiled. 'I'm terribly afraid, Corvinus,' she said, 'that was me.'

I goggled. 'It was *what*?'

'Quintus couldn't use a sling to save himself. I can, very well. And a bow, incidentally, although on that occasion I chose a sling because it was far easier to conceal.' The smile broadened. 'Don't look surprised. I was quite a tomboy when I was a child, and I always have been very good at anything involving aiming and throwing.'

'But why the hell attack me at all?'

'To kill you, obviously. Or at least hurt you very badly. It was the simplest way to stop you asking questions. If it's any consolation, however, I'm glad now that I missed. And I realised almost immediately that it had been a mistake.'

Her voice was totally matter-of-fact; we could've been talking about the price of fish. Sweet holy Jupiter! Callous was right.

I left her to her thoughts and set out for the fish-farm.

I took my time over the journey. There wasn't any hurry with that, either, and I didn't want to overtake Stentor. Things were out of my hands, too, by now, and I suspected it was better that way because if they hadn't been, unlike Penelope, I wouldn't've had any choices to make.

The guy on the gate let me in. He was white-faced, and he didn't say much. Slave grapevine: news travels fast.

They'd left him where they'd found him, in the little office. I'd thought – hoped – that when Penelope's message came he might've done a runner. I'd've been happy with that; like I say, I didn't have much sympathy for any of his victims, and to see a guy handed over to the public strangler through my doing doesn't give me any pleasure at all. But he'd chosen to kill himself instead, which was his only other option under the circumstances. Probably, for Ligurius, it'd been the only option he'd considered. A knife under the chin is quick, and he'd lost it all, anyway.

I wasn't going to go up to the villa; no *way* was I going there. Gellia could find out the results of the investigation through official channels. The same went for Nerva. I supposed I really should report to the town officer, tell him what I knew, get his congratulations and wrap the whole thing up . . .

Bugger it. The loose ends could wait. What I *really* felt like now was getting smashed out of my skull at Zethus's and then going home.

28

I moped about a bit for the rest of the day. I hadn't got completely canned in Zethus's after all: when it came to the point there didn't seem much point, as it were. I just had the half jug, told the gossip-mongering barfly-ghouls at the counter how things'd turned out – they'd hear the story quick enough through the grapevine anyway, and at least this way I could be sure of what the bastards were passing on – and called it a day at that. I didn't mention Ligurius's connection with Penelope, though: I reckoned that lady had grief enough, and the information was private. As far as Zethus's clientele were concerned he'd just been insulted one time too many, beaned the master with the fish pole and in the end killed himself to avoid an inevitable date with the public executioner. End of case, exit villain.

So, like I say, I went back home and moped around. Mother and Priscus had gone off to Neapolis again – there were still a few shops out in the sticks that she hadn't been into – but Perilla had stayed behind to give me some moral support when I got back. I needed it. It was always like this at the end of a case: you felt empty, drained. It was even worse when the guy who'd done it turned out not to be one of the bastards you hoped had.

'You think all this faffing around is worth it, lady?' I said to Perilla. We were sitting out in the garden, under the shade of a trellised vine. She was reading, I was watching a squirrel poking around beneath the big beech tree fifty yards off. Wrong time of year, pal, I thought. No nuts in July.

'What faffing around, Marcus?'

'This detecting. Half the time it only leads to trouble. If I hadn't interfered Ligurius would still be alive, so would Tattius, and the two of them would probably have got married when the old man popped his clogs.'

'Ligurius and Tattius?'

'Come on, Perilla, you know what I mean. My bet is that Penelope was just waiting for her husband to drop off his perch from natural causes. Then she'd've given her father the finger, if he was still alive himself, and married Ligurius in spite of him and her brothers. Duty done, happy ever after, and it wouldn't't've mattered if it'd taken another fifteen years because she'd've waited them out as well, and so would he. Me being here changed all that.'

Perilla rolled up her book and gave me a long, steady look. Finally she said in a hard voice, 'Don't be silly, Marcus. Ligurius was a killer. He had to be caught. And if he decided to take his own life rather than run then that was his own decision.'

'Ligurius wasn't a killer, lady. Not originally, not by nature. Murena's death was an accident. What turned the guy into a murderer was knowing I was sniffing around the corpse and being afraid I'd find out what happened. That's what I'm saying. If I hadn't interfered then it would've ended with Murena, and Murena's was no murder at all. Chlorus and Tattius would still be alive – even those bastards had some right to life – and Ligurius and Penelope would still have a future, or at least the hopes of one.'

'Trebbio wouldn't.'

That stopped me. She was right, of course: someone had to be up for the rap, and Trebbio had been it. Penelope had told me upfront that she wouldn't't've interfered. He could've got off at the trial, sure, but that wasn't likely. Praetor's reps are very *neat* about those things: a murder needs a murderer, and that's the end of it. We were still talking balances here, though: one life saved against three lost. Not good arithmetic. I said so.

'One innocent life, Marcus,' Perilla said.

'Against three guilty? One I'd grant you, just. The other two – well, Chlorus and Tattius might've been out-and-out bastards, but could you put your hand on your heart and say they deserved to die? Because I couldn't. And they died because I interfered.'

She put the book down. 'They died because Ligurius killed them,' she said.

I sighed. Yeah, well; it wasn't worth arguing, and she was right, anyway. It was just the mood I was in. I watched the squirrel for a bit, and after a while Perilla picked her book back up and carried on reading.

Ten minutes later she raised her head. 'Why don't we go to Philippus's tonight?' she said.

My eyes had glazed over. I snapped back to attention. '*What?*'

'I'm sure he wouldn't mind. He's a lovely man really. And I noticed that some of the people there were playing Robbers. I enjoy Robbers.'

Jupiter in bloody spangles! 'Perilla, that's a men-only gambling hall! Just because he let you in once as a favour doesn't mean—'

'Nonsense. We can ask, at least. I'm sure there must be some good players there. I can give you a whole row of men and still beat you hands down every time, Marcus. It'd be nice to have some decent competition for once.'

Oh, shit. What had I let loose? 'Perilla—'

'We could even persuade Vipsania to let us take Priscus along. He'd be all right with us there, and the poor man deserves a proper holiday like anyone else.'

I had to put a stop to this right now. 'Perilla, listen. Pin your bloody ears back for once and use them. We are *not* going back to Philippus's, okay? Believe me, lady, gambling's a habit that can get a real grip on you. Just don't start, right?'

She grinned at me.

Bugger. I stood up, kissed her and went inside to see if I could scare up Bathyllus and another half jug of wine.

Ah, well; maybe life wasn't too bad after all. And an evening at Philippus's might be fun.

So long as the lady didn't get a taste for it.

AUTHOR'S NOTE

I experienced another of those weird coincidences while writing this book.

The original idea was twofold. I wanted to set a story in Baiae, against a background of fish-farming, where my victim would be found in a tank of moray eels. I also wanted names (and nicknames especially) to be central to the plot.

Okay; so I started with my victim. The Latin for a moray eel is *murena*, Murena is a Latin surname, so my victim – given the 'names' idea – would be Murena. Murena is a surname of the *gens* (broader family) Licinia, so the man's name had, for the sake of authenticity, to be Licinius Murena. The first name didn't matter, so I chose one at random: Lucius. So. Lucius Licinius Murena.

Then I started to do my research, and discovered that in the first century BC – about the time of Cicero - there had been a real Lucius Licinius Murena, who had pioneered fish-farming.

Weird, right? It's true, honestly, and that's the way it happened.

Two very short background notes, for those who are interested:

Fish-farming

The Romans loved fish, but it was definitely an expensive luxury; also, where sea fish were concerned at least, it was a seasonal delicacy and not readily available in the winter months. The first person to realise that fish, or rather shell-fish, could be farmed was Sergius Orata, who constructed oyster ponds on the Gulf of Baiae in the early first century BC. He was followed by others, including the real Lucius Licinius Murena (my fictional Murena's 'grandfather') and the epicure Lucullus. When Lucullus died the fish in his ponds were sold and brought in the huge sum of four million sesterces (two and a half thousand would buy a decent slave; the cost-equivalent, today, of a mid-price new car).

One of the 'fish' fish that the Romans kept in their ponds was the moray eel; not that it tasted particularly nice (I don't know that from personal experience, mind) but because it was exotic. It was also a flesh-eater, which gave it an added *cachet*. The bit in the book about Murena feeding Philippus's father to the eels I have not made up: the Romans believed that morays fed on human flesh tasted better, and they didn't believe in waste.

Twelve Lines

'Twelve Lines' (*Duodecim scripta*) was, according to my invaluable old *Smith's Dictionary of Greek and Roman Antiquities*, the ancestor of our backgammon, with certain important differences. There were fifteen counters, and the board was marked off horizontally (either side of the vertical centre-line which – if it was physically present – provided the dividing spine with the turning-point at the end, like the *spina* in a racetrack) with twelve lines. Play, as in backgammon, was 'out and back', with the two opponents moving in opposite directions and taking the pieces off at the end. Single pieces were vulnerable, and covered pieces were safe.

So much for the similarities. There were three main differences. First of all, instead of the staggered modern arrangement, each player began the game with all his pieces arranged in three rows of five on his first three lines. Second, the Romans used three six-sided dice, not two. Third, the rule was 'one die, one piece', which meant that you couldn't, say, combine the scores of three and two on two dice to move one piece forward five lines.

I admit I may have cheated a little at the end of 'my' game by allowing Perilla (and Florus) to use the three dice for their remaining single men rather than just one; I'm not absolutely sure (Smith doesn't say), but I think that the second would be more likely. I chose three simply for reasons of pace.

My thanks (again) to my wife Rona, for her usual patience; to Ronald Knox and Costas Panayotakis of Glasgow University's Department of Classics; and to Adam Hutchison, researcher extraordinary, for finding me bits about Baiae.